THE TWO MRS. ABBOTTS

T0204381

D. E. STEVENSON

Sourcebooks and the colophon are registered trademarks of Sourcebooks, Inc.

Published by Sourcebooks Landmark, an imprint of Sourcebooks, Inc.
P.O. Box 4410, Naperville, Illinois 60567-4410
(630) 961-3900
Fax: (630) 961-2168
www.sourcebooks.com

First published in 1943. This edition created from the 1973 printing by Collins Clear-Type Press, London.

Library of Congress Cataloging-in-Publication Data

Stevenson, D. E. (Dorothy Emily)
  The two Mrs. Abbotts / D.E. Stevenson.
      pages cm
  "First published in 1943. This edition created from the 1973 printing by Collins Clear-Type Press, London."
  (pbk. : alk. paper) 1. Miss Buncle (Fictitious character)--Fiction. 2. Women authors, English--Fiction. 3. City and town life--England--Fiction. I. Title.
  PR6037.T458T8 2014
  823'.912--dc23

                              2013031051

Printed and bound in the United States of America.
POD 10 9 8 7 6 5 4 3

Chapter One
The Lady in the Drawing Room

G rrh, I'm a bear! Grrh, grrh, I'm a bear, Dorkie!"

"Oh, dear, so you are! Wotever shalladoo!"

"Grrh—I'm going to eat you up."

Dorcas raised her eyes and saw, peering through the lacework of the wrought-iron banisters, the small eager face of her beloved. She thought—as she had often thought before—that Simon was the most beautiful thing in the world. His clear skin was pale gold, warmed by the sun; his hair, thick and straight and shiny, was a deeper, richer gold, and his eyes beneath his arching golden eyebrows were true hazel. Dorcas was devoted to little Fay of course—she was the baby and babies are very close to one's heart—but Simon came first. If it would have saved Simon a moment's pain Dorcas would have lain down in the road and allowed a steam roller to pass over her recumbent body…

Silly old fool! thought Dorcas to herself.

"Go on," urged Simon. "Go on, Dorkie."

"Oh dear, wotever shalladoo," said Dorcas again, trying hard to simulate terror but not succeeding very well.

"Be frightened," cried Simon eagerly. "Say, 'I'll have to get my gun.' Go on, Dorkie."

Dorcas went through the usual formula. She should have been good at the game if practice makes perfect, for she and Simon played it every afternoon of their lives when they returned from their walk. Sometimes Simon was a lion or a tiger and sometimes he was a bear but "Dorkie's" role was always the same. Today Dorcas was less convincing than usual for her thoughts were not in her part. She was thinking how odd it was that children grew up so quickly and grown-up people remained much the same. It was only yesterday (or so it seemed to Dorcas) that she had carried Simon upstairs in her arms. Now he could run up the stairs much faster than she could. Tomorrow, or soon after, he would have grown too big to play bears—he would not need her anymore.

The game of bears had taken a little longer than usual this afternoon, and Fay, who took no interest in it, began to climb up the stairs by herself. The steps were broad and shallow, for the Archway House had been built in spacious times, and Fay went up on all-fours like a very fat monkey. Her skirt stuck up in the air and showed her behind, which was clad in frilly drawers; her legs had delicious fat creases at the knee…

Now they were all at the top and had crossed the landing and were clattering down the passage to the nursery.

"Hush!" cried Dorcas. "Not so much noise, Simon. The lady will think there's a regiment of soldiers in the house."

"What lady?" asked Simon, stopping so suddenly that little Fay bumped into him.

"The lady in the drawing room," Dorcas replied.

"Who is she, Dorkie?"

"Come along, do," said Dorcas. "We want our tea. We're late as it is…and I shouldn't wonder if the 'vacuees won't be coming up to play with you when they've done their lessons," added Dorcas guilefully.

"Grice an' 'ilda'!" cried Simon, hopping about. "We'll play at going to the Zoo and…"

"Simon, I've told you not to call them that!"

"It's what they call themselves, Dorkie," declared Simon with an impish grin. "Grice an' 'ilda' 'ill from Edgewire."

"Not now they don't. They've learnt better. Say it properly, Simon."

"Grace and Hilda Hill from Hedgeware."

"Vack-wees," added Fay in her precise little voice.

"That's right," agreed Dorcas.

"But who's the lady?" asked Simon who was of a persistent nature.

"She's a vack-wee," suggested Fay.

"She's a Mrs. Walker—that's who," replied Dorcas, who was busily engaged in laying the nursery tea. "She's sitting in the drawing room waiting for your mummy to come home."

"Why?"

"Oh dear, you are a curiosity! She's coming to give a lecture about the Red Cross and she's going to stay the night."

"Why is she going to?"

"Because it's too far for her to go home—in the dark and all."

"She should have a torch," said Fay.

"And that's all I know about her," said Dorcas firmly. "So you needn't ask any more questions."

"I want to see her, Dorkie," Simon declared.

"Well, you can't then."

"But Dorkie, I *want* to see her."

"That's enough, Simon. You go and change your shoes like a good boy and then we'll 'ave our tea...we'll have our tea," she amended, *sotto voce,* as Simon left the room.

It was not often that "Dorkie's" aitches came adrift—only sometimes when she was bothered or when such well-worn phrases as "we'll 'ave our tea" rolled off her tongue unawares—but sometimes was too often, thought Dorcas. She wasn't going to have Simon and Fay dropping their aitches because of *her.* Dorcas was elderly. She had been nurse to the children's mother, and, as a matter of fact, it did not seem very long ago. Then, when her small charge grew up she had stayed on as cook and general factotum. That stage in her career had lasted for years; it had been ended by her mistress's marriage when the faithful Dorcas had blossomed into a personal maid. Now she had reverted to her first job, and reverted with delight, for she adored children and was an excellent nurse. She possessed a calm and placid nature that was rarely ruffled—never ruffled by the children—and, although she was just a trifle too lenient with Simon, she had a certain amount of control over him and the children were moderately good and extremely well and happy under her care.

Simon went into the night nursery and removed his shoes (he tugged them off quickly without undoing the laces) and put on his slippers and ran downstairs. He wanted to see the lady in the drawing room. He wanted to *see* her—that was all.

Meanwhile the lady in the drawing room had been amusing herself quite happily; she had been provided with tea and left to enjoy it in peace. She did not mind having tea alone; in fact she welcomed the rest and solitude after her somewhat trying cross-country journey. The trains were hot and stuffy and crawled along stopping at every station—she had been obliged to change three times. At first Sarah Walker had been amused, for she was interested in people and had a sharp eye for anything funny or unusual, but after a bit her sense of humor had become blunted by exhaustion. If Sarah had known the journey was going to be so awful she would have hesitated before accepting the invitation to lecture at this meeting, but she had not known (from Silverstream to Wandlebury did not look far on the map). It was only when John came home and she asked him to look out her trains that she discovered what she had let herself in for.

"If you had asked me, first, I could have told you," said John, looking at her with his grave smile.

"I know," agreed Sarah, "but they wanted an answer and it looked quite *near.*"

"It's fifty miles as the crow flies but it will take you three hours. Need you go, Sally?"

"I must, it's all arranged. I'm to stay the night with a Mrs. Abbott. I hope she'll be nice."

"She won't be nice," said John with conviction. "They never are…but as long as she doesn't put you into a damp bed—"

"I'll sleep in my dressing gown, darling."

"Did she ask you to stay?" asked John anxiously.

"It was the committee," replied Sarah. "They just said they would find a room for me and then they rang up again and told me the address. *Mrs. Abbott, The Archway House, Wandlebury.*"

"I wish you wouldn't gad about the country like this," said John with a sigh.

"But I'm quite strong now!"

"Stronger than you were," amended John.

"It's my war work," Sarah pointed out. "I don't enjoy tearing around the country giving Red Cross lectures—but I don't suppose soldiers enjoy fighting or munitions workers enjoy standing all day long, filing nuts and screws."

John had made no further objections, but had looked up her trains for her and written them out clearly on the pad he used for his patients' prescriptions…and Sarah had followed the directions faithfully, changing from one train to another, and arriving safely—as she had known she would arrive—at Wandlebury Station. Now here she was in Mrs. Abbott's drawing room, eating Mrs. Abbott's buns and drinking Mrs. Abbott's tea out of a nice deep, well-shaped cup.

It was pleasantly quiet and cool in the shady room and Sarah felt comfortably relaxed. She had a feeling that it would be very nice if Mrs. Abbott did not come home at all—she did not feel inclined to make polite conversation with a complete stranger. What would Mrs. Abbott be like? One ought to be able to tell what she was like from the room, thought Sarah, looking around with a sudden accession of interest. The room was exceedingly pleasant, large and well-proportioned, with tall windows that looked out on to a terrace and a rose garden. Mrs. Abbott would be a pleasant hostess if she was like her drawing room, if she had made it herself and had not inherited it or got it decorated by someone else. It was a dignified room, yet it was comfortable too, with good solid furniture and restful colorings…and what a lovely Adam mantelpiece! Sarah was so pleased with the mantelpiece that she rose from her chair and crossed the room to examine it and to run her fingers over the moldings, and, as she did so, her eyes fell on a miniature hanging on the wall…

Sarah stared at the miniature. She had seen it before.

"Barbara Buncle!" she exclaimed aloud.

Yes, there was no doubt about it. She had seen that queer little picture of Barbara Buncle as a fat rosy child hanging upon the wall in the sitting room at Tanglewood Cottage! Dear Barbara, thought Sarah, and she looked at the little picture with affection—for she and Barbara had been friends, very great friends indeed until they had lost sight of each other. Barbara had left Tanglewood Cottage suddenly, she had vanished in the night and nobody in Silverstream had heard of her again. She had been obliged to go, of course, because she had written two very amusing books all about her neighbors and their little peculiarities, and her neighbors had not appreciated their portraits—quite the reverse. Sarah's lips curved into a smile as she thought of the tremendous upheaval those two books had caused in the village of Silverstream.

But what did it mean? wondered Sarah. Why should this particular miniature be here, hanging on Mrs. Abbott's wall? Sarah looked around the room again, with even more interest than before, for she wanted to see whether there was anything else in it that had belonged to Barbara. The furniture was not from Tanglewood Cottage—definitely not—it was much too large; but there were one or two odds and ends that seemed familiar to Sarah…a couple of china vases, a bronze cowbell, a sandalwood box…

The door opened and Simon walked in. He shut the door firmly and then turned and looked at the lady. He had wanted to see her and he was seeing her now. She was worth seeing, Simon thought: not young, but slim and pretty with big gray smiling eyes. He looked at her and she looked at him. Then she laughed.

"Are you the Golden Boy?" she inquired.

"I'm Simon Abbott," he replied solemnly.

"A very good name," she remarked. She was calculating rapidly as she spoke…how many years was it since Barbara had fled from the fury of Silverstream?

"I count on my fingers, too," Simon told her. "Daddy says you shouldn't, but it's the easiest way."

"Much the easiest," agreed Sarah. "I always do. How old are you, Simon?"

"Four years older than the war," replied Simon promptly. "I can remember when there wasn't any war at all. I can even remember bananas—and cream."

"They were good, weren't they," said Sarah reminiscently.

"Do you *know* Mummy?" asked Simon, who was anxious to obtain as much information as possible before some tiresome person interrupted this pleasant *tête-à-tête*.

"I think so," said Sarah.

"I wondered," he admitted. "I mean I wondered if you were a friend of Mummy's or if you were just a Red Cross person."

"I'm both," replied Sarah, for she was practically certain that she was. "I'm a Red Cross person and I used to know Mummy before she was married."

"You don't look old."

"Age is relative," said Sarah gravely. "Which really means that, although you might think me old, a person of ninety would think me quite young."

"Compared to them," agreed Simon, nodding to show that he understood.

"Exactly."

"Have you got any children?"

"Two. They're twins, which is rather fun."

Simon digested this. He said, "I'd rather just be me."

"Some people feel like that," allowed Sarah.

"Where do you live?" Simon wanted to know.

"At Silverstream."

"Is it far from here?"

"Not far as the crow flies," replied Sarah with a sigh.

Simon's questionnaire continued, "What *are* you?—besides being a Mummy, I mean."

"A doctor's wife," replied Sarah without a moment's hesitation.

"Do you help him?" Simon asked.

"I try to," she declared, smiling to herself. "I run his house and answer his telephone and amuse him when he has time to be amused. Yes, Simon, I think I'm a fairly useful wife."

Simon nodded. Then he said, "Who is the Golden Boy? You thought I was him, didn't you?"

"I thought you might be," she replied. "You see I was thinking about the Golden Boy and then the door opened and you came in."

"Is it a story?"

"Yes."

"An *interesting* story?"

"Very interesting. Even people who didn't like the story were deeply interested in it."

Sarah had resumed her seat at the table and was pouring out

another cup of tea. She was enjoying her chat with Simon; his questions did not worry her at all for she was used to her own children. They were a good deal older than Simon now, but they still asked questions—children could not learn unless you answered them sensibly, or so Sarah thought. Simon had perched himself on the end of the sofa with one leg tucked beneath him; he looked more than ever like Sarah's conception of the Golden Boy. All gold, he was. His hair and skin were different tones of gold, and his eyes were flecked with the same precious color. His face had a slightly impish look and his small flat ears were just a trifle pointed. How odd that Barbara should have produced a real live Golden Boy!

"Tell me about it," said Simon eagerly. "Tell me the story."

"It's a grown-up story," said Sarah after a pause. This was true, of course, but not entirely true, for, as a matter of fact, it was a story her own children had always adored and Sarah had told it so often in simple language that she could have told it to Simon very easily. It was the story of how the Golden Boy came dancing into Silverstream, playing on his pipe and stirring up trouble, bringing life and movement into the sleepy place...so that even the buns on the baker's counter began to hop about. Of course Simon would like it—Sarah had no doubt of that—but she felt she had no right to tell Simon Abbott this particular story. Only one person had that right.

"I think it's just a little too grown-up," said Sarah firmly. "I'll tell you about Aladdin and the Wonderful Lamp."

Chapter Two
Old Friends

Sarah was enjoying her tea and forging ahead with Aladdin when the door opened again and her hostess appeared. She came into the room uttering apologies in a conventional manner and then, with her hand of welcome still extended, she suddenly stopped. "Sarah!" she exclaimed.

The voice was so surprised, the expression was one of such utter amazement that Sarah could not help laughing.

"Sarah!" said Barbara Abbott again.

"Yes, it's me," nodded Sarah (who, although aware that one should say "it is I," could never bring herself to utter the words because for some reason or other it sounded as if one were God).

"Oh, Sarah!" cried Barbara. "This *is* a lovely surprise! It's ages since I saw you—simply ages. How nice of you to come! You'll stay to dinner, won't you? I mean supper, of course—we don't have a proper dinner now, because—"

"I think you are expecting me to stay the night," said Sarah somewhat uncomfortably.

"Of course," agreed Barbara hospitably. "Of *course* you must stay the night...Oh dear, what a pity I've got that tiresome woman coming! We could have had such a nice chat about old times. It's most unfortunate."

"I'm the woman," said Sarah, her voice shaking with laughter. Somehow this misunderstanding was "so like Barbara."

"Isn't it unfortunate," repeated Barbara, wrinkling her brow. "I'm afraid I can only give you a very small room—just a dressing room with a bed in it—because of this Red Cross woman, you see. Or perhaps I could put the Red Cross woman in the dressing room...or perhaps the Marvells would have her. No, *that* won't do because she's arrived. There's a frightful shabby old suitcase in the hall—I saw it when I came in—so I shall have to put her somewhere. I wonder where she can have gone," added Barbara, gazing around as if she expected the Red Cross woman to be hiding behind the sofa.

"Barbara...it's me..." gasped Sarah, between her spasms of laughter.

"It's you?" asked Barbara in bewilderment.

"I am the Red Cross woman," declared Sarah.

"You are? Do you mean you're going to give the lecture?"

"Yes," said Sarah, taking out her handkerchief and mopping her eyes. "Yes, that's exactly what I mean."

"Goodness!" exclaimed Barbara. "But of course you always *were* clever..."

"There's nothing clever about giving a lecture on bandaging. It's much more clever to write books."

Barbara made no reply to this. She turned to Simon and told him to go to the nursery and have his tea.

"But Mummy—"

"It's tea time, darling," said Barbara firmly.

Sarah's first impression of her old friend was that she had changed a good deal, but after a few minutes she had decided that "changed" was not the word. Barbara had developed, that was all. She was still the same natural creature, interested in other people and unconscious of herself. She was still humble-minded and sincere. She had filled out a little, of course, and she was better dressed and more assured in her manner—but these were merely surface changes. Sarah had time to notice these things while Barbara argued with her son and finally bribed him with a chocolate biscuit to depart in peace.

"I suppose I shouldn't," said Barbara, sitting down.

"We all do," replied Sarah comfortingly. "It's so much the easiest way."

"But it isn't the right way," said Barbara. "I know it isn't but I do it all the same. I do it and then I'm sorry...and the next time it's even harder."

"Why didn't you write to me, Barbara?" asked Sarah, who thought the subject unlikely to bear fruit. "Why on earth didn't you write and tell me where you were? It was really very naughty of you. You could have trusted me not to give you away."

"Oh yes, I knew that. I knew I could trust you, Sarah."

"Why didn't you write?"

Barbara smiled affectionately. "I meant to write but all sorts of things happened. I got married for one thing."

"You married your publisher?"

"Yes," agreed Barbara, blushing. "Yes, I married Arthur. He had been so kind to me about the books."

"When everyone else was unkind."

"But it wasn't only that," said Barbara hastily. She hesitated and then continued, "Really and truly I meant to write and tell you all about it, but I thought I'd wait for a little...and then I waited too long and that made it difficult. It wasn't that I didn't think about you," explained Barbara. "I thought of you a lot, and I thought of Silverstream. I even thought it would be rather fun to go back to Silverstream and see what everyone was doing, but Arthur wouldn't let me."

"He seems to have some sense," said Sarah dryly.

"I should have had to be disguised, of course," added Barbara in a thoughtful manner.

"Disguised!" exclaimed Sarah, laughing.

"Well, of course," said Barbara. "They didn't like me, did they?"

"No, but really," began Sarah who had had a sudden vision of Barbara wearing a black beard and dark blue spectacles.

"Oh, it was just an *idea*," said Barbara apologetically. "I knew it was silly all the time...I shall never go back, now. It seems like a past life—Silverstream and Copperfield and all that. Tell me about everyone, Sarah."

Sarah complied with this comprehensive request to the best of her ability, and recited the chronicles of Silverstream in her usual fluent and slightly racy manner. It was a chronicle of births, deaths, and marriages interspaced with items of gossip and reports of internecine feuds. The Hathaways had got a new baby. Mrs. Carter had got a new wig, Mrs. Greensleeves had got a husband at last—such was the burden of her tale. She was in the middle of her story and Barbara was listening with all her ears when Arthur Abbott came home.

"Oh Arthur!" cried Barbara, jumping up to greet him. "This is Sarah, Mrs. Walker, you know. She's come to give the bandaging lecture—isn't it a nice surprise?"

"Very nice," said Arthur, shaking hands with his guest. "But hardly a surprise. We were expecting Mrs. Walker, weren't we?"

"But I expected a *woman*," cried Barbara, laughing delightedly.

"Yes," agreed Arthur. He looked at Mrs. Walker again in a puzzled manner.

"We knew each other long ago at Silverstream," put in Sarah.

"Oh, I've got it now," said Arthur. "It certainly is a delightful surprise to expect a stranger and find she's a friend."

Barbara nodded with a pleased expression on her face, for Arthur had done it again. He could always be relied on to unravel her tangles and put things clearly and concisely. She was all the more pleased with Arthur for she wanted Sarah to see how clever he was—he had played up splendidly.

Arthur was quite glad to sit back in his chair while his wife and her friend chatted to each other about old times and mutual friends. Their voices had a soothing effect upon him, and he needed soothing for he had had a troublesome sort of day. Publishing was never a plain sailing sort of business but in war-time the waters were rougher than usual. He thought about a book his firm had just published—*Her Loving Heart* by Janetta Walters—and wished that the firm of Abbott and Spicer was rich enough, and haughty enough, to refuse that sort of book, though as a matter of fact there were precious few publishing firms who would refuse a book by that well-known lady. Her books sold in scores of thousands, her admirers were legion. "High-powered tushery," murmured Arthur Abbott to himself and all at once he chuckled because he had found such an apt description of her work.

"What are you laughing at?" asked Barbara with interest.

"At the idea of a book we have published."

"I like funny books," said Sarah, pricking up her ears.

"But this is not a funny book in *that* sense," said Arthur quickly. "In fact it isn't a funny book in any sense. It is—er—sentimental and romantic. I was merely—er—smiling to myself because I had found the right words to describe it."

"For the blurb," said Sarah complacently. She was rather pleased with herself for having remembered the right word.

"Er—no," replied Arthur, smiling broadly. "Just for my own satisfaction. This particular author writes her own advertisements—or at least her sister writes them. Her sister manages all her business affairs."

"I wish there were more funny books," said Sarah, looking at her hostess as she spoke, for the two funniest books Sarah had ever read had been written by Barbara Buncle.

"No," said Barbara firmly. "I'm too busy, now. I mean my mind is too busy, isn't it, Arthur? There are the children, you see, and the housekeeping—and of course the war."

Arthur smiled at his wife. "But afterwards, when the war is over and the children have gone to school, Barbara will write another book, better and funnier and more successful than the other two put together."

Barbara blushed and said, "Oh, Arthur!" in a voice that showed how truly delighted she was.

Chapter Three
Letters from Egypt

T he following morning at approximately ten o'clock Sarah was sitting in Arthur Abbott's study reading the paper and enjoying herself immensely; not that there was anything very enjoyable in the paper, of course, for the news was indifferent to say the least of it, but because it was such a treat to sit down like this at ten o'clock in the morning instead of having to wash up the dishes and dust the rooms and rack one's brains over housekeeping. It was not that Sarah disliked housekeeping, she was interested in it and did it well, but it is pleasant to have a holiday even from something one likes—so Sarah discovered—it was even pleasant to have a holiday from John.

Sarah was quite horrified at *this* discovery, for she adored John…she was trying to persuade herself that she missed John dreadfully and was longing to return to him when she heard steps in the hall and a girl suddenly appeared in the doorway. The girl looked about twenty-eight (Sarah thought); she was small and slight and was clad in riding breeches and a dark green pullover. She had no hat, and her thick, silky brown hair was blown about by the wind. Her eyes were gray and unusually wide apart and her fair skin was powdered with golden freckles. Sarah liked the look of the girl—or rather the young woman—so she smiled at her.

"Hallo!" exclaimed the young woman in surprise.

"I'm Sarah Walker," said Sarah Walker. "An old friend of Barbara's."

"Oh good! I mean I'm awfully pleased to meet you. I'm Jeronina Abbott—Jerry for short. It's rather a blot to be called Jerry these days but it was too much bother to make everyone change. My husband is Barbara's husband's nephew so I'm really Barbara's niece. Silly, isn't it?"

Sarah hesitated. She realized what the girl meant, of course. Barbara was a babe in some ways, she was the sort of person who never seems to grow old, so it seemed silly that she should have a grown-up niece—but really and truly Barbara was not so very young in years (she must be over forty, thought Sarah, calculating rapidly). Fortunately there was no need to reply to young Mrs. Abbott's question, for she came over and stood on the hearth rug and began to chat in a friendly fashion, and while she chatted Sarah had time to look at her more carefully and to mark with interest that although she was slim and small she looked tremendously strong…she looked tough—if that was not too uncouth a word to apply to an extremely attractive young person.

"I rode over from Ganthorne across the moors," said Jerry. "It's such a lovely ride. Do you like riding? Where's the woman who lectured last night at the Red Cross meeting?"

"I'm the woman," said Sarah, who was getting a little tired of describing herself thus. "I lectured to the meeting and I'm also a friend of Barbara's. I combine the two roles in my own person."

"Goodness!" said Jerry. "The last woman was frightful."

Sarah accepted the compliment without remark.

"Positively frightful," repeated Jerry. "She squashed everybody the moment they opened their mouths—Barbara was terrified of her."

"Does Barbara always put up the lecturers?"

"Nearly always. Of course the committee is supposed to take it in turns but the others find excuses and Barbara is so good-natured that she's left to hold the baby. The Marvells *always* manage to get out of it. Have you met the Marvells?"

Sarah had been introduced to a great many people at the Red Cross meeting but she could not remember the Marvells.

"You haven't met them, then," said Jerry confidently. "You wouldn't forget the Marvells. He's a great big bounding buffalo of a man with a booming voice and an odd sense of humor. He paints, of course, and I believe he's quite good in his way—at least a friend of Sam's says so. I wouldn't know. Mrs. Marvell is the sort of woman who strews herself on the sofa and makes everyone slave for her,"

"You don't seem to like them," commented Sarah.

Jerry laughed. "You've noticed that, have you? It's because they batten on Barbara. I can't bear people to make use of Barbara—she's such a dear, isn't she? So good-natured and kind. As a matter of fact she's my very greatest friend," said Jerry earnestly. "We seem to understand each other so well...but we were talking about the Marvells, weren't we?"

Sarah nodded.

"The parents are bad enough but the children are *worse*. They were like savages when they were young, rushing about the garden and laying booby traps."

"They sound uncomfortable neighbors!"

"They are," said Jerry, nodding vigorously. "Of course they're grown up now so they don't lay booby traps, but they make themselves unpleasant in other ways." She hesitated and then laughed. "I always get worked up about the Marvells— let's change the subject, shall we?"

"With all my heart," agreed Sarah.

"How did the lecture go?" asked Jerry in quite a different voice.

"All right, I think. There were a lot of people there, and

they listened quite peacefully—or at any rate they gave one the impression of listening. I don't flatter myself that they'll remember a word of it, of course. I showed them a Pott's Fracture and—"

"Oh Jerry!" cried Barbara's voice from the door. "Jerry, I'm so glad you've come. I wanted to see you because—"

"I've been talking to Mrs. Walker," began Jerry.

"I've been trying to ring you up," declared Barbara, hugging her niece-by-marriage in an affectionate manner. "They rang and rang and of course there was no answer because you were here."

"And Markie never hears the phone."

"I've got a letter from Sam."

"So have I, darling!" cried Jerry, diving into her pocket and producing a sheaf of thin gray envelopes with dark blue airmail stamps on them. "Look, Barbara, eight all at once!"

"Oh, Jerry, how lovely!"

"No letters for seven weeks," continued Jerry. "I was nearly crazy—and now eight all at once. I feel like a different woman."

"Of course you do!"

"He's perfectly fit and full of beans," said his wife proudly. "He's enjoying himself—I can tell that by the way he writes. Of course he can't tell me much about what he's doing. He just says they are in the desert now, and he's been given command of a small detachment—four tanks, he says."

"Jerry, how splendid!"

"I was reading them all night," continued Jerry, putting the letters back in her breeches pocket and patting them lovingly. "Or at least I was reading them until Markie came in and took away the lamp...we have lamps at Ganthorne Lodge," explained Jerry, turning to Sarah as she spoke, for it had suddenly struck her that Barbara's friend was being left out of the conversation.

"Markie was quite right," said Barbara firmly.

"Well, I don't know," returned Jerry in a thoughtful voice. She had perched herself on the arm of a chair and was swinging her leg and gazing at the toe of her beautifully polished chestnut-brown boot. "I mean why should we do things at the right hours? Why should we go to bed at ten and get up at seven? There doesn't seem much point in it, really."

"Arthur has to catch—"

"Oh, of *course*! It's *quite* different if you have someone coming and going and wanting meals and catching trains. I mean us."

Sarah blinked for she found the conversation a little difficult to follow but apparently Barbara found no such difficulty.

"We must, darling," Barbara told her. "And all the more if it isn't necessary—just like a man changing for dinner when he's in the jungle and there's no other white person for miles. I don't mean we always change for dinner, because now that Arthur is in the Home Guard we've given it up—and anyhow it's only supper, but that *is* a reason, isn't it?"

"Oh definitely," replied Jerry without turning a hair.

"But Barbara," began Sarah in bewildered tones.

"*And* doctors, of course," added Barbara, turning to her old friend with a brilliant smile.

Sarah was stricken dumb.

"I believe you're right," declared Jerry with a serious air. "I mean about keeping to proper mealtimes and all that. Markie and I have been getting awfully slack lately and feeding just when we felt inclined—at least that was the idea. As a matter of fact it doesn't work out that way, because quite often we don't feel inclined to feed at the same moment. For instance I come in ravenous after exercising the horses and find Markie in the middle of turning out the linen cupboard…You see," continued Jerry, turning back to Mrs. Walker and smiling in a friendly fashion. "You see, I keep horses and dig the garden so all my work is out of doors."

"And hens," Barbara reminded her.

"And hens, of course," agreed Jerry.

"She used to run a riding school," said Barbara.

"But it all fell to bits when the war started," said Jerry. "I've only got two horses left—and a pony, of course. The horses are old and not fit for hard work, you see."

Sarah saw. She said, "Do you live there by yourself?"

"I've got Markie," replied Jerry.

"Miss Marks was Jerry's governess," explained Barbara. "She came to live with Jerry because Jerry couldn't get any servants."

"Because Ganthorne is an Elizabethan house with all the Elizabethan drawbacks," said Jerry.

"Ghosts," said Barbara nodding.

"No electric light," said Jerry.

"It must be rather lonely for you," said Sarah, who felt she ought to make some contribution to the conversation.

Barbara and Jerry looked at each other and laughed.

"You had better tell her the whole story," Barbara said.

"Yes," agreed Jerry, wrinkling her brows. "Yes, I'd better. It must be awfully muddling for you. It was like this, you see. When the war started Sam joined up at once. He was in Uncle Arthur's office before that, but he had always wanted to be a soldier."

"He's a born soldier," said Barbara with pride.

"Yes," agreed Jerry. "Yes, he is, really. That was why I didn't try to keep him back...so Sam went off and Markie and I were left—not lamenting, exactly, because—well, because—and then I thought I would shut up Ganthorne Lodge and get a job. I was just on the point of signing up when suddenly a whole battalion of soldiers appeared, practically in the night."

"Like a crop of dragons' teeth," put in Barbara.

"And there I was," added Jerry with an air of finality.

"I see," said Sarah, but she said it without conviction, for why should the arrival of a battalion have prevented young Mrs. Abbott from taking a job?

"It was because Ganthorne Lodge is the only house for miles and miles," said Barbara. "That was why."

"I see," said Sarah faintly.

"Jerry runs a sort of canteen," added Barbara.

"No, Barbara, not really," objected Jerry. "They have their own canteen. I just let them come in when they like, that's all. They're in huts, you see, and it isn't very comfortable for them, especially if it's wet. The men come into the kitchen and sit there and have the wireless, and the officers use the dining room. Markie and I live and move and have our being in the sitting room."

"How good of you!" Sarah said.

"Not really," replied Jerry. "I do it for Sam, you see. I mean they're all soldiers—like Sam."

"Yes," said Sarah.

"Of course I couldn't do it without Markie," continued Jerry. "Markie looks after them. She's a very special sort of person— isn't she, Barbara? She's terribly clever, you know, and yet she's good at housekeeping, too, and does it well and likes doing it. There's practically nothing Markie can't do if she sets her mind to it. She's *good*," declared Jerry, nodding gravely. "Markie is good all through and I believe that's why she's so happy in spite of everything."

Sarah was about to inquire further regarding this paragon of all the virtues, and particularly to inquire what disabilities she suffered from to make her happiness a subject of surprise but she had no opportunity, for Jerry glanced at the clock and said she must fly and was gone in a twinkling.

Chapter Four
Shopping in Wandlebury

B arbara Abbott and Sarah Walker were so delighted with each
other and had so much to talk about that it required very
little persuasion to induce Sarah to prolong her visit for a few
days. She consulted her husband by telephone and received his
assurance that he could manage quite well without her.

"That's lovely," said Barbara. "Of course it will be dull for
you because nothing happens anywhere just now but it will be
a change of air. I think I shall ask one or two people to come to
tea tomorrow."

"Not for me," said Sarah hastily.

"Oh no," agreed Barbara smiling. "But I've been meaning to
ask one or two people for ages and it will be so nice for them
to meet someone new...and the bazaar is this afternoon, so—"

"The bazaar!"

"I shall *have* to go," nodded Barbara. "It would be nice if
you came. You needn't buy anything of course and we shan't
stay long. It's being opened by an author—one of Arthur's
authors—Janetta Walters is her name."

"Goodness!" exclaimed Sarah, who had read some of Janetta's
books and had very little use for them.

"She's a draw," Barbara explained. "They were very lucky
to get her."

"I suppose they were," agreed Sarah. (Personally she would not have gone out of her way to see the author of *Her Prince at Last*—which was one of Janetta's best known works—but she was aware that quite a number of people differed from her in that respect. Janetta's name was well known; her portrait appeared in various weekly and monthly papers—Janetta at her desk, Janetta in her garden, Janetta in her drawing room surrounded with flowers.)

The morning was bright and sunshiny and the two friends sallied forth to do the shopping, Barbara with a large basket on her arm.

"I'm afraid this is dull for you," she said as they emerged from the arched gateway, which had given the house its name, and proceeded toward the town.

"Dear me, no," replied Sarah. "I like seeing new places and it will be interesting to watch somebody else coping with food."

The town of Wandlebury consists mainly of a large square, and for some reason it seemed to Barbara today that she was seeing the square for the first time, seeing it with Sarah's eyes... the wide space, paved with cobblestones, and the fountain in the middle; the pigeons wheeling about or strutting around the stone rim of the fountain with the sun shining on their iridescent plumage.

"It's fascinating!" exclaimed Sarah, pausing and looking around.

Barbara was pleased. She, too, thought it was a fascinating place. She pointed out the county buildings that occupied the south side of the square (they had been designed by Adam and were simple and dignified). She pointed out the ancient Elizabethan hostelry, the Apollo and Boot, which occupied the western side. She pointed out the shops. As they crossed the open space Sarah continued to give vent to her admiration. "It's so spacious," she said. "It's so quiet and peaceful, so dignified. John would go raving mad if he saw those Adam buildings!"

"He must come and see them," declared Barbara, oblivious of the literal meaning of her invitation. She was—as a matter of fact—somewhat *distrait,* for she was most anxious to meet some of her neighbors and introduce them to Sarah. Sarah was so *nice*—it had always been her word to describe Sarah although she was aware that strictly speaking the word meant something different from what she meant when she used it.

"There's a young man smiling at you, Barbara," said Sarah as they made their way toward the butcher's.

"Where?" asked Barbara. "Oh yes, that's Lancreste Marvell. He's on sick leave just now, his mother told me. He's in the air force. It was because of Lancreste that the Marvells couldn't put you up—though as a matter of fact I know they have a perfectly good spare room—but I'm very glad they couldn't—or wouldn't," added Barbara, pressing her friend's arm and hurrying on.

Barbara did not want to talk to Lancreste Marvell for he had been a disappointment to her. When she first came to Wandlebury Lancreste was fifteen. He was tall and fair and beautiful and had the voice of an angel, but these endearing charms had hidden inward wickedness. Yes, he had been a disappointment. Now, of course, Lancreste was grown up; his hair had become mousy and he had cultivated a small moustache that reminded one just a little of Hitler...Barbara nodded to him, quite kindly, and dived into the butcher's shop.

"I've got two shillings and twopence," said Barbara, buttonholing the butcher who was dismembering a sheep. "What could I have for that? And could I possibly have some liver because I've got a friend staying with me."

"You 'ad a piece of liver last week," said the butcher sternly.

"Oh no," cried Barbara. "Honestly I didn't. I haven't had any liver for ages."

"Mrs. Abbott," said the voice of Lancreste from behind her.

"Mrs. Abbott, are you very busy? I mean could I—would you mind—I want to—to introduce a friend of mine."

Barbara was exceedingly busy. She was engaged upon the most important business of the day—and it was not often that one had the good fortune to get hold of Mr. Bones himself—but she relinquished Mr. Bones and smiled at Lancreste, reminding herself that Lancreste was a member of the R. A. F. and was therefore one of the few to whom the many owe so much (though to be sure he had been drafted into the R. A. F. only recently). "Yes, Lancreste," said Barbara vaguely, for she was still wondering how far the two and twopence would go amongst eight people (counting the children) and whether she could persuade Mr. Bones to give her the liver so that they could have a steak and kidney pie. Strictly speaking it would be a steak and liver pie but for some reason that sounded rather nasty. "Yes, Lancreste, of course, but if your friend could wait—I could speak to him later, couldn't I?"

"It's a girl," said Lancreste.

"Oh, I see."

"If you wouldn't mind," he continued, swallowing nervously. "I mean she's waiting outside. She doesn't know anyone at all and you're always so kind."

"Yes, Lancreste," said Barbara, her heart melting a little not only at the compliment but also at the sight of so much embarrassment and distress. "Yes, of course—but I *am* a little busy at the moment. Perhaps you could bring her to tea this afternoon. How would that do?"

"It's the bazaar," he reminded her. "I've got to go to it. Mother has roped me in. I've got to look after Miss Walters and see she has tea and all that."

"That *will* be nice," said Barbara.

"It will be frightful," replied Lancreste. "What am I to say to her? I don't know how to talk to authors."

"Talk about her books, of course."

"But I haven't read any of them!"

"You must borrow one and read it this afternoon."

"I suppose I must," said Lancreste miserably.

"Why did they choose you," began Barbara, for it seemed a strange choice. Mr. Marvell would have entertained Miss Walters very much better; he would have taken her in his stride.

"You may well ask," interrupted Lancreste. "That's what I said to Mother—I said, 'Why pick on me?'…and why on earth was I such a stooge as to say I would do it? I must have been mad."

"It will be all right," said Barbara comfortingly.

He sighed heavily and then continued in a different tone of voice, "So you see I can't do anything about Pearl this afternoon…so if you could just come *now* and let me introduce Pearl…Oh, here she is!"

Here she was, for she had grown tired of waiting outside. She stood at Barbara's elbow, waiting to be introduced and Barbara was obliged to make the best of it. She had been willing to do what she could for Lancreste's friend but when she saw Miss Pearl Besserton she had a feeling that very little could be done—even with the best will in the world—for Miss Besserton was not Barbara's cup of tea. And Barbara was aware that, unless you can find some common ground upon which to meet, there is not much use meeting a person. It was not so much her appearance—though that was startling enough, for she looked as if she had stepped straight off the stage of a third-rate music hall without having taken the trouble to remove the grease paint—it was her personality that alienated Barbara's sympathy. It's no good at all, thought Barbara as she extended her hand and murmured a conventional greeting.

"I'm okay," replied Miss Besserton.

"Pearl is staying in Wandlebury," babbled Lancreste. "She's

taken rooms. It's nice for me having her here when I'm on leave but she's finding it rather dull."

"Dull's the word," said Miss Besserton.

Barbara heard herself issuing a general invitation to come to tea any day that was convenient—she could do no less—and after a few minutes of somewhat strained conversation the two young people left the shop.

"I find I can let you 'ave some liver," said Mr. Bones, who had been waiting for the conversation to end. "It was Mrs. Dance 'oo 'ad the liver last week."

"Oh good!" said Barbara, beaming on him.

"And you can 'ave your ration in steak."

"Splendid!" exclaimed Barbara. "It's exactly what I wanted... and what about a little suet, Mr. Bones?"

"*If* I can manage it, Mrs. Habbott," said Mr. Bones grandly. "*If* I can manage it I will personally see that a few hounces of suet goes with your horder."

Barbara came out into the square and looked up and down, but there was no sign of Sarah. Sarah had vanished completely, and that was a pity because *here* was Mr. Marvell, who was one of the sights of Wandlebury! Barbara greeted him and asked him to tea tomorrow—and Mr. Marvell accepted. She met Archie Chevis-Cobbe (Jerry's brother) and asked him, too, and Archie replied that tea parties were not in his line but he would look in about six and have a chat with Arthur. After that Barbara's tea party grew rapidly, for she met "everybody," and she wanted "everybody" to meet Sarah. What was the use of having a delightful guest and hiding her under a bushel! None at all, thought Barbara as she went on her way, gathering food, meeting people, explaining about Sarah, and scattering invitations right and left. Oddly enough everybody accepted and quite a number of people said might they bring someone else—a son or daughter on leave or a sister who had come down from London for a rest—and to all these requests Barbara replied, "Yes, of course. How nice!" for she was of a hospitable nature.

Meanwhile Sarah had been prowling about the yard at the Apollo and Boot, trying hard to shut her eyes to the very modern streamlined Humber (which belonged to a visiting general and was being washed by his perspiring driver) and to conjure up in its place a coach and four resembling the illustration in John's *Pickwick Papers*. She tried so hard and stood there for so long with her eyes closed that Mr. Grace came out of the bar and asked if she were feeling poorly and suggested a small brandy or a glass of port. Sarah refused politely and said that the sun was very bright…and then she came out into the square and met Barbara face to face.

"My dear!" cried Barbara, seizing her arm. "I thought you were lost!"

Sarah explained what she had been doing—or trying to do—and added that it had not been much of a success, and Barbara, who was always ready to enter into the experiences of her friends with heart and soul, immediately entered into Sarah's.

"It's the smell," said Barbara with conviction. "The smell of petrol. Ghosts hate the smell of petrol. I've often thought that if you wanted to get rid of ghosts (to disinfect a house like they did in the papers the other day) you could do it quite easily by sprinkling petrol about. I wouldn't, of course, because it would be such a waste—and anyhow we haven't any petrol except what Arthur requires for his work—but you see what I mean." Sarah saw.

"I've been looking for you everywhere," continued Barbara. "I've been walking up and down and around and around and meeting everybody I knew—and I've asked them to tea."

"Oh, Barbara!"

"I couldn't help it," explained Barbara apologetically. "It just happened. Have you noticed that if you think of giving a party you either find that nobody can come at all or else everybody can come and wants to bring somebody else? We aren't at the end of it yet," predicted Barbara. "You'll see, Sarah. The telephone will ring and ring and the party will grow and grow."

"But what will you do?" asked Sarah in dismay. "How on earth are you going to feed them?"

"We'll make sandwiches," said Barbara, happily. "There are still some raspberries in the garden...it doesn't matter, really. People don't expect much nowadays."

Chapter Five
The Bazaar

The town hall was decorated with flags and flowers and furnished with several large trestle tables upon which was displayed a curious collection of knickknacks and infants' garments and fancy-work representing the labor of the Wandlebury Ladies' Sewing Party for the last year. As a rule this bazaar was an enormous success and earned large checks that were dispatched to deserving objects with the Wandlebury ladies' compliments but this year things had proved much more difficult, and Barbara—as she looked around the hall—decided that the check would not be as large as usual. There was no dearth of buyers—nor sellers either—the dearth was in the merchandise.

"It's a poor show," yelled Mrs. Fitch to her sister, Miss Wotton, who was as deaf as a post. "Yes, I said it was a poor show."

"It's wonderful," declared Barbara, rounding upon the sisters with flashing eyes. "It's wonderful that there's anything here at all."

"They won't make much," shouted Mrs. Fitch, who was so used to conversing with her sister that she conversed with everybody in the same stentorian tones. "It would have been better not to have it at all—that's what I think."

Barbara had been thinking the same but now she changed her mind and was about to argue the point heatedly when Sarah tugged at her sleeve.

"There will be nothing left to buy," whispered Sarah. "I mean if you want to buy anything."

They pushed on through the crowd, stopping to speak to various people Barbara knew and then pushing on again. Barbara had set out with the benevolent intention of buying something at every stall, and her encounter with Mrs. Fitch had confirmed this intention into a resolution. She bought a duck and a large turnip at the produce stall, and she bought a pair of khaki socks, which would do for Sam. She bought a basket and a black doll made out of a stocking and a tin with spills in it, which would do for Arthur to light his pipe. Sarah was much too wise to offer to relieve her friend of any of these purchases for she was aware that people who bought things at bazaars preferred to carry them, themselves. (She remembered going to a bazaar with Mrs. Featherstone Hogg and how angry she had been with that lady for insisting upon carrying everything that she—Sarah—had bought. Of course everyone had thought that Mrs. Featherstone Hogg had behaved with lavish generosity, and Sarah with unaccustomed meanness.)

Sarah had expected to be slightly bored at the Wandlebury Ladies' Bazaar, but she had forgotten that it was impossible to be bored with Barbara at your side. Barbara was a sort of magnet, she attracted funny little incidents as a magnet attracts steel, and, this being so, Sarah began to enjoy herself in a slightly malicious way. She noticed that, although Barbara's manner was more assured, she was still nervous when it behooved her to speak to people she did not like. It was therefore quite easy to discern which of her neighbors she liked and trusted and which she did not.

"That's Mrs. Dance," said Barbara, gripping Sarah's arm. "I shall have to introduce you to her."

"Why?" inquired Sarah, who felt she could do quite nicely without the lady's acquaintance.

"She's the vicar's wife," hissed Barbara. "And that's Marguerite—her daughter—*she's worse.*"

Marguerite Dance was presiding over the "white elephant" stall, which was by far the best furnished stall in the place. It was really very strange to see the collection of objects people had discarded as being of no further use to them; they ranged in size from a nursery fire-guard to a needle book—without needles in it, of course. Marguerite considered herself a "good saleswoman" and was determined to screw as much out of Mrs. Abbott as she could.

"Oh, Mrs. Abbott!" exclaimed Marguerite with a simpering smile. "I've been keeping these vases specially for you. So very striking, aren't they? Several people wanted to buy them but I managed to head them off."

"They aren't very pretty," said Barbara doubtfully.

"So striking," said Marguerite, handing them over. "And only thirty shillings for the pair. I thought of you the moment I saw them. 'Those will do beautifully for Mrs. Abbott,' I said." Barbara took them and paid for them—there was nothing else to be done.

Meanwhile Sarah, who had been poking about on her own, had discovered a delightful little seascape, its charms somewhat obscured by a cumbersome gilt frame, and as she knew a little about pictures she was not surprised when she discovered that it was signed by a well-known academician. John will like it, thought Sarah, and she asked the price.

"Half a crown," said Marguerite, glancing at it.

"Half a crown!" echoed Sarah in surprise.

"Two shillings, then," said Marguerite hastily.

Sarah was so annoyed with the girl on Barbara's behalf that she handed over the two shillings and put the picture under her arm.

"It's quite a nice frame," said Marguerite, in a patronizing tone. "You could touch it up if you got a little bottle of gilt paint."

"I shall use it for lighting the fire," replied Sarah with a brilliant smile and she hastened after Barbara, who had moved on to another stall.

After having completed this somewhat curious transaction Sarah was assailed by a qualm of conscience (for the money was to go to charity, was it not) but she soothed it away by telling herself that she would give Barbara thirty shillings for the vases and so make everything right. I can't take them home, of course, she thought with a shudder as she looked at them, tucked under Barbara's arm. I shall have to get rid of them somehow—perhaps I could leave them in the train.

"There's Jerry!" exclaimed Barbara in delighted tones. "And Markie, too. I specially wanted you to meet Markie. Isn't it lucky?"

Jerry looked different in her "dressed up" clothes. She looked just a trifle self-conscious. Beside her was a short, thick-set woman in a black coat with gray frizzy hair and a large pale face...so that's the paragon, thought Sarah with amusement. Miss Marks was talking to the vicar (there was no doubt about the vicar for he was more like a vicar than any vicar that Sarah had ever seen in her life) and as Sarah and Barbara approached Miss Marks was saying earnestly:

"But I don't think it is quite right to pray for victory. I just pray that the enemy may be frightened and run away."

"Let their bones turn to water," said Mr. Dance in a booming voice.

"Exactly," agreed Miss Marks. She stepped back a pace as she spoke, for Mr. Dance was the sort of speaker who is more bearable at a slight distance, and as she stepped back she bumped Barbara's arm and one of the hideous vases fell on the floor. It burst like a bomb, scattering pieces far and wide and frightening the bystanders considerably.

"Oh dear!" exclaimed Barbara.

"Oh *dear!*" cried Miss Marks. "Oh, Mrs. Abbott, how clumsy of me! I had no idea there was anybody behind me—I can't tell you how sorry I am. Oh dear, it is most distressing!"

"It doesn't matter," said Barbara hastily. "Please don't worry, Markie. They aren't very pretty and anyhow I've still got one."

"Oh dear!" cried Miss Marks, wringing her hands. "I wouldn't have had this happen for anything—so clumsy—and one vase is no use at all. Would it be possible for me to buy you another, I wonder."

This was a frightful thought and Sarah could not bear it. She bumped against Barbara's elbow and the second vase immediately leapt from the crook of Barbara's arm and flung itself onto the *debris* of its companion.

"There," exclaimed Barbara, somewhat inadequately—and she began to laugh. Everyone laughed, even the people who had been frightened, even Markie was forced to laugh…

Sarah recovered first, perhaps because she was feeling a little guilty. She bent down and began to collect the pieces and she was assisted in this necessary task by a large man in a tweed suit who obviously belonged to the Ganthorne party. She had not been introduced to any of the Ganthorne party, for Barbara had been much too excited to observe the conventions, but the holocaust of vases had broken the ice and made introductions superfluous. The tall man—he was very nice-looking, Sarah noticed—spread his handkerchief on the floor and began to gather the pieces into it.

"Odd, isn't it?" he said in a nice deep bass voice.

"What's odd?" asked Sarah. "Look out, that's an awfully jagged bit!"

"Odd that anyone should have thought them worth making. Must have taken hours to make, I suppose."

"Dusting them, too," suggested Sarah with a sigh.

"Nobody will ever dust them again," he reminded her.

"No," agreed Sarah, picking up two more pieces from under Mr. Dance's large flat feet.

"Their life is over," continued Sarah's assistant, rising from his crouching position and dusting his hands. "They can no longer offend the eye by their excruciating form and lamentable color. May I offer you my congratulations, Mrs.—er—"

"Walker," said Sarah, smiling.

"Oh! *You're* Mrs. Walker!" he exclaimed. "Jerry told me about you—I'm Jerry's brother—Chevis-Cobbe is my name."

"You're a little like Jerry," said Sarah, who had been wondering why his face seemed vaguely familiar.

"We're supposed to be alike, but I can't see it. Let's have tea together, shall we?"

Sarah refused somewhat regretfully. She was aware that Barbara intended to go home to tea.

"Oh well, I shall see you tomorrow," said Mr. Chevis-Cobbe. "Meanwhile I had better dispose of the body." He pushed off through the crowd carrying the handkerchief and its contents very carefully.

"That's Jerry's brother," said Barbara—quite unnecessarily of course. "That's Archie Chevis-Cobbe...and now I must introduce you to Colonel Melton—over there in uniform. He's the colonel of Jerry's battalion," added Barbara, who always referred to the 7th Westshire Regiment in this unorthodox way.

"About the vases, Barbara," began Sarah.

"It doesn't matter a bit," said Barbara firmly and she gave her friend's arm a little squeeze. "Don't worry about the vases—I don't think Arthur would have liked them."

Sarah had intended to explain that she would pay Barbara for the vases—because of the picture still safely under her arm—but she realized in time that the affair was somewhat complicated and decided to wait until they were alone.

"We must go," said Jerry, appearing suddenly from amongst

the crowd with her arms of bulb-bowls and knitted garments. "Markie and I must go or we shall lose the bus. We can't stay and see Miss Walters."

"Oh Jerry!" exclaimed Barbara in dismay.

"It doesn't matter," said Jerry. "Her books are loathsome. I'll look in and see you tomorrow on my way home from the town," and so saying she pushed her way through the crowd and disappeared from view.

"And now we've lost the colonel!" said Barbara. "It's a pity because you would have liked Colonel Melton...but never mind. I must hurry up and buy something from Miss Linton at the cake and candy stall or there will be nothing left."

There was nothing left *now*—so Sarah observed—nothing except a very handsome cake that stood upon a raised block in the middle of the table. This large cake had been baked by Miss Linton with her own hands and for its sake she had given up her personal ration of sugar and butter and dried fruit for three long weeks. Miss Linton explained all this to Barbara in an undertone, and was suitably praised.

"And this is Mrs. Cole," said Barbara, introducing Sarah to a thin toothy woman with a pleasant smile. "Mrs. Cole has done a tremendous lot for the bazaar. She's Mr. Marvell's sister...and here's Mr. Marvell, himself," added Barbara in delighted tones.

Sarah was interested to behold Mr. Marvell. He was a painter, and Jerry had described him as a bounding buffalo. He was certainly very big, and he looked even larger than he really was on account of his somewhat ungainly movements.

"Ah, a cake!" exclaimed Mr. Marvell in a voice that matched his size. "A noble cake, if I may say so!"

Miss Linton simpered. The supererogation of her rations had been hard but she was reaping her reward.

"Is it for sale?" inquired Mr. Marvell.

"No, but you can take a ticket for it, Mr. Marvell."

"A raffle, I suppose."

"Oh no, that's against the law," cried Miss Linton in horrified tones. "You must guess how much it weighs and if you're right you win it."

"And thus the law is fulfilled," boomed Mr. Marvell, fishing in his pocket for a shilling.

"Look!" exclaimed Mrs. Cole. "There she is! I *do* love her books, don't you?"

"Charming," agreed Mr. Marvell, but whether he referred to the books or to their author, who had just appeared on the platform, Sarah could not determine.

"So clean," said Mrs. Cole—and, presumably, it was the books she meant.

"Charming, charming," repeated Mr. Marvell, gazing across the crowded hall and registering admiration and delight.

Miss Walters was certainly easy on the eye. She was small and slight and graceful, and was dressed in pale pink with a frilly sort of collar and a picture hat. Her features were regular and well-formed and she had a delightful pink-and-white complexion. Pretty, thought Sarah, and much younger than I expected... nicer than I expected, too.

There were several other women on the platform—the committee of the WLSP. One of them stepped forward and introduced the speaker in the following terms:

"Ladies and gentlemen, you all know what the bazaar is for. It's for home missions this year. Home missions have got to go on in war-time, in fact they are—er—more important than ever so we want to raise as much money as we possibly can, because—er—because it's so very important to keep home missions going. We mustn't let them down. I am not going to say any more because I know everyone will do their best and of course you are all longing to hear what Miss Janetta Walters is going to say...and of course I am, too. We are all very pleased and proud to have Miss Walters here today to speak to us. She has come over from Foxstead on purpose to—to speak to us and it really is very good of her to come, because we all know how busy she is. It must take a long time to write books—especially books like Miss Walters's, which everyone enjoys so much—so it really is very good of her to spare a little time to come and speak. I'm sure you'll all agree."

Loud clapping proclaimed that everyone agreed. The chairwoman smiled complacently, waited for the noise to subside, and then continued:

"I'm not going to say any more because of course no one wants to listen to me when they can hear Miss Walters, but I just want to say how grateful we are to everyone who has helped us, and sent flowers to decorate the hall and—and decorations. And of course we are grateful to all the people who helped to decorate it. Everyone has taken such a lot of trouble, in fact everyone has been quite splendid, and I feel sure we shall raise *ever* so much more than we expect for home missions—or— well, I won't keep you any longer because I know you all want to hear Miss Janetta Walters." Miss Walters came forward. She looked a little shy, Sarah thought, and liked her all the better for it. There really was something very attractive about her, and her voice was pleasant and clear. She made quite a neat little speech, Sarah thought.

Chapter Six
Miss Janetta Walters

T here were two young men in air-force blue waiting for Miss Walters when she stepped off the platform; for Lancreste had been fortunate enough to run across a friend in the Apollo and Boot, to which hostelry he had repaired—just before the bazaar opened—to obtain a little Dutch courage for his part in the proceedings. It had not been easy to induce Tom Ash to come, but Lancreste had used all his persuasive powers, and these, reinforced by a couple of whiskies and sodas, had done the trick. Mr. Ash was a few months older than Lancreste; he was a lieutenant and sported pilot's wings. He had flown over Germany fourteen times. He had been to Berlin and Wilhemshaven. Ham, Cologne, and several other centers of Axis industry had been the worse for Mr. Ash's attentions...on two occasions Mr. Ash had descended by parachute from a disabled plane. All these things Mr. Ash had accomplished without turning a hair for they were merely part of his job—but he had never taken tea with an author before. The effect of the whiskies and sodas and of Lancreste's eloquence was wearing off and Mr. Ash was nervous. "Great snakes, I must have been dotty," he whispered to himself as he followed Miss Walters and Lancreste to the tea room.

The tea room was empty. They settled themselves at a table

in the corner and ordered tea—at least Lancreste ordered it; Mr. Ash seemed to have lost the use of his tongue.

"Ash is a pilot," Lancreste said. "Ash goes to Germany and all that. Don't you, Ash?"

"Yes," said Ash.

"How interesting!" exclaimed Miss Walters.

"Ash baled out in the drink the other day. Didn't you, Ash?"

"Yes," said Ash.

Miss Walters looked a trifle puzzled.

"Tell her about it, Ash," said Lancreste.

They waited for him to begin but, despite anguished glances from his friend and a couple of somewhat painful kicks on the shin bone, Ash remained as dumb as an oyster. If the author had been an elderly woman Ash might have been able to speak to her, but she was much younger than he had expected and quite good looking with fair hair and rather nice brown eyes. The effect was spoilt—or so Ash thought—by her fluffiness. She had fluffy hair in curls and fluffy clothes. Ash liked good lines. His bomber—he called her Sybil—had marvelous lines. She was his only love. He compared Miss Walters with Sybil to the detriment of the former.

All this time Lancreste had been struggling manfully with the conversation. He had been struggling so hard that Miss Walters had no chance of taking a hand in it and putting him at his ease, but now Lancreste had shot his bolt, he had exhausted the subject of the weather and he could think of nothing more to say. There was a jar of sweet peas on the table. Miss Walters leaned forward and smelt them.

"They're your favorite flowers," said Lancreste with sudden inspiration.

"How did you know?" Miss Walters inquired.

"Mother knew—and Mrs. Cole. She's my aunt. That's why she put them there."

"How thoughtful of her!" said Miss Walters smiling.

"I've read one of your books," continued Lancreste, swallowing nervously. "The Duke of Something or other, it was called."

Miss Walters looked a little surprised. She did not recognize her story under this curious title.

"*You* know," said Lancreste desperately. "It's about a fellow called Edward who dies of pneumonia—at least he doesn't actually die—because he takes off his coat and wraps up the girl in it."

"*Her Prince at Last,*" murmured Miss Walters.

"Yes," said Lancreste, nodding. "Yes, that was it. Aunt Edith gave it to me to read—she's my aunt, you know. I told you that, didn't I?"

"Yes," said Miss Walters doubtfully.

"I read it this afternoon," said Lancreste proudly. "I just skimmed through it, you know, and—"

"I've read two of them," said Ash in a husky voice.

They were both pleased to hear him speak—Lancreste especially.

"Which did you like best?" asked Miss Walters smiling at Ash in an encouraging manner.

"I didn't like either of them," said Ash.

Miss Walters was surprised. She was aware that the English-speaking world contained people who did not care for her work, but never before had she met one of these people in the flesh—not so far as she knew. Reviewers were sometimes unkind, but reviewers were different...Miss Walters stared at Mr. Ash with her mouth slightly open and her tea cup, from which she had been about to drink, poised in the air. Lancreste was equally surprised and much more upset. He lashed with his foot in the direction of his friend's legs but could find nothing to kick, for Mr. Ash, in his excitement, had curled his feet around the legs of his chair.

"Well, you asked me," said Ash. "I mean—well—you asked

me, didn't you? I wouldn't have read them but there wasn't anything else to read—it was in hospital, you see."

"Most people like my books," said Miss Walters faintly.

"Most people are saps," said Ash.

There was a short but pregnant silence. Miss Walters had a feeling that she ought to be angry, or offended, or deeply wounded, but strangely enough she was none of these. She was—yes, she was *interested*.

"But why—" she began.

"Oh, well," interrupted Ash, running his finger around the inside of his collar that all at once seemed to have become too tight. "Oh well—of course I know lots of people like the soppy stuff—I mean of course we know they do."

"Mother likes them," babbled Lancreste. "So does Aunt Edith. Don't listen to Ash. He's mad. Have a cake, Miss Walters."

"I'm not mad."

"You are mad. I wouldn't have asked you if I'd known. You ought to be locked up. Aunt Edith would be simply livid if she knew—if she thought."

"But Marvell."

"Hold your tongue for the love of Mike!"

"You wanted me to talk."

"I don't, now," declared Lancreste. "I've changed my mind. Have a bun, Ash."

"No, thank you."

Another silence ensued but Miss Walters felt she could not leave the subject. She had heard too little—or too much. It was a mystery—so Miss Walters felt—and unless she could clear it up it would remain in her mind and haunt her for the rest of her life.

"But why?" said Miss Walters again. "Weren't you interested in the characters, Mr. Ash?"

"They aren't real," replied Ash shortly.

"Not real!" echoed their creator in surprise.

"They're like people out of a fairy tale—not human at all…I suppose it's difficult for you," continued Ash more kindly. "I suppose you sit in your study—or wherever it is you sit—and write for hours and hours. You haven't time to go out and bump up against real live people and see what they're like. You're a sort of fairy-tale person yourself, aren't you?"

"Am I?"

"Oh, definitely. I mean look at the stir you make wherever you go: Everyone nudging each other and saying, 'There she is. That's Miss Janetta Walters, the authoress.' Everyone bowing and scraping and saying how wonderful you are…"

"Ash, for Heaven's sake!" cried Lancreste.

"As a matter of fact you *are* rather wonderful," continued Ash thoughtfully. "I mean I thought I knew exactly the sort of person you would be, but you aren't like that at all. I bet you could write something really decent if you tried."

Miss Walters hesitated. She made a considerable income by the books—so heartily despised by this extraordinary young man—and she and her sister lived in comfort, not to say luxury, upon their proceeds. She hesitated whether or not to disclose this interesting fact to the extraordinary young man but eventually decided not to do so. I don't write for money, she thought. At least…

"You must have gone off your chump," Lancreste was saying. "Aunt Edith will skin me alive if she gets wind of this. I wish to heaven I'd never set eyes on you."

"But Marvell," said Ash in reasoning tones. "She asked me to tell her. She *asked* me to tell her, Marvell."

"Shut up," said Lancreste.

"It's just the plots," said Ash. "I may as well go on—"

"If you say another word I'll strangle you."

"She *asked* me," muttered Ash.

Chapter Seven
Archie Chevis-Cobbe

B arbara Abbott's gigantic tea party was over and she and Sarah were left alone in the disordered drawing room.

"It looks as if there had been a battle," Barbara remarked.

"It feels like it, too," replied Sarah, sinking into a chair.

"Everyone enjoyed themselves," said Barbara with a sigh. "There wasn't enough food but that didn't seem to matter."

"It didn't matter in the least."

"You were splendid, Sarah. I wish I could talk to people like that."

Sarah was about to disclaim any part in the success of the entertainment when the door opened and Mr. Chevis-Cobbe walked in.

"Oh, Archie!" cried Barbara. "I'd forgotten all about you. I'm afraid there isn't anything to eat."

"I didn't come to eat," replied Mr. Chevis-Cobbe with a smile.

"You came to see Arthur," said Barbara. "I'll go and find Arthur and tell him you're here."

Sarah was quite pleased to renew her acquaintance with Jerry's brother, for the few words they had exchanged over the broken vases had given them a good start; and Sarah was anxious to explain the whole matter of the vases and the picture to the young man so that he should understand why she had felt at liberty to take such a very strong line. She explained, and Archie understood at once—which showed that she had not been mistaken in him—he examined the picture and congratulated Sarah on her find.

"Try it with a mount and a narrow white frame," suggested Archie, screwing up his eyes and looking at it in a knowledgeable way.

Having settled the fate of the picture they spoke of other matters. "What did you think of Miss Walters?" Archie wanted to know.

"I was surprised," replied Sarah. "I thought she was most attractive."

"Why were you surprised?"

"She was different from what I had expected."

Archie hesitated for a moment and then he laughed. "I went and bought all her books—all that I could get hold of—I suppose it was rather silly."

"Hadn't you read them before?"

"No, I haven't much time for reading."

"I'm afraid you may be a little disappointed," said Sarah thoughtfully.

There was no chance to say any more for Barbara returned with her husband and the children (who had been waiting in the nursery until the tea party was over and they could have their usual romp) but Sarah was so interested in her new acquaintance that, after he had gone, she asked Barbara to tell her more about him, and Barbara was only too ready to comply with the request.

Archie Chevis-Cobbe was a little older than Jerry—about thirty-two, Barbara thought. They were tremendous friends, and were really devoted to one another but sometimes they were very rude to one another and quarreled with a ferocity that was a trifle alarming.

("You never had any brothers or sisters, Barbara," put in Sarah.)

When Archie was very young he had been a gay spark and had gone the pace but now he had mended his ways and settled down. The change in Archie dated from the death of his aunt, Lady Chevis. She left him Chevis Place on condition that he took the name of Chevis—he had been Archie Cobbe before— and from that moment Archie had become a different person. It was not because he had changed his name, of course, it was because he had inherited the property and with it a great deal of money. Archie had always wanted Chevis Place and now he had got what he wanted. He was one of those people who are improved by responsibility. "He's nice, now," said Barbara, using her favorite word of praise, and she added, "Arthur likes him," which was the highest praise of all.

"Wasn't he nice before?" asked Sarah with interest.

"He was rather a nuisance," replied Barbara. "Jerry used to worry about him a good deal...but young men are often wild. There was nothing really bad about him, you know."

"Go on," said Sarah.

Barbara continued her tale. She explained that Archie was a bachelor. Barbara had done her best to marry Archie—not to marry him herself, of course, for she had a perfectly good husband already—to marry Archie to a really nice girl.

She had trotted out every girl she could lay her hands on, but it was no use. Archie was wedded to Chevis Place; it absorbed all his attention, so he had no time for a wife. It was a pity, of course, for Chevis Place needed a mistress—but what could you do?

"Nothing," said Sarah, smiling. "I mean if you couldn't find Archie a wife nobody could. You paired off everybody of marriageable age in Silverstream."

Chevis Place was well worth the care and thought lavished upon it by its new master. It was a stately mansion in the early

Tudor style, surrounded by fine old trees. Queen Elizabeth had spent a few days at Chevis Place during one of her royal progressions. Her visit was authenticated by an old account book that showed Sir Godfrey Chevis had spent a good deal of money in furbishing up his house and laying in stocks of food to entertain the royal lady and her train. Since those far-off days the house had undergone alterations. It had been endowed with bathrooms and electricity, and although this detracted from its interest it had added considerably to its comfort...And after all (said Barbara) if you happen to be the person living in the house, convenience is more important than history.

There was a great deal of land attached to Chevis Place, land that had belonged to the Chevis family for hundreds of years, and when Archie inherited the property he discovered that most of the land was leased to neighboring farmers. This might have been quite satisfactory if the land had been properly cared for by the tenants, but it had been neglected and misused and was rapidly becoming derelict. Archie could not bear to see his precious inheritance in such a condition so he decided to farm the land himself, and to farm it in the latest and most scientific manner, and gradually, as the leases expired, he took over one farm after another and got it into trim. Tractors and ploughs and reapers of the latest pattern made their appearance at Chevis Place; hedges were mended and ground that had been allowed to become a wilderness of thistles was ploughed up and made to yield crops. All this had cost money, of course, and for a time there was little return, but, after some years of fostering care, the farms began to thrive.

"Clever of him," said Sarah thoughtfully.

"More than clever," declared Barbara. "It's been terribly hard work and he's had all sorts of disappointments and setbacks, but he's never lost heart."

This was Barbara's tale, and although it was all true, it was not quite complete, for there were certain aspects of Archie's life Barbara did not know, which nobody knew except Archie himself. Only he knew of the hundred and one mistakes he had made—due to lack of experience—and of how he had taken them to heart and labored to rectify them. Only he knew how near disaster he had been, how the money had rolled out and none had rolled in until he was on the verge of bankruptcy... and then, quite suddenly, the tide had turned and he realized that he was safe. The farms began to pay and the fine herd of Jerseys that grazed in the meadow near the stream grew larger and more productive.

He was safe, but he was by no means satisfied, for there was always more to do, more improvements to be made in the working of the farms, more improvements on the land. There was the bog, for instance, fifteen acres of unproductive land in the very middle of his property—it had always been an eyesore to Archie, but he had been too busy with other matters to do anything about it. Now that he was safe he could tackle the bog; he could drain it. Archie was about halfway through his ambitious scheme when Hitler marched into Poland.

"War!" said Archie to himself. "Good Lord, what a mess! What am I to do? I must go, of course...but how can I go? Good Lord, this is awful!"

He spent several very uncomfortable days and sleepless nights worrying about the war and the farms and the bog... two people seemed to be quarrelling inside him, he was swayed first one way and then the other. At last he could bear it no longer and he decided to consult someone else, some unprejudiced person who could see both sides of the question and settle it once and for all. I shall ask Arthur Abbott, thought Archie. He's thoroughly sound. I shall leave it to him and do whatever he says is right.

Archie rode over to Wandlebury the same day—it was a

Sunday—and, finding Arthur alone in his study he explained the whole thing. "Am I to go or not?" inquired Archie. "Is it my duty to go or to stay and get on with the work?"

"Stay where you are," replied Arthur without a moment's hesitation.

"But look here."

"You're a specialist," said Arthur. "You're a valuable person."

"No."

"Oh, I don't mean valuable in yourself, but valuable to the country. You're getting twice as much out of the land as an ordinary farmer, aren't you?"

"A third more, perhaps."

"We shall need it."

"But look here, I'm perfectly fit."

"I tell you we need our farmers. Just wait till the U boats get into their stride. We shall need every ounce of food that this country is capable of producing."

"I hoped you'd say I should go," said Archie, who had just discovered this interesting fact.

"Well, I don't say anything of the kind," replied Arthur flatly.

Arthur had been right, of course—time had proved him right—but it had not been easy for Archie to take his advice and stay at home. All his friends had joined the forces; many of them had been killed. There had been a certain amount of unpleasantness to bear—hints and innuendos that had found their way to Archie's ears—but the fields had been his comfort for they had burgeoned and filled his barns to overflowing.

As for the house, Archie shut up the best part of it and retired to the gun room with his personal belongings. The house was unsuitable for a hospital or for evacuees so he was left to his own devices...he cooked his own breakfast and made his own bed and the wife of his head cowman came in daily and "did" for him. He was perfectly satisfied with Mrs. Frith and with her arrangements for his comfort, nor did he mind being alone at night for if there were ghosts at Chevis Place they did not show themselves to Archie.

The following morning, when Barbara was listening to the American news, which she always found extremely interesting, she was interrupted by the entrance of Lancreste Marvell. It was a pity Sarah was not here to talk to Lancreste, for Sarah was so good at talking to people, but Sarah had gone to Wandlebury to do some shopping and could not be expected back for some little time. Barbara turned off the wireless regretfully and welcomed Lancreste as warmly as she could.

"I don't know if you really meant me to come," said Lancreste doubtfully. "I mean sometimes people say 'come' and they don't really want you to come at all."

"Of course I wanted you to come," declared Barbara.

She disliked telling lies—even very white ones like this—but Lancreste looked so dejected.

"I meant to bring Pearl, of course," added Lancreste, who seemed to have got hold of the erroneous idea that he would have been more welcome if he had brought her.

"It doesn't matter," said Barbara hastily—and, before he could say any more upon the subject, she changed it by inquiring how he had got on at the bazaar.

"The bazaar?" said Lancreste, looking at his feet.

"You were going to have tea with Miss Walters, weren't you?" Barbara inquired.

"Yes," said Lancreste.

"Didn't you have tea with her?"

"Yes," said Lancreste.

"How did you get on?" asked Barbara in encouraging tones.

Lancreste was silent.

"Did you talk to her about her books?" asked Barbara,

pursuing the subject for the sole reason that she could think of nothing else to say.

"Ash did," said Lancreste in a husky sort of voice.

"Ash?"

"He was there too. I asked him."

"Oh, I see! You asked a friend to help you. That was a splendid idea."

Lancreste said nothing.

"A splendid idea," repeated Barbara desperately. "I'm sure you must have entertained Miss Walters beautifully—you and your friend."

Lancreste was completely dumb. He was staring at his boots as if he had never seen them before and did not like the look of them.

Oh dear, I wish Sarah was here, thought Barbara. Aloud she said politely, "How is your mother, Lancreste?"

"She's all right," said Lancreste.

"Splendid," said Barbara. "I'm so glad…and your father?"

"He's all right."

Barbara was about to express her delight at this excellent piece of news when Lancreste suddenly came to life.

"Pearl's ill," he said.

"Oh dear!" exclaimed Barbara, changing her expression rapidly to suit the case. "Oh dear, what a pity!"

"It's frightful," declared Lancreste. "It isn't only her being ill, though that's bad enough. Everything has gone wrong. You liked her, didn't you?"

"I only saw her for a few moments," Barbara reminded him.

"But you liked her—I could see that at once. Mother doesn't like her."

Barbara was not as surprised as Lancreste seemed to expect. She murmured, "What a pity!" and left it at that.

"And Father doesn't like her either."

"Doesn't he?"

"No, he was frightfully rude to her," said Lancreste miserably.

Barbara was just going to say what a pity, but she remembered she had said that before so she said, "How very unfortunate!"

"But I can't help that," declared Lancreste. "I mean I can't help whether they like her or not, I'm going to marry her."

"But Lancreste."

"I *must* marry her," said Lancreste more miserably still. "There's nothing else for it. I suppose once we're married she'll be different."

"Different!" echoed Barbara, for she could not understand the matter at all. If Lancreste did not think Miss Besserton quite perfect why did he want to marry her?

"Once we're married she'll settle down, won't she?" said Lancreste hopefully.

"Settle down!"

"And I won't love her so much."

"You won't love her so much," repeated Barbara in amazement. She knew she was behaving like a parrot but she could not help it—and Lancreste was too upset to notice.

"I know it sounds odd," admitted Lancreste, "but as a matter of fact I couldn't go on loving Pearl like I do now. I'm miserable when I'm with her and I'm miserable when I'm away from her. I'm miserable all the time. I'm sure I shall go mad. I'm mad now, of course. It's mad to come and talk to you like this but there's nobody else. Nobody understands or cares."

"Oh, Lancreste."

"Nobody," repeated Lancreste. "Nobody cares a hoot. Even Pearl doesn't care. She thinks I'm silly—I expect she's right but I can't help it. Perhaps we'd get on better if we were married."

"I don't think so," said Barbara.

Lancreste paid no attention. "She says she'll marry me if I like," he declared. "At least that's what she said this morning.

She may have changed her mind again by tomorrow—she keeps on changing her mind and it's driving me mad. I don't know where I am with her..."

"Look here, Lancreste," began Barbara.

"No," he said, interrupting her. "No, it's no use. I'll just have to marry her and hope for the best. She's ill—I told you that, didn't I?"

"Yes."

"Yes, ill in bed—and the rooms are awful. They didn't look so bad when we took them and of course we thought she'd be out most of the time. I thought Mother would ask her—but Mother won't—and there she is in bed. I don't know what's the matter with her. She won't let me get the doctor."

"I'll go and see her, Lancreste," Barbara said. It seemed the only thing to say.

"Oh, Mrs. Abbott!" cried Lancreste. "Oh, if only you *would!*"

"I'll get my hat," said Barbara.

As they walked along the street together toward Miss Besserton's rooms Lancreste continued to talk about her, and (although his tale was extremely incoherent) a sort of composite picture of the unfortunate affair formed itself bit by bit in Barbara's mind. He had met Pearl at a party in London and had fallen for her suddenly and completely. One moment she had meant nothing to him at all (she was just an ordinary girl that he had been introduced to at a party) and the next moment he was a slave. The odd thing was he appeared to have very few illusions about her; he seemed to realize she was as hard as nails and completely selfish, but still he was her slave, bound to her chariot wheels by chains of steel.

Barbara listened. She did not understand the affair in the least, but that was not her fault. She did her best for Lancreste by listening intently...and as a matter of fact she was so unselfconscious by nature that it was easy to tell her things, so Lancreste found.

Miss Besserton was lying in bed. She looked ill, but not very ill, and she had not omitted to paint her face, which was a good sign, Barbara thought. The room was awful—as Lancreste had said. It was untidy and sordid; the dressing table was covered with powder; garments lay about in confusion upon every available chair. Lancreste hovered around in an embarrassed manner, asking if he should open the window or light the gas fire or bring another pillow.

"Do go away, Lanky," said Miss Besserton, waving her hand.

"I'll wait in the hall," said Lancreste humbly and he disappeared.

Barbara moved some stockings off a chair and sat down near the bed. "I'm so sorry you're ill," she said sympathetically.

"I'm miserable," said Pearl. "Oh, it isn't because I'm ill. There's nothing much the matter with me—it's just a chill or something. I'm miserable and I'm sick of everything—you know how you get sometimes."

"Yes," said Barbara, but she said it doubtfully for she could not remember feeling sick of everything. There was always so much to do and so many interesting people to see…but of course I'm lucky, thought Barbara.

"I get like that sometimes," continued Pearl. "It's my temperament. I'm very artistic, you see. I get so as I feel I want to scream at people. Lanky drives me mad."

"He's very fond of you."

"Oh yes, I know. We're going to get married soon."

"Why?" asked Barbara.

Pearl laughed. "That's a funny question! You got married yourself, didn't you?"

"But if he drives you mad," began Barbara patiently.

"Not all the time, he doesn't. Lanky can be quite good company sometimes."

Barbara was speechless.

"I've knocked about a lot," continued Pearl. "I left home

when I was seventeen. It was too dull. Me and another girl took a flat in town—two rooms and a kitchen. We were in business," she added.

"What kind of business?" asked Barbara.

"Stockings," replied Pearl, adding defiantly, "Lots of nice girls go into business nowadays."

"Of course," agreed Barbara.

"We had a good time," continued Pearl, smiling reminiscently. "We went about a lot, but after a bit I got fed up with Joan. It would have taken a saint to live with Joan...always chipping at me, she was. Always on at me to keep the place tidy. I'd had enough of that sort of thing at home and I told her so."

There was a little silence. Barbara looked around the room. She had a feeling that she could sympathize with Joan.

"After that I moved about," continued Pearl. "Lodgings and hostels—there isn't much to choose between them as far as I can see. In hostels the girls are so nosey you can't call your soul your own. In lodgings there's always a fuss about one thing or another."

It sounded incredibly dreary and Barbara was sorry for her. "Why don't you go home?" she asked.

"I should hate it," Pearl replied. She humped herself about in the bed and added, "I don't know why I'm so unlucky, I'm shore."

Chapter Eight
Sophonisba Marks

When Jerry stated that Markie was happy in spite of everything, she had said no more than the truth. Markie was elderly and deaf, she suffered from rheumatism and was poor in worldly goods but these disabilities, which might have affected the spirits of a woman of lesser breed, had no power to affect the inward happiness of Sophonisba Marks. To understand this enigma it is essential to know something of the history of Miss Marks. Very few people knew her history—practically nobody except herself—because, although friendly, she was reserved. She was one of those somewhat mysterious people that other people take for granted. There she was—elderly, plain, and kindly—as if she had materialized from the atmosphere full-fledged. Looking at her, one could not imagine her as a child, helpless and uncontrolled. One could not imagine her as a girl, young and pretty and slim. In short one could not imagine Miss Marks in any way different from what she was in the late summer of nineteen forty-two. But of course she had a history—even the most uninteresting people have histories and Miss Marks was not uninteresting. Her history was one of hard work and abnegation, of disappointments and anxieties.

Sophonisba was the daughter of a minister in the Scottish Presbyterian Church. She was born the very day upon which

Britain secured "peace with honor" by the diplomacy of Lord Beaconsfield, but, as Mr. Marks was a devoted follower of Mr. Gladstone, this interesting circumstance was only discovered by Sophonisba when she was in a position to discover it herself. She was an only child, at a time when only children were exceedingly rare, and was brought up in a small parish in East Fife. Later she went to St. Andrews University, where she took honors in Arts and History and on the strength of these attainments she was offered an extremely good post. The skies seemed bright and clear that summer. She was busy and happy and the path of life stretched out before her in the sunshine. Then Mrs. Marks died and Sophonisba gave up her career and returned to the manse to keep house for her father.

It would not have been such a serious blow if she had had anything in common with her father, but he was a narrow-minded man and difficult to deal with. He missed his wife and Sophonisba did not fill the gap—she did not understand him. He did not understand her either, of course. He saw her going about her duties cheerfully with a pleasant smile, and it would have taken a more perspicacious individual than Mr. Marks to guess at the disappointment, the misery, the sense of frustration that warred in her bosom. Years passed and with them Sophonisba's youth. She was thirty-four when Mr. Marks became ill. She nursed him for months. They were nearer, then, than they had ever been, for they appreciated each other. He bore his pain with fortitude, with a steady courage that won him her admiration. She won his respect for her devotion to his service. When her father died Sophonisba found herself penniless (the sale of the furniture covered a few small debts and paid for the funeral). She was not surprised, of course, for she knew her father pretty well by this time; he was not the sort of man who could save; he thought it a sin to worry about the future. If anyone had suggested to him that it was his duty to provide for his daughter, who had given up her career on his account, he would have replied: "Consider the lilies of the field," or perhaps, more sternly, "The Lord will provide," but Sophonisba was not a lily, she required clothes and food, so it was necessary to toil and spin. She managed to get a post in a girls' school near Bournemouth and was there for years, teaching history and literature and other things no less important that were not set out upon the prospectus of "Wheatfield House." She had become "Markie" now.

Nobody called her by her Christian name—indeed nobody knew what it was. The girls, who found time to be interested in the matter, looked at her neat signature on their papers and decided that it was probably Susan, or Sarah—the idea that it might be Sylvia made them giggle. During those years at Wheatfield House hundreds of girls passed through Markie's life, they respected her and loved her and occasionally laughed at her, and then they left and forgot all about her. But sometimes when two or three of them were gathered together they would discuss old times and one of them would say, "D'you remember Markie? Wasn't she a dear?"

Markie stayed at Wheatfield House until the head mistress retired and a new broom was appointed in her place, and then, because she did not approve of the changes being made, she left the place and took up private teaching. Her first post was with the Cobbes at Ganthorne Lodge; she was there until Jerry grew up, and then she left and went to the Glovers at Sunbury. She went from post to post, but each time she left one post it was a little more difficult to find another. Her references were excellent and she was a highly qualified teacher but she was getting on in years and she was slightly deaf. Markie began to get a little frightened. The money she had managed to save would not last very long—it was melting away rapidly. What was to become of her? Who wanted an old deaf governess?

She was nearing the end of her tether and envisaging the future with dismay when she received a letter from Jerry Cobbe. The letter was not as cheerful as usual and was even more badly phrased and spelt—for Jerry had not profited as much as she might have done from Markie's painstaking instruction.

"*I'm in dispair,*" wrote Jerry. "*It's really desperite. I can't get servants anyhow or if I manige to get them to come they won't stay. Of course I love Ganthorne but you know what it is with lamps and everything. I don't know what I'm going to do.*"

Markie shook her head over this letter. Two spelling mistakes and a total disregard for punctuation. Jerry was incorrigible...but she was quite the dearest pupil Markie had ever had. "I wonder..." said Markie to herself in a thoughtful manner. She looked around the horrible little bedroom with its sloping roof and sliding window and decided that there was no time to wonder—she must act—and taking up her pen she wrote off at once saying that she was out of a job at the moment and, if Jerry liked, she would come to Ganthorne and help to run the house. She would come for a week or two and see how it worked. What did Jerry think of the idea?

Markie sat down to wait for a reply but she did not wait long. She received a wire the following day saying, "Come at once."

It was a great relief to find that somebody wanted her, that she was not utterly and completely useless. Of course Jerry did not want her as a governess, nor even as a companion. Jerry wanted somebody to cook and clean the rooms. Markie had no illusions at all, she was aware that she was going back to Ganthorne as a cook-general.

It is just as well that I can cook, thought Markie a trifle bitterly as she packed her box. But once at Ganthorne the bitterness vanished and she settled down to her new job. It was different work, but it was just as important in its way. She was providing food for Jerry's body instead of Jerry's mind—and Jerry was such a dear.

Nearly eight years had passed since Markie had come back to Ganthorne and she was still there. She had suggested leaving once or twice, in a tentative sort of way, not because she wanted to leave Ganthorne, but just to see how Jerry felt about it (for her greatest fear was that she might become an incubus) and each time she had mentioned the matter Jerry had implored her to stay, had implored her in such a manner as to leave no doubts as to her sincerity. Markie had suggested leaving when Jerry married Sam Abbott, and they had both implored her to stay. "We can't do without you," Jerry had declared and Sam had backed her up, saying earnestly, "If you're bored with us take a holiday, but for goodness' sake come back."

Markie was not bored with them. She adored them both. She did not want a holiday—where would she go? She was perfectly happy cooking and cleaning and mending...and of course there was no need to allow one's brain to rust because one brushed the carpets and prepared the meals—dear me, no! Markie read history (history had always been her subject); she studied ethnology and anthropology with pleasure and diligence. She delved into the works of Blumenbach, Flower, Keane, and Dixon as she waited for the kettle to boil, and digested their theories as she dried the plates and put them away on the rack. Sometimes her fine strong capable hands hesitated in their task as a particularly interesting theory and a hitherto unrelated fact clicked together in her mind...

The war, the departure of Jerry's husband, and the arrival of the 7th Westshires made changes at Ganthorne but the changes came gradually and Markie took them in her stride. She was not the only person whose life was completely revolutionized by the war and who accepted the revolution without question.

On this particular afternoon toward the end of August Markie was busier than usual for she had decided to give Jerry's bedroom a thorough clean. She had turned it out methodically—as was her way—and now she gathered up the cretonne covers, which she had taken off the chairs, and bore them down to the wash house. She was not in the least surprised to find three soldiers there (in fact she would have been surprised to find it empty). One was shaving, one was scrubbing his equipment at the sink, and the third was sitting on an upturned bucket playing "Home Sweet Home" on a mouth organ. They all greeted Markie cordially and the one at the sink—who was Colonel Melton's batman—turned around with a smile and said he was "through." He and Markie were particular friends because they had both seen light for the first time in the Kingdom of Fife—it was a strong bond between them.

"I'll wash it out for you," he said, suiting the action to the word. "I've mended the plug. I got a wee bit of chain from the quarty."

"Thank you, Fraser," said Markie, smiling back at him. She put the covers to soak and went into the kitchen, and here she found more soldiers. One was sitting at the table writing a letter, two were reading, another had taken his rifle to pieces and was cleaning the barrel carefully and whistling through his teeth. Markie sat down at the table and began to peel potatoes.

There was no real need for Markie to cook the supper in the kitchen (when she and Jerry had decided to give the soldiers the run of the back premises they had turned the pantry into a kitchenette and installed a gas cooker for which cylinders of gas were procured) but Markie was of an economical nature and it seemed to her exceedingly wasteful to use gas when there was a perfectly good fire in the kitchen range. She therefore used the kitchen for what she called "hard cooking" and the gas stove in the pantry for sauces and omelets and last minute odds and ends.

"I'll peel those potatoes," said the man who was reading near the fire. "You leave those to me. I'm a dab at the job. I always do them for the missus when I'm at home."

"How is she, Willis?" asked Markie with solicitude.

"Better. I had a letter this morning—and the baby's doing well, too."

"I expect you're longing to see them."

"Yes," said Willis. He came over to the table and took the potato knife in his large horny hand. "You leave those to me," he said.

"It's very good of you," declared Markie, getting up.

The boy at the other end of the table, who was writing a letter, seemed to be having some difficulty with its composition. He was biting his pencil and twisting himself into knots, and Markie was interested to observe that the tip of his tongue was protruding slightly and rolling around as he formed his words. She had noticed the same thing in the kindergarten at Wheatfield House when she had been called upon to take the "babies" for their writing lesson.

"'ow d'you spell man yoovers?" he asked in a hoarse voice.

Markie spelt it out to him, letter by letter and he wrote it down.

"I'd never 'ave thort of that," he declared looking at his handiwork in approval. "'Ilda won't 'arf be surprised when she sees that."

Markie would have liked to explain the roots of the word, but she curbed the impulse, reflecting as she did so that the difference one found in the intelligence of these men was extremely interesting. They all looked much the same on parade but their uniform appearance hid a multitude of individualities and idiosyncrasies. Girls in schools—of whom Markie had experience—did not show so much disparity, so much innate capacity or

incapacity for progress and improvement. Here, too, amongst
these men, Markie found many types of cephalism. She mea-
sured their heads and jaws in her mind's eye and labeled them
to her own satisfaction...and this was all extremely interesting
to Markie, who for years had lived in the depths of the country
with practically no human material upon which to try out her
theoretical knowledge of the groupings of the human race.

Two other men came in and one of them turned on the
wireless, which immediately said...

"And now we are all fairies. Listen to the music, children...
it's gay music, isn't it? But soon you will hear the raindrops
falling and you must *run* back to your places *ever* so quickly.
Fairies don't like getting their wings wet, you know. Are you
ready, children..."

None of the men smiled. Perhaps none of them heard the
sugary voice on the air...not because they were deaf, of course,
thought Markie, but simply because they kept the wireless
going full blast from morning to night and had become so used
to it that the sound did not reach their brains. Markie had been
about to take a jar of rice from the cupboard for she intended
to give Jerry curry for supper tonight, but now she paused, and
looked around. Somehow or other the voice on the air had torn
a veil from Markie's eyes..."Now we are all fairies, running
very softly," and lo and behold there was the kitchen full of
soldiers—soldiers smoking, reading, talking, writing letters, and
cleaning their rifles—and she, Sophonisba Marks, was moving
about amongst them, perfectly at home, perfectly at ease, stepping over their feet on her way to and from the range. She
thought, "How very strange! Is this I? Is this true?"

There was no time to stand and ponder, but the scene somehow printed itself upon Markie's memory. The kitchen was
shadowy; there was a red glow from the fire that made it seem
more dreamlike. Markie's eyes took in the whole effect, the

big shadowy room, the soldiers, the rain that had begun to beat against the window, and the wireless lashing away unheard. She wondered what Mrs. Cobbe would have said if she had returned from the grave and seen the kitchen thus. Mrs. Cobbe (Jerry's mother) had been rather old-fashioned, rather "particular," Markie remembered...and, before *her* reign, there had been Jerry's grandmother (probably more "particular" still), and, before her, a whole string of elegant ladies with straight backs and rigid ideas, coming down to the kitchen every morning at the proper hour to interview their cook and order quantities of luscious food for their husbands...and all that time there had been "maids" in Ganthorne kitchen, maids with starched aprons and snow-white caps.

"What a long way we've come," said Markie to herself with a little sigh of regret for the good old days that were past and gone forever.

Chapter Nine
Troubles

J erry had been to Wandlebury with the pony cart (she went twice a week and collected food and anything else that was required). These expeditions were necessary now because none of the shops had vans to send to Ganthorne. Today the task had taken longer than usual and the light was beginning to fade as she drove into the stable yard…it was a time of day that made Jerry think of Sam. If it were not for this horrible war Sam would be here—he would have returned from the office and the two of them would be walking around the stables together saying good night to the horses. If it were not for the war the stables would be full, and there would be that lovely warm horsey smell and the peaceful sound of horses feeding. Jerry's heart was heavy. It was definite pain to be separated from Sam. Sometimes the pain was bearable and sometimes it almost wasn't…tonight Jerry felt small and lonely and sad. She was missing Sam with every bit of her. Sam was so dear and understanding, he was so funny, so friendly, so good to look at. Where was Sam now, wondered Jerry, stopping in the middle of the stable yard and losing herself in thought. He was "somewhere in the desert"; that was all she knew and it was not enough. She wanted to know what he was doing at this moment, what he was thinking and feeling. It seemed all wrong not to *know* what Sam was thinking—they had lived so close to each other in body and mind.

It was not only Sam she missed—though she missed him most. She missed the work she had loved so much, the noise and bustle of the stables, the horses, the grooms. One of the grooms, Edgar, who had been with Jerry for years and was a true and steadfast friend, had been killed in the retreat to Dunkirk. Fred was a prisoner of war in Germany—she sent him parcels. Sometimes she received queer little stilted letters from Fred. Joe had chosen to be a sailor—he was only nineteen and was somewhere in the Mediterranean.

Jerry brushed away a film of moisture from her eyes and taking Dapple's bridle she went into the harness room to hang it up...and there she found Rudge, sitting by the fire eating his supper. Rudge was the last remaining groom; he was a handyman and helped in the garden. He was older than the others and had not been called up—sometimes Jerry wondered what on earth she would do when Rudge's age group was conscripted.

Rudge was eating his supper in comfort, he was looking at a newspaper as he ate, and a mug of beer stood at his elbow. He looked up at Jerry and said, "I been to Wandlebury. I got my papers."

"Oh Rudge, will you have to go?" asked Jerry in dismay.

Rudge laughed shortly. "Not me," he said. "I got exemption. I told 'em I was the only man on the place—told 'em the size of the garden and that. I put it across 'em all roight."

Jerry hesitated. She said, "But Rudge, you ought to go—if they want you, I mean."

"Not me," replied Rudge, taking another mouthful of sausage. "Why should I go? It ain't my war. I never wanted war with the Germans."

"Nobody wanted war!" cried Jerry.

"Why did they 'ave it then? They won't get me for cannon fodder," said Rudge with a grin.

Suddenly Jerry saw red. The others had all gone—all the good ones—Fred and Edgar and little Joe…and Sam, too. Edgar was dead. Fred was starving in a German prison, Sam was lost in the wilds of an African desert, and here was Rudge sitting in the warm comfortable harness room eating an enormous supper and laughing at them…

"They're doing their duty!" she cried. "They're fighting for their country."

"Let 'em," said Rudge shortly.

"No," said Jerry. "No, Rudge, it won't do. If you can get exemption that's all right—that's your affair, not mine—but I can't keep you here."

"You can't keep me!" he cried in amazement. "Who's going to do the work?"

"I am," she replied. "I'll get a woman. I'll get an old man or a little boy. I'll manage somehow."

"But they won't exemp' me unless you ask for me."

"I can't ask for you. Why should *you* be exempted."

"Why shouldn't I be?"

"I don't know," said Jerry helplessly. "I'm probably quite mad—but I just can't bear it."

Rudge hesitated, and then he said in a different voice. "I know it's 'ard for you, Mum. I mean it stands to reason you're feeling a bit under the weather—well, that's why I arst for exemption just to stay on an' 'elp you."

"No, Rudge," said Jerry, shaking her head. "I can't explain what I feel about it but you'll have to leave here. I can't bear to see you sitting there, having your supper."

"Why shouldn't I 'ave my supper?" asked Rudge, heatedly.

"I don't know," said Jerry. "Or—wait a minute—perhaps I *do* know. Perhaps it's because you aren't willing to fight for your supper. *Willing,* Rudge, that's the test. Yes, I'm glad I've got it clear."

"So I've got to go an' fight, 'ave I?" demanded Rudge in furious tones. "I've got to blooming well go an' fight because you think—"

"No," said Jerry firmly. "No, you've got it wrong. I can't make you fight if you don't want to—and anyhow you wouldn't be much use if that's how you feel about it—all I say is you can't shelter behind me. That's all, Rudge."

"They won't exemp' me unless you arsk," said Rudge again.

"I can't ask," said Jerry. She took up Dapple's blanket as she spoke and went out into the yard.

Rudge followed her. "I'm sorry I spoke like that," he said in a wheedling tone. "I was a bit 'asty. You think it over, Mum. You think of all the things I do. I don't waste my time. You'd find it difficult to get another chap 'oo would do all the things I do. You would really. Everyone can't fight, you know. We got to keep the 'ome fires burning."

"That was the last war," said Jerry gravely, as she flung the blanket over Dapple's back and strapped it into place. "Business as usual and keep the home fires burning and all that. This war is different. It's a total war, Rudge."

"It ain't my war," said Rudge.

"All right, Rudge. There's no need to say any more about it."

"I didn't want it," he said. "It didn't matter to me if 'itler took Poland. What's Poland to me? Why didn't we let 'im 'ave Poland if that's what 'e wanted."

"Poland was just the beginning. He would have swallowed Poland first and then he'd have come for us—one at a time, that was his idea."

"That's what you think," said Rudge, not rudely, but just stating the fact.

"That's what I think," she agreed. "I'm entitled to my opinion and you're entitled to yours. It's no use saying any more."

"Think it over," suggested Rudge, returning to his own case, which interested him more nearly than the ethics of the war. "See what Miss Marks ses about it. Don't do anything in a 'urry that you might be sorry for."

"No, Rudge," said Jerry. "I might think for a month and it wouldn't make any difference because this isn't a thought—it's a feeling."

⁓✕⁓

When Jerry had finished putting Dapple to bed she came out into the yard and found that it was quite dark now and the stars were shining. She was very tired, for her argument with Rudge had taken it out of her—taken something vital out of her body—strength, merit. She went across the yard to the big gates and turned up the path to the house. She walked quietly, for she was obliged to pass the cottage and she did not want to see Mrs. Boles tonight. Mrs. Boles was an evacuee. She had come from Stepney with her two children and had taken up her abode in the cottage very thankfully at first, but now the horrors of the bombing were fading from her mind and she had become increasingly discontented.

Jerry looked at the cottage as she passed. She looked at it with affection for she and Sam had had great fun doing it up and making it fit to live in—two of the grooms had lived there with Joe's mother to "do" for them. It had been a happy place in those days.

"Hallo!" exclaimed Jerry, and she stopped suddenly in her tracks for there was a streak of light showing from the kitchen window. She was tempted to let it slide, but no, that wouldn't do. She would have to go in and get the blackout adjusted. Jerry knocked twice at the door before Mrs. Boles appeared, wiping her hands upon her incredibly dirty apron. She was a thin wispy woman with a pointed nose and furtive eyes, and her hair was adorned with steel curlers. Nobody in Ganthorne had ever seen Mrs. Boles without curlers in her hair...but perhaps she takes them out at night, thought Jerry vaguely.

"Oh, it's you!" exclaimed Mrs. Boles. "That's lucky. I was wantin' to see you. The coal 'ammer's broke. The 'andle came away in my 'and when I was breakin' up the coal—so now I 'aven't got nothin' to break up the coal with."

"There's a light showing," said Jerry. "You can't have drawn the curtains properly."

"They've come orf the 'ooks," said Mrs. Boles.

Jerry sighed. "Couldn't you have sewn them on?" she asked wearily.

"I meant to, but summow I never got around to it."

They were standing in the passage and as Mrs. Boles spoke she rubbed herself against the passage wall. It was like a cat, thought Jerry, with a little shudder of distaste. Cats rubbed themselves against walls like that...but cats did not leave greasy marks on the wallpaper...

"Oh dear!" exclaimed Jerry. "I think you might have found time."

"I'm always busy," whined Mrs. Boles. "There's the 'ouse to clean an' the clo'es to wash. I'm never off my feet from the toime I gets up till the toime I goes to bed. It's crule the amount of work the 'ouse taikes to keep it toidy."

Jerry looked around the kitchen. It was anything but tidy; it was dirty, smeary, sordid, and a curious sickly smell pervaded the place. In the corner sat Elmie Boles (a child of about fourteen with a small white peaky face) she was hunched up in a curiously dejected position like a moping bird.

"What's the matter with Elmie?" asked Jerry.

"She never slep' a wink all noight," replied her mother proudly. "'Urt 'er finger—that's wot—tore it on a nile. Real narsty, it looks."

Here was another job, thought Jerry in vexation, the child's finger would have to be dressed—but first the blackout must be adjusted. Jerry borrowed some pins from Mrs. Boles, climbed onto the kitchen table, and pinned up the curtains.

"You must sew them tomorrow," said Jerry firmly as she jumped down and surveyed her dirty hands in disgust. "And I *do* wish you would try to keep the place cleaner, Mrs. Boles; it used to be so fresh and nice when Mrs. Lander was here."

"I never bin told I wos dirty before," said Mrs. Boles aggressively.

Jerry did not reply. There were many things she might have said but she could not trust herself—if she began to tell Mrs. Boles what she thought of her it would be difficult to stop—and what was the use of it? The woman was not capable of keeping the house properly.

Elmie's finger was the next consideration, but nothing could be done *here*. To begin with Jerry's hands were not in a fit condition to dress a wound...and Jerry's one idea was to get away quickly before she lost her temper.

"You had better come up to the house with me, Elmie," said Jerry a trifle wearily as she turned to go.

Elmie rose and followed her at once and Mrs. Boles came to the door with them. "Wot about the coal 'ammer?" inquired Mrs. Boles. "I carn't break up the coal without a 'ammer. The poker's no use."

"I'll remember about it," said Jerry shortly.

"That's roight," said Mrs. Boles, who had suddenly become quite pleasant and cheerful now that she had achieved her end. "That's roight. You can sen' the 'ammer back with Elmie—an' she can bring a little milk as well—jus' a few drops that you can spire. I ain't got a drop o' milk for the supper."

"I'll see if there is any," replied Jerry, edging away.

But Mrs. Boles was not an easy person to escape from. She kept Jerry standing on the step while she discoursed about her children, and it was impossible to get away without being actually rude. Jerry heard the whole story of Elmie's finger and, when that was finished, she was obliged to listen to a long account of Arrol's doings at school. Arrol was eleven, he was big and boisterous and the pride and joy of his mother's heart. His name really was Arrol—not Harold, as Jerry had thought at first—though why he had been given that name she had never been sufficiently interested to inquire. (Elmie was really Wilhelmina. It was a fine-sounding name but too grand for everyday use.)

Mrs. Boles was still in the middle of her story of what the master had said to Arrol and what Arrol had said to the master when the hero of the tale appeared on the scene looking even dirtier than usual and with one sleeve of his coat hanging in tatters from his shoulder.

"Arrol!" cried his mother in dismay. "Arrol, wot 'ave you bin doin'."

In the ensuing confusion Jerry was able to escape.

"Am I to come?" asked Elmie, following her.

"Yes, of course," replied Jerry. "We must have a look at your finger, mustn't we? Miss Marks will put a dressing on your finger..."

"Will it 'ave to be cut off?"

"Goodness, no!" said Jerry in alarm.

"There was a girl in our street wot 'ad to 'ave 'er finger cut off," said Elmie with gloomy pride.

Fortunately Elmie's finger was not in such a serious condition, but it was by no means a pleasant sight when Markie unrolled the dirty rag and displayed the festering wound. It must have been very painful, too, thought Markie, looking at her small white-faced patient with some respect. She boiled some water and put on a dressing of wet boracic lint and oil silk and tied it on firmly with the finger of an old glove.

Elmie watched the whole process with interest. Indeed she seemed interested in everything she saw. Her eyes, wide with surprise, roved around the little pantry where the proceedings were taking place. "Everything's shiny," she said at last.

"Because everything is clean," replied Markie, improving the shining hour.

"Mide of silver," said Elmie, pointing to the lids of Markie's pans, which hung on little hooks along the wall.

"Dear me, no," replied Markie. "They are made of tin, just like the pans your mother uses...but I like to keep them clean."

Elmie said no more.

"There, it is finished," said Markie at last as she tied the tape around Elmie's thin wrist. "You've been very good and brave. Come tomorrow morning and I will put another dressing on it."

"Come tomorrow?"

"Yes, twice a day until it is better," said Markie firmly.

Chapter Ten
Janetta Is Indisposed

M r. Abbott was on his way to Foxstead. He had been sent for
by Miss Walters—not Miss Janetta Walters, the well-known
novelist, but her elder sister. "You must come at once," Miss
Walters had told him, on the telephone. "You must come and
see Janetta. She isn't well."

Mr. Abbott had suggested that a doctor might be more use
under the circumstances, to which Miss Walters had replied
somewhat enigmatically that it wasn't that kind of illness. "You
must come," she had repeated—and she continued to repeat the
same words until Mr. Abbott agreed to go. Fortunately it was
not far from London, and was actually on the Wandlebury line,
so he could drop in and pay his visit on his way home.

The train was crowded but it arrived in good time. Mr.
Abbott walked up from the station and soon he was sitting in
the comfortable drawing room at Angleside talking to Miss
Walters. "Where is Miss Janetta?" asked Mr. Abbott, looking
around the room. "She isn't in bed, I hope."

"Oh no, she isn't in *bed*," replied her sister.

"Writing, I suppose."

"No. No, she isn't writing. She's out. As a matter of fact I
didn't tell her you were coming. I wanted to talk to you."

Mr. Abbott sighed. He had come here to be talked to, but

that did not make it any less boring. Miss Walters bored him.
She was not—to Mr. Abbott's mind—attractive. She was quite
nice to look at, of course, and was always extremely well turned
out, but she was too managing, too efficient, too self-assured.
He preferred Miss Janetta every time. There was something
very nice about Miss Janetta...in spite of her books.

Miss Walters had said she wanted to talk to Mr. Abbott
but she seemed to have some difficulty in starting, and during
the silence that ensued Mr. Abbott had time to wonder what
she was going to say. He felt pretty certain that it was something unpleasant—perhaps she intended to ask for a rise in
royalties on Janetta's next book—and he wondered what he
could say to head her off. Miss Walters was Janetta's agent,
and to do her justice Janetta could not have had a better one.
Mr. Abbott was aware that Miss Walters had got the upper
hand of him twice—he wished he had sent Spicer to talk to
Miss Walters. Spicer was ruthless, he was not easily rattled.
The silence had lasted so long that Mr. Abbott felt impelled
to break it.

"The book is selling well," said Mr. Abbott. "The third edition is almost sold out. When may we expect the next one?"

"That's just it," said Miss Walters in gloomy tones.

"Not coming along well?" asked Mr. Abbott in surprise, for
he was so used to the regular appearance of manuscripts from
the pen of Janetta that he could scarcely believe there was any
difficulty in their production.

"It was coming along splendidly," Miss Walters replied.
"It was the best of all, I thought. We had decided to call it
Love Triumphant."

Mr. Abbott winced, but he said bravely, "Quite in the best
tradition, Miss Walters."

"Quite," she agreed. "We were both very happy about the
book—and then, quite suddenly, Janetta lost interest in it."

"Stale," suggested Mr. Abbott. "All writers have periods of staleness."

"Not Janetta," said Miss Walters. "Janetta never gets stale."

This was perfectly true. Janetta had never suffered from any of the ills of the spirit that beset the owner of an artistic temperament. Janetta's temperament was equable. She worked at fixed hours. Stories gushed from her pen like water from a well-behaved bath tap. She wrote at high speed and her sister collected the precious sheets and typed them. The process went as smoothly as a factory—which indeed it was.

Miss Walters explained all this to Mr. Abbott (in her own words, of course) and Mr. Abbott listened patiently, for that was his business.

"I see," he said at last. "Yes, I see…and now she has stopped writing and you can't understand why."

Miss Walters nodded.

Mr. Abbott was more sympathetic now, for he perceived that Miss Walters was really very much distressed and he was a kind-hearted man. "You had better tell me all you know," said Mr. Abbott in soothing tones. "We'll put our heads together and see what can be done."

"But I know *nothing*," declared Miss Walters in agonized accents. "I only know that Janetta is quite different. I can't think what has upset her."

∽∾

It was not surprising that Miss Walters was all at sea, for Janetta had told her nothing. As a matter of fact it would have been difficult for Janetta to explain what was the matter with her even if she had wanted to do so. Mr. Ash was at the bottom of it, of course, but Mr. Ash was not the whole cause of the trouble, for Janetta was so secure in her position as a successful novelist that his criticisms of her books had not worried her unduly—not at the time. She had been interested rather than annoyed. It seemed odd that this young man should be allergic to her stories—but of course he was a very odd young man. They were both very odd, and the tea party had a curiously dream-like feeling about it. But, in spite of all that had been said, they finished tea quite amicably and parted politely. Immediately afterwards Janetta was surrounded by a crowd of Wandlebury ladies, who had been waiting eagerly to speak to her. She was petted and flattered to an almost embarrassing extent, and her books were lauded to the skies. She had then returned home, quite pleased with herself, to partake of another much better and more sustaining tea with her sister, in her own comfortable drawing room.

"Did everything go off well?" Helen had inquired.

"Very well," replied Janetta. "The committee were very grateful to me. I signed some books for them."

"Did they give you tea?"

"Not a very good tea," replied Janetta, helping herself to another piece of cake.

Helen purred. She was housekeeper as well as amanuensis and gardener and general bottle washer to her gifted sister and she took great pride in her jobs. Janetta would not get such a good tea anywhere as she got at home.

It was not until Janetta had finished her second tea and had gone into the study to put in a few hours' work upon *Love Triumphant* that she remembered Mr. Ash. She hesitated by the big solid desk, which was placed at exactly the right angle near the window, and an uncomfortable feeling assailed her. It was like a breath of cold air, blowing across her soul. "Soppy Stuff"—that was what he had said. But why should she care? He was an insufferable young man. She did not write for his entertainment. He was incapable of appreciating her books—that was all.

Janette sat down, took up her pen, and turned over the pile of manuscript that lay before her on the table, and as she did so a passage caught her eye—it was a passage she had written that morning:

"My beautiful Phyllis," cried Hector, throwing himself on his knees. "If all women were like you—so pure and good and innocent—how wonderful the world would be!"

Janetta read it twice, and then, resting her chin on her hands, she gazed out of the window. After a little while, there was a knock on the door and Helen looked in. "Am I disturbing you?" she asked in hushed accents.

"No," replied the author. "No, I was just thinking. I don't feel like writing at the moment."

"You're tired!"

"No, not really."

"What is it, then?"

There was no answer.

"What is the matter?" asked Helen, coming into the room and looking at her sister in concern.

"Nothing at all," said Janette. "But I think I shall leave it till tomorrow. There's no hurry, is there?"

Janetta slept well and arose feeling refreshed and ready for work. After breakfast she sat down at her desk, took out a clean sheaf of paper, and began to write. Her pen raced over the page in the pleasantest manner imaginable; she pulled the wires and the puppets danced to her tune. Hector proposed to Phyllis and was refused—he had proposed to her on page fifty-seven but there was no reason why he should not repeat the experiment— later, at the very end of the story he would propose again. The third time was lucky.

Suddenly, in the middle of a sentence, Janetta's pen faltered. She sniffed the air in a tentative manner and her eyes fell on a vase of sweet peas on the table beside her desk. (Helen had

gone out early and picked them for her—it was a delicate attention.) The sun was shining in at the window and the warmth
was drawing out the strong sweet perfume of the flowers—the
room was filled with their scent. Janetta looked at the flowers
and, as she looked, she seemed to see that young man's face—
that insufferable young man's oafish face—and to hear his curiously husky voice: "I bet you could write something decent if
you tried." What a thing to say! How dared he say such a thing!
"Something decent"—what an expression to use!

Janetta was so upset that she laid down her pen and went
out through the French window. She passed through the
garden without a glance at the roses and the sweet peas, which
were the pride of Helen's heart, and opening the wicket gate
at the top of the garden she wandered into the woods. The
woods were peaceful and soothing; sunshine fell in golden
rain between the leaves. Janetta sat down on a bank and tried
to reason with herself. It was ridiculous to allow that young
man to interfere with her work—quite ridiculous. She had not
liked him, he was not her kind of person, he was not worth
thinking about..."But I'm not thinking about *him*," said
Janette aloud. Neither she was. It was his words that haunted
her...and they haunted her because they found an echo in her
heart. She realized that for some time past she had been feeling
a little dissatisfied with her books.

Janetta sighed. She reminded herself that hundreds of thousands of people enjoyed her stories and showed their appreciation
by borrowing her books from libraries—or, better still, buying
them and keeping them in their bookcases. She reminded herself of the large "fan mail" that poured into Angleside from all
over the world (not only letters, but also parcels of food from
admirers in America and Canada and South Africa who were
anxious to sustain her so that she might continue to delight them
with her books). Two letters had arrived that very morning, one

from Baltimore and the other from Birmingham—letters full of praise and thanksgiving. Janetta felt in need of encouragement so she took them out of her pocket and looked at them. They began in much the same fashion by assuring Miss Walters that the writer had never written to an author before but after that they differed. The Baltimore lady declared that *Her Prince at Last* had soothed and sustained her through a sharp attack of flu. The Birmingham lady had read *Her Loving Heart* and was extravagantly delighted with it. Janetta found it very pleasant to have these timely reminders that her stories were enjoyed by people in two hemispheres, but they did not remove her discomfort—not entirely. "Most people are saps," that was what he had said, and it was only too obvious that the writers of these letters belonged to the great majority.

Several days passed. *Love Triumphant* lay upon the desk in a half-finished condition while its author wandered in the woods.

"Couldn't you finish it?" asked Helen anxiously. If you could just finish it we might go away for a little holiday."

"I can't finish it," said Janetta.

"Finish it—*do*," said Helen in wheedling tones. "There are only a few chapters to write and I can type them out in half no time. Then it will be off your mind."

"It isn't on my mind," said Janetta.

Helen pretended not to hear. "You could finish it in three days," she declared. "You have only got to let Phyllis find the letter in the bureau drawer and discover the truth about Hector—that Hector has been faithful to her all along—and then the ending. You're so good at endings."

"It wouldn't have happened like that."

"What do you mean? What would have happened?"

"I don't know," replied Janetta. "It isn't any use to try to think what would have happened because they aren't real people."

"It's a story," said Helen soothingly.

"I want to write a story about real people," Janetta said. She was quite surprised to hear herself make this statement because she had not thought of it before, but if she surprised herself it was nothing compared with the amazement and consternation her simple words engendered in her sister's bosom.

"A story about real people!" cried Helen in horror-stricken tones. "Janetta, what do you mean! You can't think of changing your style!"

"Why not?"

"It would be ruin!" Helen declared. "It would be the end of everything. Think of your reputation! Think of your public! Think of your sales! You would lose all you've gained—all these years of building up! You can't do it. It isn't fair. I've toiled and moiled to make you what you are and now you propose to throw it all away."

"You've toiled and moiled!" echoed Janetta.

"Of course I have," said Helen. "I've made you what you are. You know that as well as I do. It isn't only your books that have made your success—it's you. You're a sort of tradition—a symbol if you like the word better—and I've made you. I've worked like a slave. I've been your publicity agent. I've had you photographed and interviewed; I've chosen your clothes and the way you do your hair. I've built you up and created an atmosphere about you; I chose your name and made it a household word."

Janetta gazed at her. It was true, of course. Helen had done all that and more. Helen had created Janetta Walters—Janetta was not a real person at all.

"You're a fairy-tale person, yourself," murmured Janetta—it was extraordinary how every word that young man had said remained written in indelible ink in Janetta's memory.

"What?" asked Helen.

"Nothing," replied Janetta. "I mean of course it's quite true."

This little conversation with Helen did not help Janetta at all, and *Love Triumphant* got no further. Sometimes Janetta would rise in the morning and come down to breakfast full of good intentions to settle down and finish the story without any more fuss…but the moment she sat down at her desk and took up her pen she would discover within her bosom a loathing for the unfinished book—a loathing that, no matter how hard she tried, it was impossible to overcome. The only thing comparable with this extraordinary sensation was the loathing for food Janetta had once experienced after a sharp bout of influenza. Then (as now) she would sit down to the table quite happily and after one look at the dish before her she would rise in disgust.

Helen badgered Janetta, which was the worst thing possible, of course, for the more Helen badgered the less Janetta felt inclined to work. Helen was always asking, "What about *Love Triumphant?*" for Helen was not of the breed that can wait patiently and leave things to right themselves. She was a born meddler. In the garden, for instance, everything was directed by Helen. The raspberry canes, the sweet peas—even the ramblers were obliged to grow in the direction Helen thought best. She bent them to her will, tying them firmly to stake or trellis with pieces of green bass she carried in her pocket for the purpose. Janetta had always bent so easily—there had never been any trouble with Janetta until now.

A crinkle of anxiety became permanent between Helen's well-marked eyebrows, for the situation had perfectly appalling complications. It was Janetta's stories that kept the roof over their heads and cooked their food, and cleaned their shoes and dug their garden. She and Janetta ate the stories—and wore them. Helen had a lively recollection of the small stuffy house in Bayswater where they had lived before Janetta discovered her marvelous gift. The house smelt of cabbages—or sometimes of kippers—smuts drifted in whenever the windows were opened, children played hopscotch in the street. She remembered darning and patching and "making things do" and all the other discomforts and inconveniences attendant on poverty. And then Janetta had written her first story *Bride of May* and to their amazement it was accepted. Royalties went up by leaps and bounds and Janetta was launched upon her career.

Remembering all this and brooding over it as she went about her daily duties Helen worked herself into such a condition of alarm and despondency that she suddenly found she could bear it no longer—something would *have* to be done. Perhaps Mr. Abbott could do something about it. She must get hold of Mr. Abbott. After all (thought Helen) it was to Mr. Abbott's interest that *Love Triumphant* should be finished and another book begun. The firm of Abbott and Spicer made a good income out of Janetta's books.

Now Mr. Abbott had come. There he sat, large and solid, kindly and benevolent, obviously anxious to help.

"I *wish* you would speak to her," Miss Walters said, clasping and unclasping her hands in the extremity of her emotion. "I wish you would *speak* to her, Mr. Abbott. Tell her you want *Love Triumphant* next week. She could easily finish it by then. You *will* speak to her, won't you?"

Mr. Abbott did not reply. He realized, of course, that it was his duty to the firm, his duty to his partner, to do all in his power to keep Miss Janetta's nose to the grindstone but the issue was enormously complicated by the fact that he disliked her books. He disliked them intensely. "High-powered tushery" was the phrase he had found to describe (for his own satisfaction) the latest effusion from her pen. Mr. Abbott had been called upon to perform unpleasant duties before, but never one that went so much against the grain.

"You don't mind speaking to her, do you?" asked Miss Walters anxiously.

"I do, rather," said Mr. Abbott feebly.

"Why?" asked Miss Walters in surprise.

"Because—er—we don't care to press our authors," he replied. "It's—well—it's against our principles, you see. Besides, if you've failed to—to persuade her it isn't likely I should succeed."

"She might listen to you."

"No, I don't think so—and anyhow it's against our principles."

Miss Walters looked at him with contempt. She said, "Very well then, if you won't speak to her, I shall take the matter into my own hands."

It was a curious thing to say, and Arthur Abbott, on his way home in the train, pondered upon the words and turned them over in his mind…for hadn't Miss Walters already done all that she could? Hadn't she come to the end of her resources before sending for him?

Chapter Eleven
Conversation of Various Descriptions

J erry walked into the Archway House and shouted for Barbara, but there was no reply. I suppose she's out, thought Jerry in some annoyance. It was not often that Barbara was out at tea time. Jerry was about to depart when she heard a slight sound and she saw Simon's face staring at her between the banisters halfway up the stairs.

"Hallo!" she said.

"Hallo!" said Simon. "Mummy's out but you can come and have tea in the nursery if you like."

"Did Dorcas say so?"

"Yes," said Simon, nodding.

Jerry had had tea in the nursery before. She enjoyed the company of the young Abbotts and, although it sometimes made her a little sad to see them, she repressed the feeling and sat on it firmly. It was Fay that Jerry loved best, Fay with her entrancing curves, her sweetly serious baby face, her quaint old-fashioned remarks. Jerry would have given a good deal if she could have had a Fay of her very own—to cuddle and pet and take care of—and now that Sam was so far away she felt this more than ever. Jerry was aware that practically everyone liked Simon better than Fay—she could not understand why.

"Well now, this *is* nice," declared Dorcas. "We didn't know we were going to have company, today, did we? How is Miss Marks keeping?"

"Very well, thank you," replied Jerry, who always felt that she had to be on her best behavior in the nursery.

"How is Dapple keeping?" asked Fay solemnly.

"Silly, you don't ask how ponies are keeping!" Simon exclaimed.

"But I want to know," said Fay. "I want to know how Dapple is keeping because I love him."

"He's very well," said Jerry hastily.

"Mrs. Abbott and Mrs. Walker have gone to tea at the Marvells'," Dorcas said.

"Is Mrs. Walker still here?"

"She stayed on because the doctor had to go to Edinburgh," explained Dorcas. "It wasn't no good her going back to be there alone and it's nice for Mrs. Abbott having her. They were always great friends, the two of them."

"When?" asked Simon. "Did Mummy live at Silverstream?"

"Pass your aunt the cake, Simon."

"She isn't my aunt."

"Of course she's your aunt."

"No, she isn't any relation to me at all."

"She's a relation to me," said Fay.

"No, she isn't," said Simon firmly. "Sam is your cousin, and—"

"Jerry is my cousiness, then," declared Fay. "She's my cousiness and I love her."

"I don't love her—not like Mummy, for instance," said Simon in a thoughtful tone.

It gave Jerry such an odd feeling to be discussed like this—as if she were not there—that she changed the subject by asking what they were going to do tomorrow.

"Coming to tea with you," said Simon promptly.

"Well—I don't think so," said Jerry, slightly taken aback. "I mean—I'm—I'm rather busy. You must come some other day."

"After the war," said Fay, nodding understandingly.

"She always says that," declared Dorcas.

"Oh, before *then*," said Jerry.

"*Long* before *then*," agreed Simon. "I want to play hide and seek with Arrol, like I did last time."

"Harold," said Dorcas. "I've told you dozens of times—they *do* get into such dreadful ways of talking, Mrs. Sam."

"It is Arrol, Dorcas," began Jerry.

"You've dropped your aitch!" cried Fay, pointing a chubby finger at her.

"His name is Arrol," said Jerry very clearly. "It's A, double R, O, L. I don't know why, I'm sure, but—"

"There's a kind of motor car called that, isn't there?" asked Dorcas.

"And there's one called jeep," declared Simon. "Jeep, Jeep, Jeep—wouldn't it be funny if I was called Jeep?"

Jerry agreed that it would. She was beginning to feel the strain, for she was not used to the conversation of children.

"It's an American car," said Dorcas, who was well used to this sort of conversation and took each subject in turn with an open mind.

"I would like to be an American boy," said Simon. "I would have lots of ice cream if I was an American boy."

"You would be sick, then," said Fay dogmatically.

"I wouldn't."

"You would."

"That's enough," said Dorcas. "Drink up your milk. You haven't drunk any of it yet."

"We can't come to tea the day after tomorrow because it's Mummy's birthday," said Simon, wiping his mouth.

Jerry was disloyal enough to feel rather glad that the pleasure of her cousin's company at Ganthorne was to be put off a little longer. "Oh yes, so it is," she said. "What are you going to give Mummy for her birthday?"

Fay raised a milky mouth from her mug and said, "A pin!" and then she laughed uproariously, for she had her own peculiar sense of humor.

"It's a book," said Simon, ignoring her completely. "We've bought it between us, Dorcas and me. We're going to write in it."

"It's a Bible, really," said Dorcas. "It seems a funny sort of present, but—"

"With pictures," said Simon.

"Pictures of the devil," said Fay. She hesitated and then added, "Three devils, there was."

"Oh Fay!" cried Dorcas. "It was Shadrach, Meshac, and Abednego!"

"Why was they cooking them?" asked Fay.

"You'd think she was a heathen," said Dorcas after a moment's silence. "But really she knows *lots* of Bible stories, Mrs. Sam."

"She knows about Daniel," Simon declared. "You know Daniel, don't you, Fay?"

"The lions et him," said Fay with relish—and she took a large bite of cake to show how it was done.

"Silly, they didn't eat him!" cried Simon.

"He et the lions, then," suggested Fay a trifle doubtfully.

"Fay thinks of eating all the time," explained Simon.

"I was wondering what we should write in the Bible," said Dorcas, looking at Jerry inquiringly.

"I know what to write," Simon declared. "I've seen it written in a book before. It's the proper thing to write in a book. Daddy has a book with that written in it and he said it made the book more valuable—that's what Daddy said."

"What is it?" asked Jerry and Dorcas with one accord.

"With the author's compliments," said Simon proudly.

Jerry was stricken helpless and Dorcas was trying patiently to explain why the inscription was unsuitable, when the door opened and Barbara appeared. She was a little surprised at the sudden silence that greeted her entrance and at the strangely guilty looks of the little party.

"You're all very quiet!" she exclaimed.

Simon rose and flung himself into her arms. "We've been playing a game," said Simon glibly. "We've been playing 'Silence in the Pig Market, the Old Sow Speaks First!'"

Jerry was not sorry to see Barbara. She explained her presence and followed Barbara downstairs to the drawing room, where the conversation was better suited to her intelligence. She and Barbara understood each other beautifully. They understood what each other was driving at with a minimum of language. One might have thought, to listen to them talking, that they slipped from one subject to another illogically and without sequence—but it was not so. They merely left things out. Most people's conversation is like a local train that stops at every station and lingers there for a few moments to allow time for its passengers to embark, but when the two Mrs. Abbotts got together they roared along like an express, missing out all the small unimportant stations in their headlong career.

Arthur and Sarah were in the drawing room, too, but they took no part in the conversation. Sarah because she was not used to it, and Arthur because he had not the right type of brain.

Sarah had now been at the Archway House for a fortnight and she was going home tomorrow—home to John and the children and the troubles and trials of housekeeping in wartime—and, far from dreading the prospect, Sarah was as excited as a girl. There was no need to *pretend* to herself that she missed John. She yearned for him. She felt as though her heart were being pulled out with strings. It's been lovely, she thought. It's done me a lot of good, and Barbara is a lamb—but, oh dear, how glad I shall be to get home! Thinking all this, Sarah had lost touch with the conversation; but now she pulled herself together and tried to follow it…and sometimes she thought she had caught it up and then she found she hadn't.

"…powdered borax is best," Jerry was saying. "They can't bear powdered borax. You sprinkle it all along the wainscoting and it keeps them away."

"Keeps what away?" asked Sarah, who was determined to make an effort.

"Cockroaches," said Jerry. "And that reminds me—that's really what I came to tell you, Barbara—I'm going to have a paying guest."

"Are you?" asked Barbara in surprise. "But Jerry—"

"I know," declared Jerry. "I know all that, but she's coming with her eyes wide open—and it will be another woman in the house."

Sarah was about to ask if she had agreed to pull her weight in the house and whether she was a reasonably good cook, but Barbara got in before her.

"Oh, she's pretty, is she?" said Barbara, nodding.

"Attractive," amended Jerry, screwing up her eyes as if she were visualizing her prospective P. G. "Yes, quite definitely attractive—not that it matters much because almost anything in petticoats would do."

"How did you—"

"That was the funniest thing," declared Jerry, laughing. "I never meant to, really. I found her in Wandlebury Square, just outside Mr. Tupper's office—you know his musty old office that looks exactly as if it ought to belong to Mr. Pecksniff."

Barbara knew it well. One of the oddest things that had ever happened to her had happened to her in Mr. Tupper's office.

"I was just going in," continued Jerry. "It was really to see the old mole about the stable roof, when the door opened and she came out and stood there looking around in a vague sort of way as if she didn't know what to do next. So I said was she looking for anything and she said no—and then she said yes— and then she smiled and said she was looking for rooms."

"Mr. Tupper wouldn't help her much," said Barbara with conviction.

"He hadn't," agreed Jerry, "and of course I knew it was hopeless because the place is packed with evacuees and what not. I knew for certain because I've been trying for ages to get rooms in Wandlebury for one of my soldier's wives."

"Does he keep a harem?" asked Arthur, coming to life suddenly and peering at Jerry over the top of his newspaper.

"A harem!" echoed Jerry. "Oh, I see what you mean. You are a tease, Uncle Arthur. You know quite well I meant the wife of one of my soldiers. It was her smile I liked," continued Jerry, with a charming smile of her very own. "No, not the soldier's wife's smile. I haven't seen her except a sort of smudged snapshot, in a coal heaver's hat, surrounded with children..."

Arthur roared with laughter.

"I wish you wouldn't, Uncle Arthur," said Jerry, chuckling herself. "I wish you'd read your paper. You put me off and muddle me. It was all your fault for bringing in the soldier's wife to begin with. She doesn't come into it at all except that I couldn't get rooms for her."

"Go on," said Barbara, who wanted to hear the end of the story. "Go on, Jerry. You liked her smile."

"I like people with nice smiles," said Jerry. "So I liked *her*. So I said I had a house and I could give her a room for a bit if she didn't mind living in the middle of an army."

"Jerry," began Barbara in anxious tones.

"No, honestly," said Jerry, shaking her head.

"But you didn't."

"Yes, I did. I considered it quite a lot before I said a word. I was exactly like a drowning man. You know how a drowning man sees his whole life pass before his eyes in a few moments? Well, I saw my whole life just like that as I stood on Mr. Tupper's doorstep...Markie and myself and the cooking and doing the lamps and digging the garden...and Bobbie, of course."

"Bobbie?" asked Barbara.

"Captain Appleyard," said Jerry. "You know him, darling. He's the one with the doggy eyes. If she could just take him off my hands I would *pay* her to come."

"You never told me."

"But it's only lately," said Jerry. "I mean I can *manage* him all right, but he *is* rather a nuisance, poor lamb...all the more of a nuisance because I like him awfully. She seemed a little doubtful at first but when I told her the house was Elizabethan and we had lamps and a ghost she got tremendously keen."

"Did she!" exclaimed Barbara in some surprise, for to her mind lamps and ghosts were definite drawbacks.

"She can ride," added Jerry. "That clinched it, really. Of course we haggled over it. We went and had a cup of coffee at Cooke's and haggled like anything. She wanted to pay three pounds a week and I said I wouldn't take more than two—so then she said fifty bob and that was that."

"You won't make anything out of it," said Barbara thoughtfully.

"I don't really want to," replied Jerry. "If she fits into the scheme of things and takes Bobbie off my hands..."

"You ought to have references," Arthur said.

"She's all right. You'll like her, Uncle Arthur."

"Will Markie like her?" Barbara inquired.

"Oh!" said Jerry. "But Markie likes most people, really— unless their head is the wrong shape."

"When is she coming?" asked Sarah.

"Soon," said Jerry. "In a day or two—she said she would send me a wire."

Chapter Twelve
Exit the Boles Family

I think you should try to keep it cleaner," said Jerry, trying hard to make the words sound like a friendly suggestion.

"Keep it cleaner!"

"Yes, there's a sort of smell in the house, Mrs. Boles. It can't be good for you—or the children."

"It's them smelly lamps, that's wot," declared Mrs. Boles in truculent tones. "I'm just about fed up with this plice. You can't go outside the door without gettin' yer feet allover mud. I never go out 'ere."

"You ought to go out."

"Wot for? I ain't got no frens an' there ain't no shops nor no pictures."

"And there are no bombs," Jerry reminded her.

"There 'asn't bin no bombs in Stepney for munce. The luff-water's finished, Mr. Boles ses."

"I don't think he's right," said Jerry mildly.

"'E knows better than you," declared his wife. "'E's workin' in an aircraff factory, Mr. Boles is…any 'ow I'm packin' up an' leavin' 'ere before I gets moldy allover."

Jerry hesitated. She was ashamed of the pleasure and relief that surged over her at this unexpected news. She said gently, "I'm sorry, Mrs. Boles. I'm afraid it must have been rather dull for you here."

"Dull!" echoed Mrs. Boles. "Dull ain't the word. It's like bein' buried alive."

"But you have the children."

"They ain't no company."

Jerry sighed. She said, "You don't really mean you're going back to London, do you?"

"I'm fed up with this plice."

"But what about the children?"

"They'll 'ave to taike their chance. That's one of the reasons I'm goin'—it's bad for the children bein' 'ere."

"Bad for them!"

"They're bein' spoilt," declared Mrs. Boles. "They're bein' took away from me. It's 'igh time we wos 'ome in our own plice."

"Who's taking them away from you?" asked Jerry in surprise.

"I dunno," she replied vaguely. "I can't expline. They're bein' taught different. Wot's goin' to come of it—that's wot I want to know."

"I don't understand," said Jerry doubtfully. "You're all living here together."

"It's the other kids," explained Mrs. Boles. "It's them country brats. Arrol comes 'ome from school an' ses the other kids 'ave soup for their dinners an' why can't we? 'E ses they 'ave stew with carrots an' turnips an' wot not. Then Elmie chips in an' ses, 'Why can't we 'ave puddin' sometimes?'"

"Well, why can't they?" asked Jerry.

"They never wanted it before."

"It's easier to give them bread and jam or fish and chips but it isn't so good for them, you know."

Mrs. Boles sniffed. She said, "I'd loike to see Bert's faice if I started givin' 'im fancy cookin'—an' wot's good enough for Bert is good enough for them."

"Food isn't everything," said Jerry.

"It's a lot," replied the woman. "And it ain't only food,

neither. It's clothes, too. 'I want thick shoes,' Elmie ses. 'I want a skirt an' a jersey loike wot the other girls 'as. I want a night-dress'...it's *I want* all the toime. She's gettin' too big for 'er boots, that's wot."

Jerry felt inclined to smile, but only for a moment. She realized that this was no smiling matter to Mrs. Boles. Indeed it was a vital problem and one that was being encountered all over the country...and she could find no answer to it. She had never liked Mrs. Boles but at this moment she *almost* liked her, for she understood, as she had never understood before, what Mrs. Boles was suffering.

Mrs. Boles was waiting for an answer, or at least some sort of reaction to her complaints, and Jerry was forced to speak. She said without much conviction, "Why not try to give them what they want?"

"Because they didn't ought to want it," replied Mrs. Boles.

"I wonder," said Jerry thoughtfully. "I think you should be pleased if Elmie wants to be like the other children."

"Ho, do you!" cried Mrs. Boles. "You think I ought to be pleased that my own kid looks down on me! I'll teach 'er to look down on me. We're goin' back 'ome. She'll soon ferget 'er fancy ideers when we gets 'ome to Stepney."

The exodus of the Boles family took place two days later. Jerry had said good-bye to them in the morning, had reminded Mrs. Boles that a small van was coming for them at two o'clock to take them and their luggage to the station, and had given them a little present to pay their fares and other expenses of the journey. It was not necessary to give them anything, of course, for she had given them more than enough already—one way and another—but she gave it to them, hoping that it would salve her conscience, which was behaving in a most extraordinary way. Her conscience said, "You shouldn't let them go home. There may be a raid on Stepney. They may be killed and it will be all your fault," and her conscience continued to say these uncomfortable things although it must have known perfectly well that Jerry had done all she could to make Mrs. Boles stay: had talked until she was tired and bribed her with offers of more coal and free milk and vegetables from the garden. In fact Jerry had done everything to make Mrs. Boles stay at Ganthorne Cottage, everything short of binding the woman hand and foot and locking her in the toolshed, so it really was extremely odd that her conscience should keep on bothering her like this. I suppose it's because I'm glad they're going, thought Jerry. I *am* glad, of course, but I can't *help* being glad...

Markie had not said good-bye to the Boles family in the morning, for she intended to be on the spot when they left. Markie had no illusions about Mrs. Boles, partly because Markie was naturally a good judge of human nature and partly because Mrs. Boles had a curiously shaped head. Markie was very much interested in Mrs. Boles's head—she would have liked to measure it.

It was just after two when Markie arrived at the cottage; the van was already there, and, as Markie approached, she saw a large roll of dark red material being carried down the steps.

"Those are Mrs. Abbott's curtains," said Markie in her mildest voice.

The vanman, who was carrying the bundle, hesitated— and at that moment Mrs. Boles appeared in the doorway and demanded what was up.

Markie could not reply immediately. She was struck dumb by the magnificence of Mrs. Boles. She had seen the woman slopping about in torn and dirty garments with her hair in curlers and her face smeared with soot, but today, for the first time, she beheld Mrs. Boles in war paint. Mrs. Boles was wearing a black satin coat and a hat with a red feather in it, and high-heeled patent leather shoes with steel buckles on them. Her hair was frizzed to the limit (and no wonder after nearly two years confinement in steel curlers); her face was thickly powdered; her hands were encased in gray kid gloves.

"The lady ses these belongs to Mrs. Abbott," said the vanman. "Are they to go in the van or not?"

"You put them in the van," said Mrs. Boles firmly. "Mrs. Abbott sed we could 'ave them."

"I think not," said Markie, finding her voice. "I am afraid you must have been mistaken. We require the curtains for the blackout, you see...and that kettle belongs to Mrs. Abbott, too, *and* the large saucepan."

"I never thort she'd grudge us a kettle!" exclaimed Mrs. Boles, more in sorrow than anger.

Markie took no notice. She was aware that if Jerry had been present the things would have been given to Mrs. Boles without a murmur, but Jerry was not present and it was Markie's duty to look after her interests—besides it was quite impossible to replace the things. Money wouldn't buy blackout curtains or saucepans; kettles were as rare and difficult to obtain as rocs' eggs.

"And that is Mrs. Abbott's rug," continued Markie, still in her gentlest voice. "It's the hearth rug from the kitchen, isn't it, Mrs. Boles? You may take those pillows if you like—they won't be any use to anybody—but the door mat must be put back... and the coal hammer, of course."

"Nosey!" cried Mrs. Boles. "Nosey Parker—wot's it got to do with you! Mrs. Abbott wouldn't mind me taikin' one or two little things. Mrs. Abbott's a real lidy—and that's more than you are!"

Markie was too busy to listen to these insults. She had opened an untidy bulging sack and was sorting out its contents. Mrs. Boles had intended to take all the cutlery back to Stepney with her...

"They're only Woolworths'," declared Mrs. Boles in disgust.

"But they are not yours."

"I wouldn't be seen dead with them. You can 'ave them an' welcome."

Markie sighed. It was a most unpleasant job but if everything were removed from the cottage it would be impossible for anyone to live there—at any rate until the war was over and the things could be replaced.

"You'd better hurry or we'll lose the train," said the vanman, looking at his watch. "The train won't wait for you—nor anyone. Is this all that's to go?"

Mrs. Boles lifted her voice and screamed for her children, and after a moment's delay they came running out of the cottage. Elmie looked much as usual except that her hair, which was usually straight and lanky, had been tortured into a frizz, but Arrol presented a very odd appearance, for his best clothes—which he had not worn for some months—were now so much too small for him that he could scarcely move.

"Wot's that you've got 'old of, Arrol?" inquired Mrs. Boles.

Arrol displayed a glass jam jar full of tadpoles. "I'm takin' them 'ome with me," he said.

"No, you don't!" cried his mother. "We don't want no country trash."

"My tadpoles!" yelled Arrol, dodging behind the van and clasping the jar firmly against his chest.

Mrs. Boles pursued, and, after a short tussle during which Arrol received a box on the ears, she managed to get hold of the jar and empty it onto the path.

"My tadpoles!" screamed Arrol. "My tadpoles!"

"Shut up, do," said Mrs. Boles, not unkindly. "You won't want no tadpoles at Stepney. You'll be goin' to the pictures and playin' with the other kids. Don't raw like that, Arrol. Jus' think wot a noice toime you're goin' to 'ave!"

But Arrol continued to roar. He was still roaring when he

was dragged into the van and the door was shut. He was still roaring when the van lurched away down the drive.

Markie watched until the van was out of sight and then she shook her head and sighed. "Most unfortunate!" she said.

The cleansing of the cottage reminded Markie of the fifth task of Hercules, so she decided; but the Augean Stables had been tenanted by animals that, compared with Mrs. Boles, were clean…"All the same it has got to be done," said Markie firmly as she tied on her apron and got to work.

Chapter Thirteen
Wilhelmina

I t was fully a week before the cottage was cleaned to Markie's satisfaction. She did a little each day, washing the curtains and carpets as she went along—indeed she washed everything in the place and Fraser came in and gave her a hand whenever he could manage it.

"I wish you would leave it to me, Fraser," declared Markie when she saw him on his knees scrubbing the kitchen floor. "You have your own work and your leisure should be spent in recreation."

"Hoots," replied Fraser. "This puts me in mind of home. You'd not grudge me a wee bit of pleasure."

"It cannot be a pleasure to scrub a floor!"

"It is. I like fine to see the place looking clean and to think I've had a hand in it. I was vexed when I saw the way yon woman misused the wee house—fushionless slawpie that she was."

"She was, indeed," agreed Markie, who had not heard these terms for nearly thirty years. "She was indeed."

"And the bairns," continued Fraser. "I was vexed for the bairns. What's to become of them!"

Markie did not know.

"Something should be done," continued Fraser, as he

scrubbed industriously. "Folks like that are not fit to be trusted with bairns."

"What could be done?" asked Markie. "The children are her own. You would not take them away from her."

"I ken fine what I'd do if I had my way," he replied. "I'd put her in the duck pond and keep her there. Maybe she'd be cleaner when she came out of it."

"She could hardly be dirtier," agreed Miss Marks with a sigh.

They worked in silence for a little. Markie polishing the window and Fraser scrubbing the floor...and presently as Markie stooped to pick up her shammy she perceived a packet of Jackal cigarettes lying at her feet.

"Oh!" exclaimed Markie, looking at them.

"You've not had your fags lately," said Fraser.

It was rather a curious way of making a presentation, but it was Fraser's way. Miss Marks had been given cigarettes before by her fellow countrymen and they had always been conveyed to her obliquely. Sometimes she discovered them in the pocket of her overall (which usually hung behind the kitchen door); sometimes she found them in the coal scuttle. There was never any doubt as to the donor, of course, for Miss Marks and Fraser understood each other.

"Oh, Fraser!" exclaimed Miss Marks, looking at the packet of cigarettes in dismay, "Oh, Fraser, how very, very good of you—but really."

"D'you like them?" asked Fraser.

"Well, Fraser," said Markie. "To tell you the truth I always smoke one particular brand of cigarette—when I can obtain it, of course."

"These are not much use to you, then?"

"If you want to give me something that I should value very highly, give me matches," said Markie.

"They're not easy to come by."

"I know," agreed Markie. "I know that well. Matches seem to have vanished from the face of the earth, and, as we have no electricity in the house, I am often at my wits' end for a means of lighting the fire."

"Have you not a lighter?"

"No, I am sorry to say neither Mrs. Abbott nor I possess a cigarette lighter, and they are not to be bought. We have tried all over Wandlebury and Gostown. It really is a problem. Once the fire is lighted we can manage with tapers, of course. It is the fire that is the trouble. You know, Fraser, it is a very curious thing that we have become so dependent upon the match."

"That's so," agreed Fraser, kneeling back and looking up at her. "We didn't think much of them when we had them. What did folk do before they were invented?"

"They used flint and steel. As a matter of fact I have been experimenting with flint and steel myself."

"Did you get a spark?" inquired Fraser.

"Not a satisfactory one," she told him. "My experiments have been unsuccessful, but I shall go on trying."

"You'll need a special kind of contraption," said Fraser thoughtfully. "Maybe I could make one for you—I'll have a go at it."

Markie expressed her gratitude. She was delighted to see that the packet of cigarettes had been returned to Fraser's pocket, and even more delighted to think that these tokens of his esteem would not embarrass her again. If Fraser could manufacture some sort of "contraption" that would serve to light her fire Markie would be his debtor for life—she had not exaggerated the gravity of her matchless condition. It was all the more strange (thought Markie as she polished the cottage windows) because Ganthorne had been built in a matchless age. Our forefathers had never depended upon matches. Markie had done her best with flint and steel and she had tried other methods as well.

She was widely read and was aware that savages obtained fire by rubbing two sticks together—Markie had rubbed two sticks together until her hands were full of splinters, but no fire had resulted.

The problem was acute and exceedingly inconvenient but it provided Markie with food for thought—and very interesting food. She realized, for the first time, how very important fire was. We lost sight of the meaning of fire when it was easy to produce. Fire was one of Heaven's best gifts to man. Fire was life. Markie began to realize the meaning of the Vestal Virgins who tended the sacred fire night and day and never allowed it to die.

These philosophical reflections were worthwhile in themselves, but they bore practical fruit, and the next time Markie went to Wandlebury, she bought a box of nightlights that relieved the situation a good deal. Ganthorne was now a place of sacred fire and this sacred fire would not be extinguished until Fraser evolved his contraption of flint and steel. A classical education was not altogether useless, as some people were apt to imagine.

The day came when the Augean Labor was completed. The cottage was once more spick and span—fresh and clean as soap and water could make it—and every trace of that queer sickly smell had vanished in the breeze that blew in through the widely open windows and set the curtains jangling on their rings. Markie stood on the doorstep and looked at the sky. The light was fading. A purple cloud hung above the stable roofs and, behind the cloud, the sky was pure saffron. It was very peaceful and very beautiful. Markie was tired and a pain that had begun to bother her a little was nagging in her side, but in spite of this she felt happy. The thought that she had banished a plague spot from her beloved Ganthorne gave her intense satisfaction.

She was about to shut the door and go home when she saw

somebody cross the path in front of her and disappear in the direction of the stables. The light was too dim to see who it was, but she was certain it was not Jerry—it was too small and somehow a trifle furtive. Jerry walked boldly; she did not slink like that. After a moment's hesitation Markie followed and she arrived in the stable yard just in time to see the mysterious figure disappear into Dapple's loose box. She pushed open the door and peered about in the gloom. "Who is there?" she said.

"It's only me," said a small voice, and Elmie Boles emerged from behind the pony's back.

"Elmie!" exclaimed Markie in dismay.

Elmie began to sob. She did not cry like an ordinary child, but with deep half-strangled sobs that seemed to shake her small ill-nourished body with the violence of earthquakes.

"Don't cry like that!" exclaimed Markie in alarm.

"I can't—'elp—it," gasped Elmie.

"What has happened? Why have you come back?"

There was no reply.

"Come out and let me see you," said Markie firmly. "There now. That's better. What's the matter, Elmie?"

"I couldn't—bear it—that's wot," declared Elmie between her gasps.

"What couldn't you bear?"

"'ome," said Elmie.

"Goodness me!" exclaimed Markie, and her heart sank into her boots.

"It was 'orrible," declared Elmie with a gulp.

"I thought you were quite pleased to go back to Stepney. Your mother was pleased."

"Not me. I might of thort I would be, but I wasn't. I couldn't bear it another minute—so I come back 'ere."

"But why?" asked Markie in exasperation. "Why did you come back *here*?"

"'Cos I 'adn't got nowhere else to go."

"But, Elmie—"

"An' you did my finger for me," added Elmie, looking at her finger, which, though perfectly healed, still bore the scar of her wound.

Markie was too kindhearted to wish that she had not cured Elmie's wound, but she *almost* wished it. She reflected that things worked in an odd way in this odd world. It was because she had taken a good deal of trouble over Elmie's finger that Elmie had returned to cause more trouble at Ganthorne Lodge. "How did you come?" asked Markie with a sigh. "Who brought you?"

"Nobody brought me. I stood in the road an' pointed."

"Did your parents know you were coming?"

Elmie shook her head. "We 'ad a row," she said. "Gor' it was a row, too! We wos all shoutin' fit ter rise the roof...then Dad ses, 'Orl roight,' 'e ses, 'if my 'ouse ain't good enough you can get out an' stye out.' So I ses, 'Okay,' an' I walks out."

"Goodness!" said Markie in dismay.

"I won't go back, neither," said Elmie.

"I'm afraid you'll have to go back."

Elmie began to sob again. "Nobody wants me," she wailed. "Nobody wants me an' I don't want nobody—I'd be better dead."

"Blow your nose, Elmie," said Miss Marks, handing over her own large clean pocket handkerchief. "Wipe your eyes and don't talk nonsense. We must think what is to be done."

"I'll do anything if you let me stye," declared Elmie, coming closer and laying a thin grimy hand on Markie's arm. "I will reelly. I can sleep in the stible with Dapple so I won't be no trouble...an' I don't need much food, just a few scraps that you can spare...I'll work, too. I will, reelly, if you'll jus' let me stye..."

The hoarse eager voice went on, making all the promises its owner could think of, making the most extravagant promises of hard work and good behavior…so much so that Markie's heart was touched and she began to wonder whether it could possibly be arranged. The parents would have to be informed and their consent obtained, of course…

"Well, anyway, we cannot do anything tonight," said Markie at last. "You had better come up to the house and have something to eat."

"Just a crust," said Elmie. "That's all I want—an' I can 'ave it 'ere—an' I can sleep 'ere with Dapple. I won't be no bother to nobody."

"You will do as you are told," said Markie firmly.

∽∾

Jerry had been spending the evening at the Archway House. It was late when she got home and she expected Markie to be in bed, but she found Markie sitting by the fire, smoking like a chimney and reading the morning paper.

"I had no time to read it before," said Markie, laying it down. "Not that it matters because there is very little news. Everything seems to have reached a sort of deadlock…and the government is being urged to start a second front."

"It would be a seventh front," replied Jerry. "At least that's what Uncle Arthur says. He says it's wrong and silly and dangerous for people to go on screaming for another front."

"Mr. Abbott's views are always extremely sound," declared Markie. Jerry nodded. She said, "But what on earth have you been doing with yourself if you haven't had time to read the paper. I suppose you've been working at the cottage, cleaning up the Boles's mess—I wish you wouldn't, Markie. Isn't there anybody you could get to help you?"

"Fraser helped me," replied Markie. She sighed and added, "I have done a good deal of cleaning today, one way and another."

"Thank goodness we're rid of *famille* Boles!"

"But we are not. Wilhelmina has returned."

"What! Elmie!"

"I think we should call her Wilhelmina."

"Call her what you like—why on earth has she come back?"

"She did not like Stepney."

"Markie, don't be so mysterious!" cried Jerry. "You sit there like a heathen idol, smoking and smiling to yourself. Tell me what's happened. Where *is* the child?"

"In bed," said Markie, smiling more broadly than before.

"Not in *this* house, I hope!"

"She's perfectly clean, dear. I washed her thoroughly with carbolic soap and cut her hair. Really she is quite a nice-looking child. You wouldn't know her."

"I certainly wouldn't," agreed Jerry. "Not if she's clean."

"The point is," continued Markie, lighting another cigarette and inhaling deeply. "The point is what are we to do with Wilhelmina."

"Send her back to her parents, of course."

"Yes, dear. That does seem the solution at first sight, but I do not think she will go. I tried to reason with her, of course, but she seems adamant. She threatens to throw herself into the river if we turn her away—and I really believe she might carry out the threat."

"But Markie—"

"There is much to be thought of," continued Markie, who had given the matter a good deal of attention. "It is not such a simple problem as it appears. The child has run away from home, but her home is not what it should be. She has run away from her parents, but her parents have done little for her except to give her birth."

"Markie, listen," began Jerry, trying to interrupt this flow of reasoned judgment.

"No, dear," said Markie. "I have thought it out and I want to give you my views. After I have finished I shall be delighted to listen to you. Wilhelmina has been brought up in squalor but now she realizes there is a better way of living; she has come back and is clinging to Ganthorne as a drowning man clings to a raft. Are we justified in pushing her back into the sea and allowing her to drown?"

"What are you going to do with her?" asked Jerry, brushing aside all question of drowning men and rafts and coming straight to the point.

"That is for you to decide."

Jerry laughed. She said, "What's the use of me deciding when you've already decided. I hope it isn't kidnapping or anything."

"My dear!" exclaimed Markie in horrified tones.

"Well, it's something like that. We aren't justified in keeping her without her parents' permission, and I don't suppose they would give it, would they?"

"She thinks not," said Markie, looking a trifle embarrassed. "In fact she obtained my promise not to write to them."

"Won't they be anxious about her?" asked Jerry. "I should think they'll be in a most awful stew when they find she's disappeared—they'll put the police on her track or something."

"I raised that point with her," replied Markie. "But Wilhelmina is quite certain that we need not envisage trouble of that nature. In fact the idea that her parents might seek help from the police seemed to amuse her considerably."

"Not 'arf they won't," said Jerry, smiling.

"Those were her exact words," nodded Markie, returning the smile somewhat ruefully. "Her choice of idiom is deplorable."

"You'll soon sweat it out of her," said Jerry.

"Really, Jerry!"

"It explains exactly what I mean," declared Jerry. "Honestly it does. I couldn't think of any other way of expressing it. Oh, of course, I know you haven't been very successful with me, but Elmie's young and green. You'll—er—get her to talk like a book before you've had her very long. She must work, of course," continued Jerry. "We're all workers, here—and I won't have her carrying on with the soldiers."

"I shall look after her," said Markie. "I shall give her a little instruction—just a few little simple daily—"

"That's another thing—what about school?"

"She has left school," replied Markie. "The child is fourteen and in the eyes of the law her education is complete. In my opinion, of course—"

"I know," said Jerry, interrupting hastily, for she knew Markie's opinion on this point and had no wish to hear it again. "I know all that, Markie. You'll be able to teach her things, but you mustn't let her bother you."

"It will be no trouble," declared Markie. "No trouble at all."

In this statement Markie was perfectly sincere, for if there was one job she enjoyed more than another it was the job of improving people, of working with human nature in a malleable form. Girls were Markie's specialty, young unformed characters, the women of the future—here was the very best material given into her hand.

"I suppose her head is all right," said Jerry as she rose and snibbed the window preparatory to going upstairs to bed.

"It is well-shaped, dear," replied Markie seriously—"and the ear is well formed and set. I think we shall have very little trouble with Wilhelmina."

Chapter Fourteen
Enter Miss Watt

Markie was preparing supper in the pantry. It was to be a particularly good supper tonight because Miss Watt would be here…what would she be like, Markie wondered. It was just like Jerry to ask her to come, in that impulsive way, and of course Jerry had a perfect right to ask anyone she liked; but supposing Miss Watt were like cocoa (thought Markie as she stirred some of that useful and nutritious beverage into her custard and watched the whole pudding turn pale brown) supposing Miss Watt had a strong flavor and changed the whole atmosphere of their lives. Most people were like some ingredient—weren't they?—and a pudding was never the same with an added ingredient. Sometimes of course the flavor of the pudding was improved (as Markie hoped the addition of cocoa would improve her pudding), but the question was whether the flavor of Ganthorne Lodge *could* be improved. Markie thought not.

Jerry had described her prospective P. G. and Jerry—in her own peculiar way—was rather good at describing people, so Markie had quite a definite idea of what Miss Watt would look like. She could not remember the exact words of the description but from it she had envisaged a nice-looking young woman, rather dressy in a mild way, with fair curls and brown eyes and a pink and white complexion, so when she saw the pony cart coming up the drive and hurried into the hall to welcome the guest and help with the luggage Markie was very much surprised. Miss Watt certainly had fair hair and brown eyes—an unusual combination—but there the resemblance between Markie's conception and the real Miss Watt ended abruptly, for the real Miss Watt was certainly not "dressy" even in the mildest way. She was clad in a gray tweed suit and a blue viyella shirt with a collar and a tie, and when she removed her perfectly plain gray felt hat Markie saw that her hair was short and straight. (As short as a prewar man's hair, thought Markie a trifle vaguely.) There are women, of course, who look "right" in mannish clothes and mannish haircuts, but Miss Watt looked odd—so Markie thought.

"This is Markie," said Jerry. "Miss Marks, Miss Watt...I've told you all about each other and Markie will give you some tea while I put Dapple away...or perhaps sherry if it's too late for tea. Have we any, Markie?"

"Of course," said Markie. "Do come in, Miss Watt. There's a good fire in the sitting room...or would you rather go straight up to your room? Supper will be ready in about half an hour."

Markie waited anxiously for Miss Watt's answer to this inquiry—not that it mattered a pin whether she came into the sitting room and partook of sherry or went upstairs and unpacked, but because it mattered a great deal what sort of voice she had. There were some people who spoke clearly, with a sort of bell-like note in their voices (Jerry was one of these) and there were others who mumbled and muttered and ran their words together in a hopeless jumble of sound.

A good deal depended upon Miss Watt's voice—everything as far as Markie was concerned—for if Markie could not hear what Miss Watt said (or hearing, could not understand) life would be most uncomfortable. Oddly enough Markie had not noticed voices very much until she became deaf, but now voices were more important than anything else. This was one of the reasons she enjoyed the company of the soldiers...when she was with them she forgot she was deaf.

Miss Watt replied quite audibly in a pleasantly modulated voice that she would love a glass of sherry if it really could be spared, and followed Miss Marks into the sitting room.

"What a perfect room!" she exclaimed, standing in the doorway and looking around. "It looks so *right,* doesn't it?"

Markie knew what she meant and agreed. She was aware that strictly speaking the room was not right as regards period (the Elizabethan age was by no means a luxurious one and a room furnished strictly in period would have been uncomfortable to say the least of it), but the sitting room at Ganthorne seemed to strike the right note; the cushioned window seat, the few good pictures, and the well-worn, well-polished furniture harmonized with the oddly shaped, low-ceilinged room and the lozenge paned windows. Perhaps this was because they had all been here so long and grown old together.

Supper was set for three on a gate-legged table and Markie explained that she and Jerry always had their meals here.

"I know," said Miss Watt. "Mrs. Abbott told me everything." She sat down on the window seat as she spoke and looked around again. "How peaceful it is," she added.

"You may find it dull," Markie suggested.

"I don't think so," replied Miss Watt. "I need peace."

"You've been living in London, perhaps?"

"No, I'm used to the country. It wasn't that sort of peace I meant. It was inside peace, really. Peace to be myself."

Jerry came in at that moment and they drank their sherry and chatted in a friendly way, but when Miss Watt had been conducted upstairs and left to wash for supper, Jerry seized Markie's arm in a vicelike grip and dragged her into her bedroom and shut the door.

"Well, Markie?" said Jerry anxiously.

"My dear," began Markie in doubtful tones. "My dear child, if you mean what do I think—"

"Of course I do. Markie, she's quite different."

"Different?"

"Quite, quite different," said Jerry earnestly. "She's like a different person, if you know what I mean."

"Different from what?"

"From the person I met on Mr. Tupper's doorstep."

"Do you mean she is not Miss Watt?" asked Markie in alarm.

"No," replied Jerry. "No, of course not. I mean she's changed."

"But Jerry—"

"Honestly, Markie, she's—she's got a different *smell*," declared Jerry, wrinkling up her whole face in her effort to explain.

"She seems very pleasant—" began Markie.

"You don't like her!" exclaimed Jerry. "I can *see* you don't like her. Well, in that case, she'll have to go—that's all. Nobody's coming to live here that you don't like."

"I didn't say I disliked Miss Watt."

"No, but you meant it."

"No," said Markie. "No, you are too apt to jump to conclusions. Let us withhold judgment," added Markie, nodding her head gravely. "Let us withhold judgment."

"What a bore!" said Jerry with a sigh.

Markie could not help smiling. Jerry was impatient of delays, she liked everything settled; Jerry was too fond of dividing people into sheep and goats and too fond of carrying out this arbitrary division without due consideration.

Supper was a pleasant meal. It consisted of stewed rabbit and mashed potatoes followed by the pale brown custard pudding Markie had been making when Miss Watt arrived. "Rabbit!" said Jerry in surprise.

"Fraser gave it to me," replied Markie smiling. "He got it

yesterday when they were doing a tactical exercise on the moor. But perhaps one should not say too much about it."

"Mum's the word," agreed Jerry with an answering smile. "It's like this, you see," she added, turning to Miss Watt. "Fraser was born in Fife so he likes giving Markie presents."

Markie was about to elucidate Jerry's explanation—which seemed to her inadequate—but she found there was no need.

"So you're a Fifer, too!" exclaimed Miss Watt, turning to Markie. "No, I'm afraid I wasn't actually born there, but my father was, and we used to spend our holidays at St. Andrews."

"Brothers and sisters?" asked Jerry with interest.

"One sister a good deal older than myself," replied Miss Watt. "Our parents died when I was quite small. I scarcely remember them."

"Your sister brought you up?" asked Markie.

"Yes," replied Miss Watt.

She said no more about herself and Jerry returned to the subject of Fraser. "He's Markie's best boy," she declared.

Markie smiled for she was used to Jerry's teasing.

"He gives Markie packets of cigarettes," said Jerry, nodding. "But unfortunately Markie is addicted to Turkish cigarettes—it's her one extravagance—so Fraser's particular brand isn't much use to her…Which will you have?" added Jerry, for by this time they had finished supper and were partaking of coffee by the fire. "Will you have one of my gaspers or a Turk from Markie?"

After a moment's hesitation Miss Watt accepted a gasper and they all three lighted up with a spill from the fire.

Cigarette smoking is so universal that one is apt to forget it requires a certain amount of practice, so when Markie and Jerry beheld their guest coughing and watering at the eyes they ascribed these unpleasant symptoms to a choking fit. But when the symptoms continued (and Miss Watt, holding her weed as far away from her as possible, took swift mouthfuls of smoke and expelled them still more swiftly with pursed lips and an expression of pained surprise) they realized that they were watching a novice at the game.

"Throw it away," suggested Miss Marks, pointing to the fire and exuding a cloud of warm gray smoke with the words.

Miss Watt threw it away at once. "I didn't know you had to learn," she said in a regretful tone.

Her companions had not known either. The memory of their first cigarettes was lost in the mists of time.

"But why learn?" asked Jerry. "I mean they're so scarce, now, and so frightfully expensive."

"I thought it would be nice."

"And why cut your hair?" asked Jerry, for somehow or other she had a vague feeling that the two things went together.

"Oh!" said Miss Watt in a somewhat embarrassed manner. "Oh, I don't know. I just thought...so I had it cut off. I look awful, don't I?"

"You have a very well-shaped head," said Markie.

"*There!*" exclaimed Jerry. "And Markie *knows* about heads—she'll tell you what your racial characteristics are. Markie is brilliantly clever. She knows ethnology and anthropology—"

"Jerry!" cried Markie in dismay. "How often have I told you not to exaggerate my attainments! Miss Watt will think we are most extraordinary people—"

"I look awful," repeated Miss Watt sadly.

"You don't," replied Jerry comfortingly. She didn't look awful, exactly, thought Jerry, but she certainly did look a little strange. Jerry glanced at Markie and tried to catch her eye, for she longed to know what Markie was thinking—but Markie would not rise.

The following morning Markie started to turn out the sitting room but before she had got very far Miss Watt appeared and, seizing a broom leaning against the wall, she signified her intention to join in the operations.

"There is no need," said Markie. "I can do it myself. Why not go out and have a look around—"

"There's plenty of time for that," replied Miss Watt.

It was obvious that Miss Watt was not used to domestic work, but she was doing her best to help, and Markie gave her credit for her good intentions.

"You are not used to housework, Miss Watt," said Markie as she rolled up the hearth rug.

"No, but I can learn—and please don't call me Miss Watt," said Miss Watt, seizing the rug in her arms.

"Jane?" inquired Markie doubtfully.

"Yes, Jane. What shall I do with this?"

"Take it outside and beat it."

"Of course—how silly of me!" said Jane and she bore it away.

"You like housework, Miss Marks," said Jane when she returned with the rug.

"Yes," said Markie. "Yes, it does not trouble me. Fortunately one can think of other things...don't start dusting the mantelpiece until I have finished sweeping the floor."

"How silly of me!" exclaimed Jane.

"Not silly at all. You are not used to this sort of work. I have no doubt there are a great many things you can do well. Perhaps you paint?" suggested Markie.

"No," replied Jane.

"Are you musical?"

"I like music," replied Jane. "I don't play or sing—if that's what you mean."

"Are you interested in history?"

"Er—yes, of course," replied Jane in a tone that disabused Markie of the hope that she might have found a kindred spirit.

This curious catechism was not being made for pleasure. Markie was not an inquisitive person, she was too fond of her own privacy to pry into other people's affairs, but she had a feeling that she ought to find out a little about Miss Watt—it was her duty to do so.

"Do you know this part of the country?" she asked, trying a different gambit.

"I've driven through it in the car once or twice."

"It is very pretty."

"Most attractive...and once I came over to Wandlebury to—" She paused.

"Yes?" asked Markie.

"To tea," said Jane.

They worked away for a little in silence.

"I have a feeling I have seen you before," said Markie suddenly.

"Oh no," said Jane hastily. "No, I'm sure you're wrong. I should have remembered you at once."

"I did not mean that we had met," Markie explained. "Merely that I have seen you somewhere."

"Shall I start dusting, now?" asked Jane.

"You are interested in Christian Science," said Markie, handing her a duster...she had found a book upon Christian Science in Jane's room when she went in to make the bed.

"Yes," said Jane. "At least I don't know much about it. I just thought it might help to—to clear up something in my mind."

"Perhaps it may," agreed Markie. "There was a mistress at Wheatfield House who practiced Christian Science and she had an extremely lucid mind..." Here Markie knelt down upon the hearth rug and began to lay the fire in the empty grate. "She was agreeable and cultured," continued Markie. "I liked her very much and I was much interested in her conversation."

"Did she convert you?" Jane asked.

"No, dear. If I have a pain I just take an aspirin in a little water. There is no need to bother God about it."

Markie had now made up her mind about Jane. She liked her. If she had not liked Jane she would not have called her "dear." She liked Jane but she had not learnt much about her, and what she had learnt made her more mysterious instead of less...for now it was obvious to Markie that Jane had a secret.

Markie was perfectly certain she had seen Jane before, and she said so to Jerry; but Jerry disagreed.

"I haven't, anyhow," said Jerry. "I should have remembered her, I'm sure. She's so unusual, isn't she? So unusual to look at, I mean."

"Perhaps she was not always so unusual," said Markie thoughtfully.

Chapter Fifteen
New Tenants for the Cottage

Nearly a week had passed since Wilhelmina Boles had returned to Ganthorne and nothing had been heard of her parents. Jerry was not quite happy about the affair, for she felt that the parents should be informed of their daughter's safety, but whenever the subject was mentioned to Wilhelmina she began to sob in that horrible strangled way—which had frightened Markie at their first encounter—and declared between her gasps that nobody wanted her and she would drown herself in the river. Jerry might have written a note to Mrs. Boles on her own account but she did not know the address and Wilhelmina refused point-blank to disclose it—"Mrs. Boles, Stepney," was obviously insufficient to ensure the delivery of a letter to Wilhelmina's maternal parent.

Markie took no part in the struggle, for she had made up her mind to keep Wilhelmina and make her into a useful citizen. She had not expected much trouble with Wilhelmina, but neither had she expected so little. The child was clever and anxious to learn. She knew nothing, of course, but if you showed her how to do a thing she remembered it and did it correctly—and went on doing it.

"You must keep yourself clean," Markie told her. "That's the first thing to remember because, if you are not clean yourself, you cannot keep other things clean."

Wilhelmina nodded. "Okay," she said.

"Say 'Yes, Miss,'" said Markie.

Wilhelmina said it obediently.

"Whatever you do, do it well," said Markie. "If you respect yourself you will be too proud to do it badly. I want you to respect yourself, Wilhelmina."

"Yes, miss," said Wilhelmina. "I want to be clean an' noice. I do reelly."

Markie had found some old dresses that had belonged to Jerry when Jerry was a child. They had been put away in a box in the attic and forgotten, but now Markie resurrected them and altered them to fit her protégée. She took a good deal of trouble over their fit, for she wanted the child to look well—it was all part of the plan. Wilhelmina was delighted with the frocks; she wore them with pride and washed them and ironed them herself.

There was a long mirror in Jerry's room and one day when Jerry went into the room she found Wilhelmina standing in front of the mirror looking at her reflection in the glass.

"Well, what do you think of yourself?" asked Jerry.

"I think I look nice," declared Wilhelmina, who already, under Markie's tutelage, was beginning to pronounce her vowels in a more conventional manner.

"I think so, too," said Jerry smiling.

She looked well and she looked happy. Her eyes were brighter and there was a faint tinge of pink in her cheeks. Her hair had improved, too; it was smoothly brushed and tied at one side with a piece of blue ribbon Markie had bought for her in Wandlebury.

"You look very nice," said Jerry, nodding. "And you're very useful to Miss Marks. I've decided to pay you wages."

There were now two extra people at Ganthorne—Miss Watt and Wilhelmina—and Markie found herself with leisure for reading. It was real leisure (not just little snippets of time while the kettle boiled or the sausages were frying in the pan) but Markie did not enjoy it quite so much as she expected, nor did she get so much hard reading done, because she was beginning to get uneasy. The pain in her side bothered her more often and her panacea—an aspirin in a little water—did not always have the desired effect. Sometimes the pain was bad and sometimes it was so slight that she forgot about it, but it was never really absent...and it frightened her. Supposing she got ill, what would Jerry do? Jerry would keep her and look after her tenderly—Markie never doubted that—but Markie did not like the idea of being a burden. In fact it was a frightful idea. Markie began to get thinner and her skirt bands became so loose that her skirts went around and around. It's because of the war, said Markie to herself, but she did not believe it. She was aware that the sensible thing to do would be to go to the doctor and ask him what was the matter with her, but supposing Dr. Wrench found it was something serious, thought Markie. Supposing he said she must remain in bed! He might discover that it was—no, it could not be that. She would not even think of it. Thinking things brought them to you—at least some people said so.

Markie was in the sitting room, trying to read *Blumenback's Manual of Comparative Anatomy and Physiology* and finding it a little less absorbing than usual when the window was suddenly darkened by a large body. Markie looked up and saw that it belonged to Colonel Melton.

"It's about the cottage," he said, leaning his arms on the window sill. "Is it to let, Miss Marks?"

"I don't think Jerry has thought of it," said Markie in surprise.

"Do you think she would let it to me?"

"To you!"

"For my daughter," he explained. "Melanie is very anxious to come to Ganthorne and be here with me."

"It wouldn't be nice enough," objected Markie. "It isn't that sort of cottage."

"Fraser thinks it would do," interrupted Colonel Melton. "Fraser is really at the bottom of the whole thing. He told Melanie about the cottage and Melanie has written to me saying I'm to take it. The fact is Fraser has been with me for so long that he practically runs me," declared Colonel Melton smiling. "I run the battalion and Fraser runs me. It works quite well, really. Fraser is tremendously loyal and trustworthy; he's a benevolent autocrat; he likes people to do exactly what he tells them and to be happy in the way he thinks best. His organizing ability is amazing, his energy is beyond belief. In short—"

"He comes from Fife," said Markie, smiling.

Colonel Melton also smiled. "Well, that's how it is," he said. "Fraser and Melanie have combined forces over the cottage so I haven't much choice in the matter."

"You had better see the cottage. I'm afraid you will be disappointed, for it is not at all well-furnished. Just wait a moment and I will get the key."

Colonel Melton waited and presently Markie appeared with the key, and together they examined the cottage with a view to Miss Melton's requirements. Colonel Melton surprised Markie a good deal, for she was not used to gentlemen who took an interest in domestic affairs (Markie's father, for instance, had scarcely known one end of a broom from the other and never noticed his surroundings unless he found cause to complain of them). The colonel looked at everything. He looked in the cupboards and beneath the carpets, he noticed that one of the bars of the range was broken and made a note of the fact. He lighted a piece of paper and put it in the grate to see if the chimney were clear. He examined the sink with meticulous care and suggested that it required a new draining board..."I'll get it done," he added hastily. "There's no need for Mrs. Abbott to bother." The bathroom window would not open easily and, when open, refused to remain in its position. "It's the weights," said Colonel Melton. "Fraser will put that right in a jiffy."

"I am afraid the bath is in a very bad condition," said Markie in apologetic tones.

"Looks as if your previous tenants had been keeping coal in it," said the colonel, laughing.

Markie did not laugh. She thought the idea by no means an improbable one.

"Never mind," said Colonel Melton. "A couple of coats of enamel will work wonders. You won't know the bath when Fraser and I have had a go at it."

"Do you really think it will do?" asked Markie anxiously.

"Of course it will do—Melanie won't mind a little inconvenience. You see we want to be together while we can. I may be sent abroad at any moment." He hesitated and then continued. "Melanie and I have never had much chance to be together. My wife died when Mell was five and I had to go to India and leave her with my sister. She was quite happy, and my sister was extremely good to her but of course it wasn't like having a home of her own. She's eighteen now—though I must say I find it difficult to believe. She's been nursing in a hospital in the north but it was too much for her and she got ill—she isn't very strong—so they sent her home to my sister for a long spell of sick leave. I want to have her near me and see something of her."

Markie nodded. She realized that there was a good deal left unsaid in this short *résumé* of Melanie's history, but she was able to fill in some of the blanks. "I wish it were better furnished," she said.

"It's beautifully clean," replied Colonel Melton. "We can bring a couple of comfortable chairs. Melanie will be quite happy here."

They had finished their tour of the cottage and were coming out of the door when Jerry came up the drive in the pony cart and stopped to speak to them.

"What have you been doing?" she asked. "You have a slightly guilty air about you as if you had been up to some mischief. I hope you aren't making off with the knives and forks—Markie has rescued them once already."

"It's the house I want," replied Colonel Melton. "The whole place—lock, stock, and barrel—not only the knives and forks."

"For target practice, I suppose!"

"No."

"Street fighting then?"

"For a purely domestic purpose."

"As a love nest?" asked Jerry seriously.

Colonel Melton laughed and after a little more cheerful badinage he explained his purpose—as he had explained it to Markie—and asked if he might have the cottage on a lease.

"Of course you can," said Jerry. "You can have it as long as you want—it used to be a nice little cottage when Mrs. Lander was here."

"Thank you very much," he replied. "Just think it over and let me know what you want in the way of rent." He hesitated and then added, "You really are most awfully kind to us. I don't feel I have thanked you half enough for your kindness to the men, but we do appreciate it. I hope they behave themselves. If there's any trouble you must let me know at once."

"It's Markie, really," said Jerry. "She has all the bother."

"They are no trouble at all," declared Markie hastily.

"You see," said Jerry gravely, as she gathered up the reins and prepared to drive on. "You see, Markie is *used* to that sort of thing. She taught in a girls' school for years and years…"

Colonel Melton choked. He tried hard not to laugh but the thing was beyond his power. He laughed until he was sore…

and all day long whenever he thought of it, and visualized Jerry's serious face and Markie's astonished one, he laughed again.

∽◇⌐

Markie worried about the cottage all night. She had cleaned it, of course, but had she really cleaned it thoroughly? Should it be cleaned all over again before Miss Melton arrived? I must go down and see, she thought, as she turned over in bed for the fourth time. I might distemper the hall and see if I can get rid of that queer greasy mark on the wallpaper...

It was afternoon before Markie had finished her household work and had found a pot of distemper and a couple of brushes. She told Wilhelmina to get tea ready at the proper hour, put on an overall, tied a red and white duster over her hair, and set forth. When she reached the cottage, she saw, with surprise, that the chimney was smoking. She hesitated and looked at it, and as she looked she was assailed by the appalling idea that Mrs. Boles had returned. Perhaps there had been a raid on London and Mrs. Boles had decided that it was better to moulder than to burn, perhaps Mrs. Boles had discovered that Wilhelmina was at Ganthorne and had come back to fetch her...but it was no use standing and looking at the smoke, Markie would have to go in and see who was there. She opened the door and went into the hall.

The door of the kitchen was ajar and, looking in, Markie saw a young girl kneeling on the hearth rug, blowing up the fire. She was so intent upon her task that she had not heard the front door open and Markie was able to have a good look at her. Pretty, thought Markie, in approval. Very, very pretty, but far too thin...as if a breath of wind would blow her away.

The girl laid down the bellows and turned. She saw Markie and bounded to her feet with one lithe movement.

"Oh!" she exclaimed. "Oh, I do hope it's all right moving in like this. Daddy telephoned last night—so I just came. Daddy was quite horrified when he saw me. He didn't really mean me to come till next week. He said he hadn't fixed it up properly with Mrs. Abbott—about the rent and everything. Are you Mrs. Abbott?"

"I'm Miss Marks," said Markie.

"Is it all right?" asked Melanie anxiously. "Will Mrs. Abbott mind? Do you think I had better go away again?"

Markie assured her that it was all right and that Mrs. Abbott would not mind in the least—she was so delighted to find that Mrs. Boles had not returned that she would have done anything for Miss Melton.

"You were going to paint something?" Miss Melton suggested, looking at the brushes and the pot of paint Miss Marks had placed on the table.

Miss Marks explained what she had meant to do, and she also explained about Mrs. Boles and her family, but she toned down the Boles family a good deal; for if Miss Melton were going to live in the cottage—and obviously she had made up her mind to do so—it would be more pleasant for her not to know the less civilized habits of its former occupants. And it *is* clean, now, thought Markie. It really is perfectly clean. I've washed *everything*.

"You can't think how happy I am," Melanie was saying. "It will be so lovely to have a little house of our very own—Daddy and I together. You see we have crowds of relations and we have always stayed with them when he had leave—they were very kind, of course, but I've always wanted to have Daddy all to myself—for my very own."

Markie nodded. She understood this quite well, for she had a great admiration for Colonel Melton.

"I've wanted it more than anything on earth," added Melanie

in a dreamy voice. She was leaning against the table, now, in an attitude of unconscious grace.

She was like a flower, Markie thought—like a spring flower, young and fresh and innocent. There was something pathetic about her youthful delicacy. Markie was quite angry with herself when she found herself indulging in such foolish sentiment so she gave herself a little shake and asked, somewhat bluntly, if Miss Melton could cook.

"Quite well, really," nodded Melanie.

"Everybody should be able to cook," declared Markie, thinking of her own case.

"Of course they should," agreed Melanie with a smile.

Chapter Sixteen
"Darling Sam"

D arling Sam," wrote Jerry.

"I never seem to have time to write in the daytime
and really it is better to write at night because there are
no interruptions and I get on quicker. I have just been
listening to the midnight news and it says, 'patrol activity
in Egypt'—and that's all it says about Egypt. I wonder if
you're on patrol and what it's like and what you think
about. It seems funny not to know. It was so lovely getting
your letters. Eight of them all at once. But I haven't got
any since so I expect you're busy or else they have been
sunk on the way. I have been writing to you regularly so I
hope you have got some of my letters all right. You sound
very cheery in your letters darling. I'm so glad you're
having an interesting time and that you have tanks of your
own now. But don't be too rash. You need not worry
about me. We are getting on splendidly. Markie and I are
both well and cheery."

(Here Jerry paused to brush away a tear.)

"Of course I miss you awfully but I am too busy to feel
dull and if I do feel dull I go over and see Barbara. She is a

cheering person as you know and I always feel better after a chat with her. You say in one of your letters, 'Tell me more about Bobby Appleyard. You seem to be seeing a lot of the fellow.' You aren't jellous of him, are you Sam? That would be silly because you are the only person that matters to me at all. Of course I see him a lot. I couldn't help seeing him unless I shut my eyes because all the officers are all over the place all the time. Their huts are in the meadow near the stream and they keep two horses in the stable. I told you about our P. G. in my last letter but I couldn't tell you much about her because she had just arrived. We were rather doubtful about her at first but now we both like her. She is a great success. Very quiet but sees a joke and has a nice laugh. I think she and Bobby Appleyard have taken a fancy to each other..."

(Jerry paused again and read over what she had just written. It looked very definite written down in blue-black ink... and, as a matter of fact, she had little grounds for her assertion. She wished it, of course, wished it with all her heart. If only those two would take a fancy to each other it would be nice for everybody: nice for them—they were both dears—and nice for Jerry, and, most important of all, it would relieve Sam's mind. For Sam *was* slightly "jellous" of Bobby—Jerry was sure of it. Of course it's all my fault, thought Jerry, biting the end of her pen. I shouldn't have mentioned Bobby to Sam, I shouldn't have driveled on about Bobby in my letters—I just did it to amuse Sam because there's so little news—and now, whatever I say, Sam will worry. If I tell him things about Bobby he will worry, and if I don't mention Bobby he will worry all the more. Having thought all this Jerry looked again at what she had written and decided to let it stand.)

"I rode over to Gostown this morning. I went across the moor—our favorite ride, Sam, and I thought of you all the time—it was such a lovely day and the bracken is just beginning to turn brown here and there. Soon the moors will be all over brown—that lovely chestnut color. You know how lovely they look. Old Cæsar went well. He seems much better—more life in him. I think the tonic has done him a lot of good. Starlight is very well. She is quite skittish these days, which is wonderful when you think of her age. Do you remember when you rode Starlight in that point-to-point? I was thinking about it this morning—how excited I was when I saw you gallop in first past the post! It seems funny only to have the two horses left—and Dapple of course—but it is just as well really because Rudge has gone…"

(Jerry hesitated again. Would Sam worry if he knew she had nobody left to help her? But I must tell him, she thought. I promised to tell him everything. I should hate it if he didn't tell me things because he thought I would worry.)

"…I didn't feel it was right to ask for Rudge to be exempted. I could have of course but I just felt it was wrong when all the others had gone. Why should Rudge stay at home comfortably and shelter behind me? That's what I thought. Do write and say you understand. There isn't much to do and I can always get Colonel Melton's batman to give me a hand if I want any extra help. That reminds me I must tell you Colonel Melton asked if he could rent the cottage so I said he could. His daughter has come to live there. She is very pretty and attractive and young, really a charming girl. I think she might do for Archie. I know you always laugh at me for trying to find a wife for Archie and say he doesn't want one but I'm sure he would be happier if he was married. Melanie Melton would be the very person for him. I'm going to do what I can about it in a tactful sort of way. I must stop now, darling Sam. There is no more news and it is very late. Markie would have a fit if she knew I wasn't in bed. Lots and lots of love, darling darling Sam from your loving— "JERRY."

There was no more news and it was very late. Jerry turned out the lamp and got into bed. "Good night, darling Sam. God keep you safe," she whispered as she laid her head on the pillow.

⚬≫⚬

Sam was not having a good night, or at least not a peaceful one. The desert was very quiet, of course, but this quietness was sometimes deceptive. Sam and his tanks were right out beyond the front line and it was an odd eerie sort of feeling…One gazed at a rock, and, if one gazed long enough, one could almost swear that it had moved, and one's hand went unconsciously to the revolver in one's belt…

It was very quiet. Not a sound broke the stillness and the stars were simply terrific; they seemed twice the size of the stars one saw at home…but of course they were the same stars, really. Sam wondered if Jerry were looking at the stars… but it was late; Jerry would be asleep. He thought of Jerry lying in bed with one hand under her cheek—she often lay like that. He could *see* her lying in the big bed with the empty space beside her. What would he give to be there? What would he give to be there for one short night, to lie beside her and feel the kind friendly warmth of her dear body? All he had. Everything.

Sam moved uncomfortably. There was sand beneath his shirt, sand in his boots and in his hair—even his eyes felt gritty.

In the light of the stars he could see the little encampment he had made. The shallow trenches with the men asleep in them, the four tanks standing around, camouflaged with nets stretched out to their fullest extent and pinned to the ground. They were properly done, for he had seen to it himself. It was difficult to get the men to understand the *principle* of camouflage, which was not only to cover the tank, but also to disguise its shape so that it did not look like a tank from the air. It was the shadows that gave you away—the shadows on the glaring sand.

This was the first time that Sam had been in command of a patrol and he was just a little anxious. His sentries were posted, of course, but he did not feel like sleep. It was cold, now. It felt colder than it really was after the heat of the day—you felt the cold more when you had been baking and boiling in the sun...

Maiden approached. Maiden was Sam's subaltern and an exceedingly good one. He was also an exceedingly fine fellow.

"Hallo, Maiden!" said Sam.

"I thought I heard something, sir."

Sam cocked his head and listened. There was a slight sound—it was a drone like a hive of bees far, far away. "A plane?" said Sam, doubtfully. "No, not a plane."

"I don't think so," agreed Maiden.

"Better rouse them," said Sam, standing up. "We can't take risks."

"Very good, sir."

The short conversation had been conducted in quiet tones—almost in a whisper—for the desert had that effect upon one, it was so quiet, so vast, so empty. It made one feel like a midget, it sapped one's confidence.

Sam left Maiden to rouse the men and walked up a little slope so as to obtain a wider view. The desert was not flat—as one had always imagined—it was a rolling plain, a plain that the force of the prevailing wind had brushed into ridges—ridges that reminded one of the ripples left on the shore by a receding tide, but magnified a thousand fold. Standing on his ridge Sam clamped his field glasses into the sockets of his eyes and swept the horizon…at first he could see nothing, but after a few moments he *did* see something away to the northwest. It looked like a very small beetle coming over a rise in the ground…and it was followed by another beetle…and another. There were five of them…no, six.

"Not ours," said Maiden's voice at his elbow.

"Can't be," agreed Sam. "Coming the wrong way for one thing."

"Going south," said Maiden.

"Yes," said Sam. He hesitated for a few moments considering his best move. The enemy tanks were passing from north to south and it was obvious that they might pass without seeing the little outpost in no-man's-land. Sam might send a message asking for reinforcements but by that time the enemy tanks would have passed. He was aware that Maiden was waiting anxiously for his decision.

"Send a message," said Sam. "Say we're attacking."

"Yes, sir," said Maiden joyfully.

Sam stood where he was for a few moments longer, looking at the lie of the ground and then he went down the slope at the double.

The tanks were ready now. The men were standing by waiting for orders.

Their eyes were eager, shining, they were fixed on Sam.

"We're attacking," he said. "There are six of them. Don't open fire till I give the signal—remember to keep together if there's a scrap. We fight as one unit."

A few minutes later the great squat monsters were surging forward across the sand.

Sam's plan, which he had evolved as he stood upon the ridge, was to make for a point where he could head off the enemy. He had seen the whole thing as a triangle—one leg of the triangle stretched from his ridge to the spot where the enemy tanks were now, and the other two legs bisected the spot where he intended to meet his enemy and offer him battle. He would make what use he could of the slight depressions in the ground but he could not hope to surprise his foe completely.

Sam was excited. His teeth were chattering a little in his head. He had experienced exactly the same sensation when he was about to ride in a Point-to-Point and wanted desperately to win.

The tanks were roaring along, rattling and bouncing over the uneven ground. The noise was frightful. It seemed all the more frightful in the silence of the desert plain. Sam had opened his turret and had wedged himself firmly in the opening for he wanted to see exactly what was happening. Away to his right he saw the enemy tanks, still heading due south, and he had to make up his mind whether to risk a shot now or wait a little longer. The light had improved; the sky was faintly gray; the stars were paler. Dawn would come soon and come swiftly, for there was no long twilight here. Was it worth it? Yes, for the enemy tanks offered a better target, they were more vulnerable if you got them sideways on, and a lucky shot might put one out of action before they turned. Sam gave the signal to fire and almost immediately the guns spoke...the tank rocked with the recoil, but Sam wedged himself tighter and riveted his glasses on the enemy. He saw the shells burst all around them...fountains of sand rose in the air, hiding them from view. When the cloud of sand subsided the enemy tanks had changed course and were heading straight for the British...all except one, which had stopped.

Sam waved to Maiden, who was wedged in the turret of the second tank, and Maiden waved back and pointed excitedly.

"I know," said Sam in a voice nobody could hear—not even himself—"I know, you ass, but there are five more…"

The odds had shortened and the range was shortening, too, for now the two units were heading toward each other at full speed. Sam had lost all signs of nervous excitement and gave his commands with confidence, for he knew exactly what he was going to do. The rattle of the tanks, the roar of the guns, the whine of the enemy shells as they flew past were scarcely heard by Sam. His blood coursed swiftly in his veins…he found himself shouting.

Almost before he knew it they had met the enemy and gone right through, keeping together in a compact mass as they had been trained to do…and now Sam rallied his force and turned sideways and raked the enemy with machine-gun fire…and then with another wave of his arm he charged the enemy again. Smoke from the guns and sand from the churning tracks combined in a thick cloud and amongst this cloud the tanks wheeled and turned and maneuvered like prehistoric monsters…and fire belched from their guns in a constant shattering roar.

For a few minutes it was pandemonium—Sam could not see what was happening—it was difficult to know friend from foe—and then quite suddenly it was over and three of the enemy tanks were in retreat, lumbering off at full speed across the plain. Of the other two (both of which had stopped firing), one lay on its side and the second was on fire. As Sam watched he saw the crew jump out and hold up their hands. The battle was over.

There was time now to take stock of his own casualties. Two of his crew were slightly wounded—that was all. He wondered how Maiden had fared and the other men. Maiden's tank had a slightly battered appearance but the crew seemed unharmed; there they were, jumping out and examining the tanks. It would be sad if the tank was badly damaged, for they would have to leave it here and send for help—but he had bagged three Germans so he mustn't grumble. It was a good show, really, thought Sam.

He climbed out of his tank and went across the sand to meet Maiden and see what was what. It was suddenly quite light, the sun was rising, and the pall that had shrouded the battle was drifting away on the breeze.

Chapter Seventeen
Five Riders on the Moor

W hen Jerry had invited her P. G. to come to Ganthorne she had made it clear that no entertainment need be expected, "We're all workers," Jerry had explained, and Miss Watt had replied that she desired no entertainment, she could amuse herself…but after a day or two Jerry discovered that it was rather nice to have another young woman to talk to, rather pleasant to do things with Jane. They got on very well, for Jane was a good listener and Jerry liked talking…soon Jane knew practically all there was to know about Jerry, but Jerry still knew very little about Jane.

One morning Jerry decided that the horses needed exercise and she invited Jane to accompany her for a ride on the moors. Jane accepted with delight and soon the two of them were walking down to the stables together. On the way they called at the cottage to leave some eggs for the Meltons, for Jerry was of the opinion that Melanie needed extra nourishment—she was far too thin. It was pleasant to call at the cottage nowadays, and to see Melanie's happy face. It was delightful to see the cottage looking clean and comfortable. The Meltons had brought a few of their own things: a couple of basket chairs, some gaily colored cushions, and a Persian rug. These additions made an astonishing difference to the living room—it looked cozy and pretty, it looked like a home.

"I've brought you some eggs," said Jerry, handing over the little basket. "There are two for you and two for the colonel...and mind you eat yours, Melanie. I've written your name on them."

Melanie laughed, for Mrs. Abbott amused her a good deal. She said, "How did you know I gave the others to Daddy?"

"A little bird told me," replied Jerry gravely. "And I was very angry. If you give these to Daddy they'll poison him."

This alarming prophecy left Melanie unmoved.

"This is my lucky day," she said, nodding. "I got a parcel from America this morning and now eggs from you."

"What did you get?" inquired Jerry, for she, also, had a generous friend upon the other side of the Atlantic and occasionally received exciting parcels, full of luscious food.

"I got butter," replied Melanie, "and sugar, a tin of spiced ham, a tin of marmalade, and a box of candy and some hairpins."

"Marvelous!" cried Jerry, opening her eyes very wide.

"Yes, isn't it?" agreed Melanie. "I mean everything is just exactly right. It was frightfully clever of her, wasn't it? The worst of it is you aren't supposed to write and thank people. It seems a funny idea—she'll think it is ungrateful if I don't write to her."

"You can write and say thank you very much for your kind thought," suggested Jane. "Tell her she guessed right; that's what I always do."

They both looked at Jane. "I suppose you've had parcels, too," said Melanie.

"Dozens," replied Jane.

"Have you got cousins in America?" asked Jerry—for this seemed the obvious explanation.

Jane blushed. She said, "Er—no. No, I haven't really..."

Jerry was a little surprised. There had been no parcels since Jane came to Ganthorne and, now that Jerry thought of it, no letters either—no letters at all—and why had Jane blushed? She realized all of a sudden that she knew very little about her P. G. She must encourage Jane to talk about herself. It's because I talk all the time, thought Jerry. I talk so much that Jane hasn't a chance.

They were standing on Melanie's doorstep, saying good-bye, when there was a clatter of hooves, and a man on a tall raking chestnut came galloping up the drive.

"It's Archie!" exclaimed Jerry, adding, for the benefit of her two companions. "There's nothing wrong. Archie always rides like that."

Archie dismounted at the gate and was introduced by Jerry to her friends.

"It's funny you haven't met them before," she declared. "It just shows what a long time it is since you came over to see me."

Archie replied that he had been busy with the harvest but that now it was safely in his barns he had time to think of matters of less importance. For instance he had time to think of Jerry. "I suppose I can stay to lunch," he said confidently.

"I suppose so," agreed Jerry, who was secretly delighted at his visit. "You may not get much to eat, of course."

They stood there, chatting. Now that Archie had reached his destination he showed no signs of restlessness or haste. Jerry noticed that he and Melanie were hitting it off very well—they had taken to each other at once. Jane was a little out of it (thought Jerry). She was taking no part in the conversation; after one brief glance Archie had ignored her completely. It was rather naughty of Archie to show his preference so clearly, but Jerry forgave him because it was exactly what she had hoped. Yes, Melanie was the very girl for Archie; they were of the same breed and understood one another perfectly—and what a splendid couple they made, standing there together in the sunshine. Archie so big and broad and robust, Melanie so slight and ethereal...

"What are you dreaming about, Jerry?" asked Archie. "You haven't heard a word I was saying, have you?"

Jerry had not. She admitted the fact with some embarrassment.

"It was about the trees," said Archie, looking around. "They've grown too big and the cottage is shadowed by them. You ought to have them thinned out."

"Oh no!" cried Jerry, who hated to lose a tree.

"Don't be silly," said Archie in a brotherly way. "It's bad for the trees to be left so thick and the cottage would get more light and air if they were tidied up and the bushes cut back. I'll come and do it for you if you like."

Jerry was about to voice a refusal, but the last sentence made her pause, for if Archie were to come over and cut down the trees he was bound to see a good deal of Melanie.

"Very well," said Jerry with a sigh. "But you must come yourself, Archie."

"Of course. I'm not so busy now that the harvest is over. The trees will burn so you'll score all around."

They were still discussing the matter and Archie was deciding which trees should be felled and how far the bushes should be cut back, and Jerry was trying to restrain his ardor, when Bobby Appleyard came down the drive, attired for riding. There was no need to introduce him, for he knew everyone.

"Hallo, are you riding this morning?" he asked, looking at Jerry as he spoke.

"Are *you*?" countered Jerry with a smile.

"Let's all ride together," suggested Archie.

"Of course, what fun!" cried Jerry. "We'll all ride over to Gostown. Melanie can have Dapple; he's quite up to her weight."

"I've got thousands of things to do," began Melanie in doubtful tones.

"But this is a holiday," declared Archie. "I'm having a holiday today and you can have one too."

After some argument Melanie was persuaded. She ran upstairs to change and the rest of the party drifted down to the stables to get the horses ready. It was only then that Jerry counted heads and realized that she had no steed to offer Bobby Appleyard.

"I'm awfully sorry," she said. "I never thought—you see we used to have heaps of horses."

"I've got one of my own," said Bobby proudly. "You said I could keep it here, didn't you, Jerry."

"Of course—but I never thought you'd manage to get one," replied Jerry in surprise.

Bobby disappeared into the stables and after a few moments he returned leading his horse. It was a broken down hunter, long in the tooth and incredibly bony, with ribs that reminded Jerry of a concertina.

"Where on earth did you get it?" she inquired.

"In Wandlebury," replied Bobby, gazing at her with his sad brown eyes. "It was the only one the man had—and I wanted some kind of a horse to ride with you on the moor—it's a horse anyhow," added Bobby.

"Are you sure?" asked Jerry scathingly. "It looks more like a brontosaurus."

Jerry's treatment of Captain Appleyard was peculiar. She liked him very much, so her natural manner was friendly and kind, but sometimes when he looked at her with his doggy eyes it gave her an odd sort of feeling—rather like an electric shock—and she pulled herself up with a jerk and was disagreeable. These alternating showers of hot and cold threw the unfortunate young man into a frightful state of confusion and instead of choking him off (as was intended) increased his devotion to Jerry's person. He never knew where he was with Jerry, and he thought about her all the time, reviewing his own behavior and searching for his faults. Jerry was perfect, of course, so if she was cold to him he must have offended her, he must have said something unpardonable—what on earth had he said? Since the arrival of Miss Watt, things had gone from bad to worse, for Bobby—though by no means clever—was intelligent enough to perceive that he was being thrown at that lady's head...and he had no use at all for Miss Watt. There was something odd about Miss Watt, and she was dull and uninteresting. Being rather quiet and shy himself, Bobby liked people who were gay and forthcoming, people who had plenty to say...in short he liked Jerry.

Melanie did not take long to change her clothes; she arrived at the stables before the horses were ready...for Bobby and Archie were so anxious to be helpful that they delayed matters a good deal. They rushed about, finding the wrong saddles and strapping them firmly onto the wrong horses and getting in one another's way. Jerry could have done the whole thing herself in half the time, and done it much better. When it was finished and they were ready to start Jerry discovered that her own particular saddle was on Cæsar's back. She had intended to ride Starlight and give Cæsar to Jane—but it seemed silly to make a fuss.

The five riders mounted and rode off. As each of them had his or her own ideas of how the cavalcade should be formed there was a good deal of maneuvering for places. At one moment Jane was riding beside Jerry...and then Bobby on his brontosaurus pushed in between them. Melanie, riding ahead by herself, was joined by Jane—and then by Archie. Jerry pushed on and tried to ride off Jane. It was not until they reached the moor that Jerry accomplished her design, namely to pair off Archie and Melanie and keep the other two by her side. She was on the point of congratulating herself on her success when Melanie dropped her crop and Archie dismounted to pick it up for her. The others stopped politely and the whole party was tangled up again.

Now that they were on the moor and the horses felt the springy turf beneath their hooves they began to jog, for they were used to cantering here and were anxious to be off, but Jerry was doubtful of giving the word for she had begun to feel a trifle anxious about Jane. Jane had said she could ride, and so she could; her seat was good and her back was commendably straight, but Starlight was in one of her skittish moods and seemed to be giving a good deal of trouble. Starlight pranced about as if she were five years old instead of nearly twelve. She curveted gracefully and sidled like a crab—and then, suddenly perceiving a small bush at the side of the track, she decided it was a dangerous foe and broke into a headlong gallop.

"Stop! Don't follow her!" cried Jerry to the others, for Jerry was aware that none of the other horses had the speed to overtake her, and if Starlight heard the thunder of hooves behind her she would merely increase her pace.

"I'll catch her!" cried Archie. "This brute has a good turn of speed," and so saying he bounded away in pursuit.

Jerry's frame of mind was not enviable; she was alarmed and annoyed. She was alarmed about Jane—would Jane be able to stick on until Starlight ran herself out? Would Jane have the sense to keep to the high ground? If not, she might find herself floundering in a bog. Jerry was annoyed with herself for letting Jane ride Starlight before making sure that she could manage her—Jane would have been perfectly safe and comfortable on old Cæsar. Jerry was annoyed with Jane, and with Archie and with her two remaining companions; she would have liked to say a good deal and would have done so if Melanie had not been there.

"Don't worry," said Bobby comfortingly. "She'll be all right. She's got quite a good seat and there's no vice in Starlight."

Jerry was not in the least soothed by these remarks. She would have been better pleased if Bobby had shown anxiety and alarm.

"Of course I'm worried," said Jerry crossly. "You would be worried if you had a grain of imagination."

"I mean—" began Bobby, but he spoke too late.

Jerry had shaken Cæsar into a canter and was pursuing the others over the moor.

All three riders had now disappeared around the corner of the wood and Bobby and Melanie were left. Their steeds were slow (Dapple because he was too fat and the brontosaurus because he was too thin). They walked along together in silence, for Bobbie and Melanie were very old friends and did not have to make polite conversation.

"I shall apply for the Glider Corps," said Bobby at last.

"Don't be silly, Bobby," replied Melanie. "You know quite well Daddy needs you in the regiment. He was saying the other day what a good adjutant you were."

Even this tribute failed to raise Bobby's spirits. "There are plenty of others who would do just as well," he said.

"You wouldn't be happy if you left the regiment."

"I'm not happy now," said Bobby with a sigh.

"You'll get over it."

"What?"

"You'll have to get over it, Bobby."

"I don't know what you're talking about."

"Oh yes, you do. What's the good of beating about the bush? You're in love—that's what's the matter with you."

"Melly!"

"I don't blame you, of course," continued Melanie. "Mrs. Abbott is a perfect lamb—but you'll just have to get over it."

Bobby hesitated. He knew Melly so well and of course she always said exactly what she thought—she had no inhibitions whatever—and somehow it was a relief to talk to someone about his troubles. They had been pent up for weeks with no outlet at all. "It's true, of course," said Bobby at last. "I know

I'm a fool but I can't help it. That's why it seemed a good idea to go away."

"Nonsense," said Melanie firmly.

"She's perfect," said Bobbie. "Nobody could help loving her. It isn't loving her that makes me unhappy. I wouldn't mind so much if only she liked me a little."

"She does like you," said Melanie.

"Do you really think so?" asked Bobby in surprise.

"It's because she likes you that she's horrid to you, Bobby."

He could not understand that. "But, Melly," he began.

"She likes you," said Melanie. "But she doesn't love you and she never will. She's devoted to her husband, absolutely devoted."

"I'm not a rotter," declared Bobby earnestly. "I mean I don't want her to love me—not really. I just want a little friendship, that's all."

"Be friends with her, then. Be proper friends. Be sensible, Bobby. *Don't moon.*"

Bobby was silent for a moment or two and then he chuckled. "Well, I asked for it," he said.

"You did, didn't you?"

"You're like the colonel," added Bobby. "I mean he can say the most outrageous things..."

Meanwhile Jerry had cantered on around the corner of the wood and on to the wide plain that sloped gently up to the hills near Gostown. She had expected to see Jane and Archie ahead of her but there was no sign of them. The moors were empty. She reined up on the top of a rise and looked all around, up and down the stream and far away toward the distant hills... what could have happened to them? She envisaged all sorts of horrors. Perhaps Starlight had put her foot in a rabbit hole and Jane was lying somewhere with a broken neck...but where was Archie? They couldn't both be sinking in the bog—or could they? She was beginning to get quite frantic and had almost decided to go home and organize a search party when she suddenly saw the whole party emerge from the wood, they were talking and laughing and appeared quite unharmed. When they saw Jerry they all waved to her gaily and Archie shouted, "*There you are! We thought you were lost.*"

Jerry was delighted to see them, of course, but all the same there was a queer lump in her throat. I wish Sam were here, she thought as she rode down to meet them.

Chapter Eighteen
The Trees Are Felled

Jerry was on her way down to the stables next morning when suddenly she heard the sound of an axe—the dull, rhythmic sound of steel biting into wood. It was Archie, of course. She had not expected him to start so soon. Her feelings were mixed for she was fond of her trees, but, on the other hand, she was even more fond of her brother, and it was her darling wish to see Archie happily married…I must just bear it, thought Jerry, as she quickened her steps and came around the corner of the cottage.

Archie was hard at work. He had brought a man with him, but he was wielding the axe himself, wielding it easily and grace-fully with a fine free swing of his powerful shoulders. He was wearing brown canvas trousers and had turned up the sleeves of his shirt—altogether he presented a very workmanlike appearance. Jerry was delighted to see that the show was not being wasted—Melanie Melton was leaning on the fence watching Archie at work.

"Hallo!" cried Melanie, waving to Jerry. "Come and watch. It's splendid. I've got lots to do but I can't tear myself away."

"You can do your housework later," said Jerry, and she too, leant against the fence and watched the proceedings.

"Your brother is very strong," said Melanie.

"Yes," agreed Jerry. "He works very hard on his farms. It's very kind of him to spare the time to cut down the trees."

"You didn't want it done."

"No," replied Jerry doubtfully. "At least—"

"Why did you let him do it?"

"Oh," said Jerry, somewhat taken aback. "Oh well, it has to be done. I mean Archie knows all about trees."

They were silent for a few moments. Archie was giving the man a lesson, showing him exactly how a tree should be felled, and he was far too busy to notice Jerry's arrival.

"I wish I could paint," said Melanie suddenly. "It would make a lovely picture—the trees and the two men and the sun glittering on the axe—"

Jerry agreed with her.

"I haven't washed the breakfast dishes," added Melanie with a sigh.

"It doesn't matter," replied Jerry hastily, for she was anxious that Melanie should stay and watch Archie. "You've all day before you. The breakfast dishes can wait."

She had scarcely spoken when there was a loud rending noise and the tree fell to the ground. Archie stood, leaning on his axe and looking at his accomplishment with a satisfied air.

"Pretty good, Stannard," said Archie—and his voice came clearly to their ears.

"That's right, sir," agreed Stannard. "It's fallen exactly where you said. Could I have a try now, sir?"

"They love it, don't they?" said Melanie in a low voice. "They haven't any sort of—regrets—"

"No," agreed Jerry. "Men are like that, you know. Much more sensible than we are. I mean if the trees are to come down they may as well enjoy it. "She felt her words were a bit mixed but Melanie seemed to understand. "I think I shall go now," added Jerry, for as a matter of fact she felt that she could bear no more.

"I must go, too," said Melanie. "I must get on with my work. Mr. Chevis-Cobbe is coming to lunch. Daddy asked him."

☙

Archie worked pretty hard for about an hour and then he left Stannard to get on with the job and went up to Ganthorne Lodge. He walked smartly as if he had a definite purpose, but every now and then he stopped and looked back. It seemed as if he could not make up his mind about something. When he reached the house he decided to go in by the back way, for he had not been in the kitchen premises for years…not since he was a little boy and had coaxed the nice fat cook for a jam tart or a slice of rich gingerbread, hot from the oven. It would be interesting to see the old place again, thought Archie, as he pushed open the back door. He knew, of course, that the Westshires used the kitchen as a sort of club room, for Jerry had told him all about it, but he was surprised all the same. The place was stiff with soldiers; soldiers washing themselves, soldiers cleaning their equipment, soldiers shouting to each other, singing, whistling, hammering. It was an extraordinary and not a pleasant experience, and it gave Archie quite a shock. He had put on the coat of his brown canvas overalls and the men took little notice of him, they pushed past him in the passage as if he were not there, but when he laid his hand on the red baize door, which led into the front part of the house, there was a sudden chorus of indignant protests.

"'ere, where d'you think you're goin'!"

"Hi, you can't go in there!"

"And who *are* you, anyway?" added a blond giant, laying a detaining hand on Archie's shoulder.

"I'm Mrs. Abbott's brother," replied Archie, wrenching

himself from the giant's grasp. "Do I have to obtain your permission to visit my sister?"

"I'm sorry, sir," said the giant, stepping back defeated by the unmistakable voice of authority. "I'm *very* sorry, sir. I wasn't to know, was I?"

"We've been told to look out for suspicious characters," added another man, coming to the help of his friend.

Archie smiled. He was not angry now. "Do I look like a suspicious character?" he asked.

"But they don't," declared a third man who had joined the group. "They look natural-like. That's what Major Cray said."

"Oh, you've been warned to look out for somebody, have you?" asked Archie in surprise.

"That's right, sir."

"What sort of a person?"

"We don't know," said the first man.

"We're just to keep our eyes open," said the second.

"We've to stop anyone snooping around the camp," said the third.

They seemed to know no more of the matter—at any rate no more information was forthcoming—and Archie pushed open the baize door and went into the front part of the house. He hesitated for a moment in the hall, then he opened the door of the sitting room and peeped in. Miss Watt was the only occupant of the room; she was sitting by the fire darning her stockings.

"Oh!" said Miss Watt in surprise. "Oh, I'm afraid Jerry has gone out—"

"Has she?" said Archie.

"I could find Markie. I think she's in the pantry."

"Don't bother," said Archie. He came in and sat down in the other chair and took out a cigarette. "Do you smoke?" he inquired.

"No," replied Miss Watt firmly.

"From principle?" inquired Archie, raising his brows.

"Because I can't," said Miss Watt, smiling. "It makes me cough. It makes my eyes pour with water..."

"Curious!" said Archie.

"Yes, isn't it?" she agreed.

"I hope you aren't any the worse for yesterday," said Archie.

"Not physically," replied Miss Wait. "My self-esteem is somewhat the worse for wear."

"Starlight has always been temperamental," declared Archie. "She didn't know you—that was all. It was rather silly of Jerry to let you ride her."

"Jerry can manage her—"

"Of course. She knows Jerry. That's why."

"My self-esteem feels better, thank you," said Miss Watt, laughing.

There was a short silence (it was a peaceful silence). Miss Watt darned her stockings and Archie smoked. Presently Miss Watt raised her eyes and saw Archie looking at her. She said hastily, "You've been cutting down trees."

Archie agreed that this was so. He began to talk about trees and, now that he had found a subject, he talked quite a lot. He explained how important it was that trees should have plenty of space to grow, and that woods should be carefully thinned out. But it was a great mistake (said Archie) to cut down the outer trees of a wood for, in so doing, one exposed the inner trees to the fury of the wind. The outer trees were used to the wind (said Archie), toughened by years of exposure, and if they were removed the inner trees that had grown up in the shelter of their neighbors were often blown down.

Miss Watt was interested. "You know a lot about it," she said.

"I've learnt," replied Archie, throwing away the stub of his cigarette and rising to go. "I knew nothing when my aunt died and left me Chevis Place, so of course I made a good many mistakes. I had to learn about farming too. You know," said Archie, a trifle uncomfortably, "you know I'm a farmer—I mean that's why I'm not a soldier—it isn't because—"

"Of course not!" exclaimed Miss Watt vehemently.

"I wouldn't like you to think."

"Of course not!" exclaimed Miss Watt more vehemently than before.

"I just thought I'd explain," said Archie, looking at the toe of his shoe. "I mean some people—don't quite—understand."

He went away.

⚭

Miss Watt was correct in her surmise that Markie was in the pantry (somehow or other nobody had learned to call it the kitchenette). She was preparing an apple pie for supper and Wilhelmina was receiving a lesson in the art of making pastry. When Markie had finished her job she walked across the hall and looked into the sitting room and saw the couple sitting by the fire. She could not hear what they were saying, of course, but Archie seemed to be talking very earnestly and Jane seemed to be hanging upon his words, and altogether they looked so intimate sitting there together by the fire that Markie had not the heart to disturb them. She withdrew silently and stood in the hall for a moment, nodding her head and smiling. Then she went upstairs.

Archie and Jane, thought Markie. Well, why not? Jane is a dear. She would make him a very nice wife. I shan't tell Jerry, thought Markie. Better not. Jerry is apt to be impatient, she has very little tact. People dislike being thrown at each other's heads. Of course there may be nothing in it—nothing at all—but then, again, why not? Jane is very nice-looking (thought Markie as she dived head first into the linen cupboard and began to count out clean sheets): such nice brown eyes, such a lovely complexion, such pretty hair. I thought she looked a little odd, at first, but now she doesn't look odd. Is it because I have got used to her appearance or because her hair has grown? (Markie hesitated with the pile of sheets in her arms.) Because her hair has grown, decided Markie. That nice wave in front makes all the difference.

Chapter Nineteen
Tea in the Nursery

A fortnight had passed since Barbara's visit to Miss Besserton and a good deal had happened in the interval. Miss Besserton had recovered from her indisposition and had departed to Bournemouth to visit a friend and left Lancreste lamenting. Barbara, who was really sorry for Lancreste, did all she could to brighten his lot, inviting him to tea and taking him to the pictures, but she was aware that she was not much use to Lancreste—she was too old for him. If only there had been somebody else, thought Barbara, some young girl who could talk to Lancreste in his own sort of language…but there was not. Wandlebury was bereft of young women; they were all in the forces.

Lancreste mooched about miserably for a day or two and then he began to recover. On the fifth day after Miss Besserton's departure there was quite a difference in him; Barbara was beginning to congratulate herself and to hope for a complete cure when suddenly Miss Besserton returned. Her return threw Lancreste into ecstasies. He came around to see Barbara at half-past nine the next morning and walked about the room, talking like a lunatic and declaring that Pearl was marvelous and they were going to be married at once.

"At once!" cried Barbara in dismay.

"Yes, that's what I came about, really," declared Lancreste. "We're going up to town to arrange everything. We're going to have a party at the Magnolia Tree the night before the wedding—just a few special friends—and—"

"But Lancreste—"

"It's a secret, of course. We aren't going to tell anyone—"

"Lancreste," said Barbara, firmly. "Lancreste, listen to me a moment. What about your father and mother—what do they think?"

"I'm not going to tell them a thing," declared Lancreste. "They were rude to Pearl—they were frightful to her. You can't expect her to ask them to her wedding when they were frightful to her."

"Oh, Lancreste!" said Barbara, appalled at this. "Oh, Lancreste, you can't—"

"Pearl doesn't want them. She doesn't want anyone except you."

"Me!" exclaimed Barbara more dismayed than before.

"You've been so decent to Pearl," explained Lancreste. "You understand her. It isn't everyone that understands and appreciates her."

"Oh goodness!" exclaimed Barbara, who neither understood nor appreciated Pearl. "Oh, Lancreste, I couldn't..."

"We're depending on you," continued Lancreste, who was imbued with the idea that he was conferring a favor upon Mrs. Abbott and was deaf to her protests. "Pearl is depending on you. She says you can stay the night at the boarding house with her—the night before the wedding—and help her to dress and all that sort of thing. It's you she wants."

"Is it?" said Barbara in amazement. "But why? I mean it's very nice of her, but—"

"Yes, isn't it?" said Lancreste, smiling. "She says she'd rather have you than anyone."

"But I can't," declared Barbara, who saw the trap closing and realized that her only chance of escape was to be really firm.

"You can't?"

"No, it's quite impossible."

"Why?" asked Lancreste in amazement.

Barbara knew why it was impossible. She did not approve of the marriage (for not only were the principals unsuited to each other, but they also were entering upon the state of matrimony unadvisedly and for the wrong motives). The marriage was doomed to failure—complete and absolute failure—and what on earth would the Marvells say if they heard she had aided and abetted Lancreste in his mad scheme? All this Barbara knew, but she could not explain it to Lancreste, for she was not good at explaining things and she was not ruthless enough to attempt to state her feelings in plain words.

"Why?" asked Lancreste again.

"I couldn't," said Barbara. "Your parents wouldn't like it—and you're too young."

"I've been in love with Pearl for years—well, nearly a year—"

"Yes, I know, but—"

"I thought you understood."

"Couldn't you wait? Couldn't you think it over?"

"No, she might change her mind," said Lancreste desperately. "I've told you before how she keeps on changing her mind."

"That's just why—"

"And she's got to turn out of the boarding house," continued Lancreste. "And I may have to go back to duty at any moment. We must get married at once—it's the only thing to do."

"But, Lancreste—"

"And Joan is getting married at the end of the month—you know who I mean, the girl she used to have a flat with—and of course Pearl wants to be married before Joan."

"Why?" asked Barbara.

"Because—because—I don't really know," said Lancreste

vaguely. "I only know she *does*. Perhaps it's a bet or something." Barbara was speechless.

"So you *will* come, won't you?" said Lancreste in wheedling tones. "It will make all the difference if you're there—and Pearl is depending on you to see her through. It's rather an ordeal for a girl, isn't it?"

"She must get someone else—"

"It's you she wants. I mean she said I was to come around and ask you and I don't know what she'll say if I go back and say you've refused. She'll be terribly hurt, Mrs. Abbott."

"I can't," repeated Barbara. "Honestly, Lancreste. She must get someone else—or else wait and arrange things properly."

"But we can't wait!" cried Lancreste, and he began to explain all over again why it was impossible to postpone the wedding.

They talked for a whole hour—Lancreste did most of the talking—and at the end of that time Barbara was so exhausted and confused that she did not know whether or not she had made Lancreste understand her point of view. She was just trying to collect her wits for a final effort when the door burst open and her cook appeared, slate in hand, and inquired if Mrs. Abbott wanted the remains of yesterday's stew made into a curry for dinner. Cook was not a patient woman—as Barbara knew to her cost—and she had got tired of waiting in the kitchen for her mistress to appear, so she had taken the somewhat unconventional course of pursuing Mrs. Abbott to the study and breaking in upon her conversation. The curry was merely an excuse, for she knew quite well that practically the only thing to do with the remains of the stew was to convert it into curry, but any excuse was better than none, and cook was angry. She was very angry indeed and there was such malignance in the gaze she turned upon Lancreste—who had kept her back in her work and wasted her time—that he took fright and departed in haste with murmured apologies.

"Thank goodness!" said Barbara as the door closed behind him, and she held out her hand for the slate and entered upon the daily discussion of food without more ado.

For three whole days Barbara did not set eyes upon Lancreste. She was grateful for the respite, but she could not help thinking about him and wondering what he was doing. Had he gone to London with Pearl and got married, or had Pearl changed her mind again? Perhaps his parents had got wind of his intentions and managed to put a spoke in his wheel. Barbara was not sure whether or not it was her duty to reveal Lancreste's plans to his parents. On the one hand it seemed dreadful to keep the matter to herself and allow Lancreste to wreck his life without raising a finger to save him, but on the other hand the Marvells were so odd, so unlike ordinary sensible people, that you never knew how they would take things—and however they took the news that Lancreste was bent upon matrimony they could do nothing to prevent him carrying out his intention. Barbara tried to imagine herself sitting in the Marvells' drawing room and telling the Marvells—telling them all she knew—but she was unable to imagine the scene, she was unable to imagine the Marvells' reactions. Last but not least Lancreste had trusted Barbara, and, although she could not remember making any sort of promise, she was aware that he depended upon her to keep his secret.

Arthur, when consulted, seemed to take the matter very lightly. "Don't get mixed up in it," he said.

"But I *am* mixed up in it," Barbara pointed out. "The fact is I seem to get mixed up in everything that happens—when all I want is a quiet peaceful life."

"Of course you do," agreed Arthur, smiling in his kind way. "It's because you're interested in people."

"Then you don't think I ought to tell them?"

"If I were you I should keep clear of this particular mess up."

"As clear as I can," agreed Barbara in doubtful tones.

"Tell Lancreste I won't let you go to London," suggested Arthur, and he took up his paper as if that settled the matter comfortably.

But there was no need for Barbara to use this excuse (which married women in every age have found so extremely useful and of which they will continue to avail themselves until the marriage vows are altered), for on the fourth day Lancreste appeared at tea time with a woebegone countenance. One glance at him showed Barbara that this was no bridegroom who had come to her for congratulations; in fact Lancreste bore much more resemblance to a funeral mute. It so happened that Dorcas was out; she had taken the bus to Camberley to see her niece who was the wife of a sergeant in the Green Buzzards, and Barbara was looking after the children in her absence. Barbara explained this to Lancreste and invited him to come and have tea in the nursery, hoping with all her heart that he would refuse...but Lancreste accepted and soon they were all sitting around the nursery table indulging in bread and margarine, raspberry jam and buns.

Dorcas rarely went out, so, when she did, it was a treat for everybody (they all loved Dorkie, of course, but still it was a treat), and if Lancreste had not been there Barbara and Simon and Fay would have had great fun together and enjoyed themselves immensely. They might have had a story—the children loved stories and Barbara was a very good storyteller—or they might have played a game Simon had invented and was known to the initiated under the descriptive title of "Eating Like Pigs." This game was the more delightful because Simon and Fay and Barbara were all aware that it was "naughty" and that Dorkie would disapprove of it most heartily.

All day long Simon and Fay had been looking forward to tea time with keen anticipation, but now the treat was spoiled. The treat was completely ruined by Lancreste's appearance at the table. There he sat, toying with a bun and talking on and on, talking to Mummy and paying no attention to Simon and Fay—which seemed a funny sort of way to behave when he was having tea in their nursery.

Barbara was thinking much the same thing, and already she had begun to regret her impulsive invitation to Lancreste, for Lancreste was talking exactly as if he and Barbara were alone, or as if the children were deaf and dumb. They were dumb, of course (though how long they would remain dumb nobody could foresee), but they were by no means deaf. Their eyes dwelt upon Lancreste—large, round, inquiring eyes. What were they making of it, wondered Barbara anxiously.

"Yes, she's gone," said Lancreste in lugubrious tones. "She went to London this morning. She said I wasn't to come with her and of course she isn't going to marry me after all—I told you that, didn't I. It's quite definite this time. She's fed up with me. She's been fed up with me before, of course, but never so definitely fed up. I mean there's always been a vague sort of hope before...I don't suppose I shall ever see her again. The worst of it is I don't really know what it was all about—we had a bit of a row. At least she got fed up with me all of a sudden. One moment everything was all right and the next moment it was all wrong, and I don't even know what I did. That's the worst of it, if you see what I mean—because I don't know what to do. I mean if I knew what it was all about I could do something, couldn't I? I could put it right if I knew. Well, of course, I tried to put it right but that just seemed to make it worse. What do you think I ought to do, Mrs. Abbott? Do you think I ought to write and say I'm sorry, or do you think I ought to go to London and see her? You see I don't know what I did to offend her—or what I said. Perhaps she would be angry if I went to London—"

"She's the cat's aunt," said Fay loudly and clearly—and then she laughed in her usual explosive way.

Lancreste was brought up short. He looked at the children as if he had not seen them before.

"That's what Dorkie says," explained Simon. "Dorkie says it's rude to say 'she.' Dorkie says, 'She's the cat's aunt.' That's what Fay means. Don't you, Fay?"

"M'hm," said Fay, nodding.

"Drink your milk, darling," said Barbara, who had learned this useful phrase from the faithful Dorcas.

There was silence—complete silence except for the sound of Fay drinking. She drank long and deep. Presently she withdrew her face from her mug and said, "Did you hear me? I was drinking like a pig."

"We don't do that when we have visitors," said Simon with conscious rectitude.

"I do," said Fay.

There was another silence, much more protracted and profound.

"You aren't used to nursery tea, are you, Lancreste?" said Barbara brightly.

"No," said Lancreste.

"And he doesn't like it," added Simon, looking at him thoughtfully.

"He could go home," suggested Fay in hopeful tones.

"But perhaps he doesn't get raspberry jam at home," objected Simon, eyeing the large spoonful of preserve Lancreste was in the act of conveying to his plate.

Barbara did not know what to say. She could tell the children to be quiet, of course, but that would only make it worse... besides it did not seem fair on the children. Why should they be squashed just because Lancreste was too silly to see the joke? The children did not mean to be rude; they were just talking to each other in a perfectly natural way. Barbara decided that the only thing to do was to make Lancreste do all the talking. This was not a difficult feat to perform. The difficulty was to stop him…he was so dreary, poor soul, but she would have to bear it.

"Is Miss Besserton quite well?" asked Barbara.

"Oh yes," said Lancreste. "She's very well indeed. We had a good time when she was here. There was a dance at the town hall. Of course it wasn't like the dances she goes to in London but she enjoyed it. She likes dancing. There was a fellow there she danced with a lot—I'm not very good, you see. He was very good, so of course she liked dancing with him."

"Can she dance the hornpipe?" asked Fay.

"Er—no," said Lancreste, looking at Fay in astonishment.

"Simon can," said Fay with a complacent air.

"I'll show you after tea," said Simon.

"How much longer leave have you got?" asked Barbara, passing the buns to Lancreste.

"That's just it," said Lancreste miserably. "I mean I don't know. I've been passed fit but I haven't got my orders. It's so upsetting not to know how long you've got. I might hear any day and that's one of the reasons why I want to see Pearl. I mean if I get my orders I shall have to go, and how can I go without having all this cleared up? I mean the mess. If I just knew what I had done to offend Pearl—"

"Why don't you ask her?" inquired Barbara.

"Oh, I did," replied Lancreste. "She just said I knew, and I was being stupid on purpose. It made it worse, really. I hope I shall get my orders tomorrow. I can't stand it. There's nothing to do except think about her all the time. If only I could get my orders. Why haven't they sent me my orders? D'you think the War Office has forgotten all about me, Mrs. Abbott?"

Barbara had no idea whether or not this was possible and was about to make a noncommittal reply, but Simon got in before her.

"Perhaps they don't need you," he suggested.

"Perhaps they think they can win the war without you," added Fay.

The wretched Lancreste looked at Simon and then at Fay—and, being met by the stare of two pairs of large innocent eyes, he looked away again.

"Oh no, it can't be *that*," said Barbara hastily—far too hastily, for of course she had merely made it worse. She was really at her wits' end by now and entertained wild thoughts of putting the children to bed, and getting rid of them. But I couldn't *make* them go to bed, thought Barbara, looking at her offspring in despair. They haven't been naughty—and they wouldn't understand—and Simon argues so! (Simon argued—as Barbara knew to her cost—but Fay was really the more devastating of the two. Her voice was so clear, her enunciation so concise, her remarks so very much to the point.)

"I shouldn't worry, Lancreste," said Barbara, trying to find something that would put things right and soothe Lancreste's injured feelings. "I expect the War Office is looking for a suitable job for you."

"Perhaps they will give you four tanks, like Sam," said Fay, imitating her mother's comforting tones with ludicrous effect.

"I'm an observer," said Lancreste rather crossly.

"He flies in an airplane," Barbara explained.

"Like this!" cried Simon, seizing his mug and making wide swooping movements with it through the air.

"And he drops bombs on the Germans like this!" cried Fay, taking her bun and dropping it onto her plate with a thud.

"Simon! Fay!" cried Barbara. "That's naughty. You must behave properly. I don't know what Lancreste will think of you."

"He doesn't like us already," said Simon, stating the fact without rancor.

"And we don't like him," added Fay.

⁓

Barbara felt a little depressed that evening; she had had a difficult time getting the children to bed. Having been baulked of their fun at the proper time they seemed determined to get their money's worth before settling down to sleep. They had both been naughty—really naughty—but Simon had been very naughty indeed and Barbara had discovered to her dismay that she had practically no control over him. She had tucked him into bed twice, and each time he had leapt up again the moment her back was turned, and, pursuing her down the nursery passage, had "booed" at her in the dark and startled her considerably. The first time, Barbara had taken it as a joke—though not a very good joke—but the second time she had been really angry. She was tired and hot and disheveled and she could not manage Simon.

"It isn't kind," said Barbara, as she tucked Simon into bed for the third time. "It isn't any fun at all to frighten people."

"I like it," said Simon frankly.

"You wouldn't like someone to frighten you."

"No, but that's different," said Simon.

"It isn't, really," said Barbara. "We ought to do to others what we should like them to do to us. That's the golden rule, Simon."

"You don't," said Simon.

Barbara was a little taken aback at this counterattack.

"I try to, Simon—" she began.

"But, Mummy," said Simon, raising himself on his elbow and looking at her with wide eyes. "But Mummy, you wouldn't like to go to bed *now,* would you?"

"Yes, I should," replied Barbara with conviction. "It's exactly what I should like to do. I'm very tired indeed."

"I'm not tired at all," declared Simon. "I'd like to get up and dance about and come down to supper with you and Daddy."

"You know quite well—"

"Yes, but why?" asked Simon. "Why must children go to bed when they aren't tired?"

"We'll talk about it tomorrow," said Barbara, who was far too exhausted to enter into an argument with her son. "Shut your eyes and go to sleep like a good boy."

"I can't go to sleep like a good boy."

"Why not?"

"Because I'm naughty—you said I was naughty."

"You're good now," said Barbara firmly and she turned out the light. There was a chuckle in the darkness from the direction of Simon's bed. "I don't think I'm very good yet," said an impish voice.

Barbara pretended not to hear. She was aware that if Simon lay still in the dark for two minutes he would be fast asleep and she would have no further trouble with him. She waited outside the door and listened but there was absolute silence—Simon had dropped off to sleep before he had time to plan further wickedness.

It was very worrying, of course, for Simon was getting out of hand. Barbara could not manage him at all and Dorcas was only a very little better at the job. Arthur could manage him, but Arthur was away all day and when he returned from his office in the evening Barbara liked him to enjoy the children—not to have to play the part of policeman. Something will have to be done, thought Barbara, as she tidied herself and washed her hands for supper. I shall have to talk to Dorcas. We shall have to be very strict with Simon...

Worrying about Simon made Barbara feel depressed so it was natural that her thoughts should turn to Jerry, for the cheering-up process worked both ways—there was nothing one-sided about it.

But I shan't say a word about Simon, thought Barbara as she picked up the telephone receiver.

The two Mrs. Abbotts chatted of one thing and another and agreed that they had not seen each other for ages—not since Monday morning.

"Far too long," said Barbara. "You had better come over to tea."

"It's your turn to come to Ganthorne," said Jerry's voice eagerly. "Come tomorrow and bring the children. I promised to have them one day."

"I don't think so," said Barbara doubtfully. "I've had the children all day long. Dorcas went over to Camberley, and—"

"Come yourself, then," said Jerry's voice. "That will be lovely. I'll ask Melanie Melton to come too. I told you about Melanie, didn't I?"

"You said she was charming."

"She's a perfect dear, very young and pretty. You'll love her, Barbara."

"Would you mind if I brought Lancreste?" Barbara inquired.

"Lancreste!" exclaimed Jerry's voice in amazement.

"Lancreste Marvell. He's in the Air Force, you know. It's very dull for him at home. I've been trying to—to cheer him up a little."

"Why?" asked Jerry's voice. "I mean why…"

"Perhaps you'd rather not have him…"

"Of course you can bring him if you want to," said Jerry's voice unenthusiastically.

Chapter Twenty
Jerry's Tea Party

It was now Jerry's turn to experience the growing powers of a tea party. She saw it as a snowball rolling down a hill, gathering size with every yard, and she said as much to Markie at the breakfast table next morning.

"Hardly a snowball, dear," said Markie in doubtful tones. "I think one might find a better metaphor."

"Well, anyhow, it's a nuisance," declared Jerry. "I meant to have Barbara. I wanted to talk to Barbara and now we shan't be able to talk properly. I meant to have Barbara and then I thought of Melanie, and then Barbara suggested Lancreste—goodness knows why—and now Bobby wants to come. It *is* like a snowball, Markie."

"Archie will be here, too," said Markie. "You remember he said he would finish the trees today."

"Eight!" exclaimed Jerry in dismay.

"Never mind," said Markie. "I'll bake some scones. I think we had better have tea in the dining room, and if any of the other officers happens to be there he can have a cup of tea with us. It is a pity that I used all the sugar we had saved to make damson jam—I cannot make a cake, I am afraid."

"Oh, isn't that *lucky*!" Jerry exclaimed. "There was a recipe for a sugarless cake on the Kitchen Front this morning and I scribbled it down just in case." She produced a torn envelope covered with hieroglyphics and presented it to Markie with pride.

"Yes dear, how nice!" said Markie, assuming her reading spectacles. "Let me see now...where are we? '*Turn the mixture into a greased tin*—'"

"No, Markie, it begins on the other side. It begins *there*," said Jerry, leaning over Markie's shoulder and pointing with her finger. "You see, Markie—*four ounces of scraped carrots, three ounces of margarine*—and it goes on *here* and it ends on the other side of the envelope in the corner. I'm afraid it isn't terribly clear."

"I shall manage," said Markie, turning the paper this way and that, and peering at it anxiously. "I think I can follow it..."

"They go so fast," said Jerry apologetically.

"I know, dear. You've done splendidly. What's this word, I wonder."

"Rice, perhaps," suggested Jerry, in doubtful tones.

"I scarcely think so."

"Beans, then—it's quite a short word, isn't it?"

"Not beans," said Markie firmly. "Beans are exceedingly useful but I feel they would be out of place in a cake."

"Could it be bread?" asked Jerry. "Yes, I believe it's bread crumbs. The crumbs are on the other side because there wasn't any room for them there. Bread crumbs, Markie, that's what it is," said Jerry triumphantly and she gathered up her letters and swung out of the room whistling in a cheerful manner.

The tea party was a great success. It was held in the dining room and, as the latest joined subaltern happened to drop in at the right moment, nine people sat down to the table. Markie's scones were excellent, of course—they always were—and the cake looked very nice indeed, though unfortunately it did not taste as nice as it looked.

"It is a trifle wersh," declared Markie, anxiously. "I was afraid it might be."

"It's my fault, of course," said Jerry hastily. "You see I heard the recipe on the wireless and I probably left something out—nobody need eat it, of course."

"I think it's excellent," declared Bobby Appleyard, helping himself to another slice.

He really *is* in love with Jerry, thought Barbara in alarm.

Lancreste did not shine at the tea party. He was awkward and *distrait* but Barbara saw him looking at Miss Melton and her hopes rose high. Barbara was a believer in "the expulsive power of a new affection" and she had brought Lancreste here today with the idea that the charms of Miss Melton might help to cure Lancreste of his complaint. If anything could cure Lancreste Miss Melton should, thought Barbara. Miss Melton was all and more than she had been led to expect. Nobody who took the trouble to look at Miss Melton could find any pleasure in Miss Besserton—so Barbara decided.

"Have you caught your suspicious character?" asked Archie suddenly. His words fell in the middle of a silence and everybody looked around.

"You heard about that, did you!" said Bobby.

"Perhaps I shouldn't have said anything."

"Oh, there's nothing hush-hush about it."

"What are you talking about?" asked Jerry. "If there's nothing hush-hush I suppose we may know the mystery."

"Of course, but it isn't anything much," replied Bobby. "Several people have seen a strange man hanging about the place and we've been warned by the police to look out for him."

"A spy!" exclaimed Jerry, opening her eyes very wide.

"Might be," agreed Bobby.

"What harm could he do here?" Barbara inquired.

"Well, there's us," said Bobby smiling. "I mean a camp is just the sort of target the Bosche likes."

"I suppose the fellow might signal to bombers with lights," suggested Archie.

"That's the idea," agreed Bobbie. "It has been done in other places, you know. There was a camp in Essex; they had camouflaged it pretty neatly, but the Bosche came over and dropped some bombs in the very middle of it. Afterwards they found the fellow who had given it away. He had a wireless outfit and signaling lights...but I shouldn't worry," added Bobby, who had suddenly become aware that he was spreading alarm and despondency and was anxious to make amends. "Our fellow is probably just a tramp. They get these scares every now and then; they get the wind up and warn everybody."

"The girls shouldn't go out by themselves," said Archie, anxiously.

"No, perhaps not."

"You don't really mean that, do you?" asked Melanie.

"Just for a day or two," said Bobby. "Just until we've caught the fellow."

"It would be all right if you had someone with you," added Archie.

Melanie said no more but she looked somewhat downcast, for she enjoyed walking on the moor by herself.

As tea went on the conversation became more animated, there were only three people who made no contribution to the noise. Jane Watt never talked much, but she was a good listener, she looked happy and interested. Lancreste was completely silent and looked miserable. Markie was the third. She was debarred from taking part in the conversation because she could not hear what was being said—all that Markie heard was a confused noise punctuated with bursts of laughter. She could not hear, but she could see and she used her eyes to good effect, she watched her companions and was happy to see that they were enjoying themselves. Jerry had been rather silent for a bit (Markie noticed) but now she suddenly came out of her shell and began to talk hard...and the others were all listening and smiling so she must be telling them something funny, or at least telling them something in a funny way. The new subaltern was playing up to Jerry. He was leaning forward in his chair and talking back at her, and his eyes, which were extremely blue, were sparkling with mischief—he really was a very nice boy, Markie thought. But Bobby would not like it...no, Bobby was not liking it at all. Poor Bobby, what a pity it was! Could one say anything to Bobby? Would it be any use?

Once or twice the whole party laughed heartily—and even Lancreste smiled—and Jane, who was sitting next to Markie, turned to her and repeated the joke; but jokes are never very funny when repeated without their context and Markie found it difficult to laugh.

"Don't trouble, dear," said Markie in a low voice. "I'm quite used to it and it does not worry me. Just see if Mrs. Abbott will have a little more tea and pass the scones to Miss Melton."

There was no reason why Markie should not have done this herself, for if she was deaf she was certainly not dumb, but Jane was only too delighted to help Markie to look after the guests so she did as requested.

After tea Jerry suggested a walk. She did not intend to go, herself, of course, but it would be nice for the others...and the sitting room was not large enough for such a large party.

"Melanie likes walking," said Jerry in her usual forthright way.

"I don't mind at all," declared Melanie hastily.

"But it's a lovely evening for a walk, isn't it? You go with her, Archie. Take her up through the wood and show her the view."

"I expect she's seen it," said Archie.

"Lancreste would like to go," said Barbara. "You'd like to go, wouldn't you, Lancreste?"

"I don't mind, really," said Lancreste without enthusiasm.

"You go with them, dear," said Markie to Jane.

"I was going to help you to wash up," replied Jane.

After some little delay the four of them started off—they could not avoid their fate without being positively rude—and, as the officers were obliged to return to the camp and Markie was helping Wilhelmina to clear the table, the two Mrs. Abbotts were left alone in the sitting room.

"Lovely!" exclaimed Jerry. "Just what I wanted. We haven't had a proper chat for ages—and it's all the nicer because I didn't expect it. I mean I didn't see how we were going to get rid of them."

"I don't think they wanted to go," said Barbara doubtfully.

"They'll enjoy it," declared Jerry with conviction.

"Do you think so, Jerry?"

"Yes, of course. You have to take a firm line with people. If I hadn't made them go they would just have sat here in a bunch and there aren't enough chairs for them."

The four victims walked up the hill abreast, with the girls in the middle. They had been sent out for a walk and they had come. None of them had wanted to come and each of them was aware that his or her companions would have got out of it if they could. For this reason the conversation was somewhat strained—Melanie and Archie bore the brunt of it. But the evening was so lovely and the sunshine so mellow that gradually they began to thaw...Archie was struck by a brilliant idea.

"I was telling you about trees," said Archie to Miss Watt. "You were interested, weren't you?"

"Very interested," replied Miss Watt—what else could she say?

"Perhaps you would like to see an oak that was blown down last winter?" suggested Archie. "It's a very fine specimen—must be about three hundred years old."

Miss Watt signified her desire to see it.

"You two can walk on," said Archie firmly. "We'll catch you up in half no time."

The party split up. Archie and Jane Watt found the oak and examined it, and sat down upon a convenient branch.

"I thought I did that rather neatly," said Archie.

"Did what?" asked Jane.

"Got rid of the children, of course. You didn't want them tagging along, did you?"

"I'm very fond of Melanie."

"Oh yes, she's a dear," agreed Archie. "But I hate going about in droves. Jerry is a nuisance sometimes."

These few sentences put the matter in a nutshell, and having cleared up any misunderstanding that might be lurking in his companion's mind Archie proceeded to light a cigarette.

"We mustn't sit here long," said Jane in alarm.

"They won't mind," replied Archie. "They can talk to each other. As a matter of fact they'll get on much better without us. Two's company, don't you agree?"

"Yes, I think I do," said Jane smiling.

Archie was emboldened by the smile. He said, "Have I known you long enough to call you Jane?"

"You've known me for a week," replied Jane in some surprise.

"Much longer than that," declared Archie. "I knew you long before you came to live at Ganthorne."

Jane looked at him, her eyes wide with dismay.

"Yes," said Archie nodding. "Yes, I know all about you... but don't worry, Jane. I can keep a secret, you know."

"You won't tell anyone?"

"Not a soul," declared Archie, smiling at her.

"How did you know—"

"I recognized you, of course. Oh yes, you look different but I knew you at once. I was interested, you see."

"I don't want you to think—"

"But I don't!"

"I want you to understand."

"That's nice of you."

They were silent for a moment. The woods were very quiet. The sun was going down through a haze; it looked like a big round orange ball caught amongst the trees.

"I ran away," said Jane at last. "I suppose it was cowardly but I couldn't think of anything else to do. I had got caught up in a sort of wheel that kept on turning—it was like one of those wheels you see in a mouse cage. I wanted to get out of the cage—to get right away from everything and try to find out what I was and what I could do. I wasn't myself," declared Jane earnestly. "I had been made into something else—and I'm not myself now. Myself is something between the two."

"That's what I think," said Archie.

"Do you mean you understand?"

"Yes."

"How?"

"Because I've read your books."

"But they aren't me!" she cried in alarm. "It was because I hated my books that I ran away—because I suddenly realized they were no good at all."

"I like them," said Archie. "Yes, honestly I do. There's something very charming about your books. I don't mean that you couldn't do better, of course. I believe you could...if you knew more about life."

"I'm trying to learn," said Jane.

"And more about love," said Archie boldly and with that he put his arms around her and kissed her in a most satisfactory way.

"Archie!" exclaimed Jane, when she could speak. "Archie—really—I don't know what to say—"

"I want to marry you," said Archie. "You will, won't you?"

"No, of course not."

"Of course you will," he declared.

"I don't know you," cried Jane. "I mean I never thought—"

"Well, think about it now," said Archie. "I assure you I'm perfectly respectable. I have no bad habits and I'm clean and tidy and pleasant about the house—"

"Really—" said Jane, half laughing.

"Honestly," said Archie seriously. "Honestly, Jane, I'm quite a decent sort of fellow—and I adore you. I feel all sentimental about you—"

"No—"

"Yes, really. But I'm not going to talk like the fellows in your books. You don't want me to, do you?"

"No," said Jane with a shudder.

"Well, that's settled, then."

"What's settled?"

"We're engaged of course."

"No," said Jane.

"Why not?"

"Because—because it's absurd. I hardly know you—"

"That can be remedied—"

"I'm going home next week."

"Going home?" asked Archie in dismay. "Going back to Foxstead? But, Jane—"

"I must go back," declared Jane. "I've been thinking about it a lot and I've come to the conclusion that you can't just cast off all your responsibilities like a cloak. I thought you could, but I was wrong. Helen depends on me and I owe Helen a good deal."

"Helen?" asked Archie.

"My sister," replied Jane. "We lived together, you see."

"I've got plenty of money, Jane."

"It isn't money—not altogether. Besides it wouldn't do."

"But, Jane—"

"I'm not happy," said Jane, turning and looking at him with her big brown eyes. "I feel I've behaved badly."

"I suppose you couldn't tell me the whole thing?" inquired Archie with some anxiety.

"There isn't much to tell. Helen wanted me to go on writing, but I couldn't—I tried quite hard but it was impossible—she kept on saying that if only I would finish the book we would go away together for a holiday. At last I could bear it no longer and I told Helen that I wanted a holiday at once and I wanted to go alone. She was very angry," said Jane, shaking her head. "I had never seen Helen in such a rage. She rushed out of the room saying that I was ungrateful and unkind and that we would both be ruined. It was true, of course," said Jane thoughtfully. "I knew it was true, but I couldn't help it. I felt as if I were going mad. I *had* to get away."

"What happened then?" asked Archie. "Did you finish the book?"

"No, I couldn't. I hated the book and all the people in it. I didn't care what happened to them."

"How did you persuade Helen—" began Archie.

"I didn't," said Jane. "I told you I ran away."

"Did you leave a note on the pincushion?"

"Of course."

They looked at each other and smiled.

"I'm glad you left a note on the pincushion," said Archie, nodding. There was silence for a few moments and then Archie said, "But honestly you can't go back. The same thing would happen all over again, wouldn't it?"

"No. Helen must be made to understand that if I go back to Angleside I go back as myself—as Jane Watt. Jane will be able to stand up to Helen—Janetta couldn't."

"Jane is your real name?"

"Yes, Jane Watt. The other was Helen's idea—in fact Janetta was Helen's creation."

"Is Janetta dead?" asked Archie in regretful tones. "I liked

Janetta, you know. I saw Janetta when she spoke at the bazaar and I thought she was a dear. I went and bought all her books—every one that I could lay my hands on—and I read them carefully."

"I've told you they aren't me," said Jane in a low voice.

"There are bits of you in them. There are, really. I put the bits together and Janetta came to life. There she was, sitting in the big chair opposite me, darning my socks—"

"You're talking like Edward!" exclaimed Jane in dismay.

"I'm sorry," said Archie. "It won't happen again."

"If you were so fond of Janetta—" began Jane.

"But that was just it!" cried Archie. "I loved Janetta dearly—and then I saw Jane."

"It must have given you a shock."

"Just for a moment," he admitted. "Just for a split second it *did* rather take my breath away. That was the reason I couldn't speak to Jane."

"But you recovered quite quickly."

"Yes, for all at once I saw the explanation: Jane and Janetta are the two halves of the apple and the real you is the whole fruit."

"But Archie—"

"I never did like half an apple," said Archie in reminiscent tones.

"But I must go back," said Jane. "I really must. Helen doesn't know where I am. She'll be getting anxious about me."

"You mustn't go back," said Archie firmly. "I want you so badly. I need you far more than Helen does. I'm very lonely at Chevis Place all by myself. Listen, Jane, you must marry me at once. I shan't interfere with your writing; in fact I can help you a lot."

"I don't need—"

"Yes, you do. I can teach you all about love—"

"Archie!"

"No, it's all right," he declared. "I'm merely making a

perfectly plain straightforward statement—Edward never did that. I can teach you about love and I can show you life. After the war we shall travel. We'll go around the world, stopping where we feel inclined and meeting all sorts of interesting people. Then we'll come home and settle down at Chevis Place and you'll write your book."

"No," said Jane, but she said it a trifle regretfully.

"Don't be silly," said Archie, taking her hand. "You would like it—you know you would. It would be fun being married to me. What's the use of making a sacrifice of yourself—a sort of burnt offering—"

"You mean a baked apple!" exclaimed Jane, laughing hysterically.

"A baked apple," agreed Archie gravely. "Don't be a baked apple, Jane. I can't bear them. I don't believe Helen likes them either."

"It isn't any use talking," replied Jane. "I've made up my mind about it—but I'm not going to sacrifice myself. I shall make Helen understand that I must be allowed to write what I want."

"Where do I come in?" demanded Archie.

"You don't come in, I'm afraid," said Jane.

⁂

The other two pedestrians did not go much farther. They found a little pool and sat down beside it on a convenient rock. Lancreste began to throw stones into the pool in a listless sort of way.

"Don't," said Melanie at last. "There may be fishes in it."

Lancreste stopped at once.

"What did you think of Miss Watt?" asked Melanie, who felt she must say something to break the deathly silence.

"Miss Watt!" said Lancreste. "Oh, I didn't look at her, really. I haven't much use for women who wear men's clothes."

"She doesn't," said Melanie.

"Well, mannish-looking clothes," amended Lancreste.

"What do you think they're doing?" Melanie inquired.

"Oh, I don't know," replied Lancreste. "Talking about the tree, I suppose. What do people like that talk about? They're quite old, aren't they?"

"Old?"

"He must be about thirty-five," said Lancreste. He hesitated and then added, in a miserable voice, "I've been wanting to talk to you all the afternoon and now I can't."

"Why can't you?"

"I don't know," said Lancreste. He picked up another stone and was about to throw it into the pool...and then he remembered about the fishes. "But I don't think there are any fishes there," he said.

"There are tadpoles, anyhow."

"Tadpoles!"

"Why should we be unkind to tadpoles?" said Melanie. There was silence.

"I saw you looking at me," Melanie said at last.

"You didn't mind, did you?"

"No, I was sorry for you because you seemed so unhappy."

"I am," said Lancreste.

"I used to be unhappy," said Melanie slowly.

"You aren't now."

"No. You see I've got what I want."

"I wouldn't be happy if I got what I want," declared Lancreste miserably.

"Perhaps you want the wrong thing."

Lancreste was silent. "Yes," he said at last. "Yes, I suppose that's true—but I want it all the same."

"You're beginning not to," she told him. "I mean if you can see it's the wrong thing—"

"It's a girl," he said.

"I thought it might be," nodded Melanie.

Lancreste hesitated. It would be a relief to tell her all about Pearl, to tell her everything, but it was not a very pleasant story and Melanie was so young and innocent. It wouldn't be fair, thought Lancreste, looking at her.

"I suppose she's very pretty," said Melanie suddenly.

"Yes," said Lancreste.

"And very, very nice."

"No," said Lancreste. "No, she isn't, really. I mean I don't like her—but I love her dreadfully. It's funny, isn't it?"

"It sounds—queer," she agreed in doubtful tones.

"She isn't very kind," said Lancreste, "and she's rather— rather deceitful, but I love her all the same."

Melanie considered this. She said, "That's *very* difficult to understand."

"I don't understand it myself," admitted Lancreste. "Of course I liked her at first, you know. I thought she was per- fect...but now I see she isn't...sometimes she says she'll marry me and sometimes she says she won't."

"Poor Lancreste!" exclaimed Melanie, looking at him wide-eyed.

"It's awful, really."

"It must be awful."

"I can't talk to anyone about it—that's the worst of it," declared Lancreste, quite forgetting Barbara's patient acceptance of his complaints.

"You must talk to me," said Melanie, smiling kindly at him.

Lancreste smiled back. She was quite different from Pearl. He did not love her—no, not a bit—but he liked her immensely. There was a strange sort of peace to be found in the nearness of Melanie, a sort of comforting balm. Just to sit beside her, and listen to her voice, soothed him and stilled his restlessness.

"Come and talk to me whenever you like," said Melanie. "We live at the cottage, Daddy and I, and we're very happy together. I've always wanted to live with Daddy."

"*That's* what you wanted?"

"Yes."

"I see," said Lancreste thoughtfully.

Chapter Twenty-One
Colonel Melton's Problems

Colonel Melton was worried. He did not know how to tackle the problem that had suddenly presented itself to his notice. The last three evenings when he had returned to the cottage about six, after his day's work, he had found a young man sitting with Melanie in front of the fire—an odd sort of young fellow with sleek hair and a horrid little moustache—and the moment Colonel Melton had appeared this odd young fellow had risen and said he must go—and had gone with unseemly haste, scarcely waiting to reply to Colonel Melton's civil conversation. It was bad enough to have a young fellow hanging about Melanie—thought Colonel Melton ruefully—but the mere fact that the fellow went tearing off like a lunatic and would not stay and talk showed that he was up to no good. Colonel Melton had not seen much of him, of course. He had exchanged a few brief words with him on his way to the door—that was all—but what he had seen of the fellow he didn't much care for. It was most worrying. Perhaps he should not have brought Melanie here. Perhaps he ought to send her back to her aunt, where she would be properly looked after. He was away all day and could not keep an eye on Melanie—she was too much alone—she was very young and innocent and absolutely defenseless. If Colonel Melton had found one of his own officers with Melanie he would not have minded—or at least he would not have minded nearly so much—for he knew them, and knew what they were like, but this strange fellow...

He was in the Air Force, too, and this fact added to the colonel's uneasiness, for, although Colonel Melton respected the R. A. F. and gave its members their due for the skill and gallantry with which they performed their duties, he was aware that fellows in the Air Force were apt to be a bit reckless and hot-headed, a bit irresponsible...and Mell was so young.

I shall have to speak to Mell, thought Colonel Melton as he tried, for the third time, to read and understand an account of a brilliant bomber raid upon one of Germany's most important industrial towns.

"Anything interesting in the paper, Daddy?" asked Melanie as she began to lay the supper table.

"No, nothing," replied her father.

"I thought you seemed very intent on it," she continued. "I meant to listen to the news at six but of course I couldn't."

Colonel Melton cleared his throat. "Er—Melanie—" he began, but he did not get any further for she put down the knives and forks and came and sat on the arm of his chair and leaned against him.

He put his arm around her.

"Daddy," said Melanie. "I want to ask you something."

His heart seemed to miss a beat. "What is it?" he inquired.

"I'm afraid you won't like it. I'm afraid it's going to be rather a nuisance for you, darling."

He was thoroughly frightened now. "Mell," he began.

"I know," said Melanie, stroking his hair. "I know you don't want to be worried and bothered when you come home tired and try to read the paper—but it really *is* important. In fact I should have told you before. I've been putting it off and putting it off because I *do* hate worrying you."

He couldn't speak. He couldn't find breath enough to ask her what was the matter. Why couldn't she tell him quickly, so that he would know the worst?

"It's the pans, Daddy," said Melanie, regretfully.

"The pans!"

Melanie nodded. "They're old and they haven't been properly looked after. I'm afraid the woman who was here before wasn't very—very careful. Miss Marks told me she wasn't, as a matter of fact."

"*Pans*," repeated Colonel Melton.

"They're all singed, Daddy—every one of them and of course once a pan has been singed it's so apt to burn the food. We could ask Mrs. Abbott for new ones, I suppose, but I don't like to do that because she has been so kind to us, hasn't she?"

"Why did you frighten me, Mell?"

"Frighten you?" she asked.

"I thought it was something to do with that young fellow that was here."

"Lancreste!"

"Is that his name?"

"He can't help it," Melanie pointed out. "He didn't choose it, darling."

"I don't like him," said Colonel Melton frankly.

"No," said Melanie. "No, I didn't think you would. That's why I told him to go away when you came home."

"What?"

"I told him," explained Melanie. "I said he could come to tea but he must go away whenever you came in."

"You told him that!"

"Yes, darling, I had to, really. He's rather the type that stays on and on and doesn't know when to go away. You didn't want him to stay, did you?"

Colonel Melton was dumb.

"*Did* you?" asked Melanie, looking at him in surprise.

"No-o," replied her father doubtfully. "Not exactly—but I like to—to know your friends."

"You wouldn't like him," repeated Melanie, rising from her perch and walking toward the door.

"Do *you* like him?" asked Colonel Melton.

She hesitated at the door with a thoughtful look. "Part of me does," said Melanie slowly.

Colonel Melton looked at her across the room. I wish she had a mother, he thought. Aloud he said, "How much, Mell?"

"Quite a lot," she replied. "You see I'm so sorry for him and I'm trying to help him. You can't help a person without liking them."

"You don't—love him, do you?"

"Oh *no*," cried Melanie. "No, of course not. Lancreste is in love with someone else...and she's a beast," added Melanie. "She's an absolute beast. I haven't seen her but I know she must be."

"I don't like it," said Colonel Melton. "It isn't a good thing to encourage the fellow to come and talk to you, Mell."

"Oh Daddy, how funny you are!"

"Funny?"

"Yes, you're afraid I shall fall in love with him, I suppose. As if I should ever fall in love with poor Lancreste!"

"No chance of it?"

"None," declared Melanie, shaking her head violently.

Colonel Melton smiled. He said, "I'm glad to hear he isn't your idea of a suitable husband."

"Poor Lancreste!" said Melanie again—and said it with such a pitying smile that every trace of anxiety vanished from Colonel Melton's mind. If Melanie could speak of him in that kindly, but somewhat disparaging, manner there was no need to worry; Melanie was safe.

Colonel Melton was so pleased at his discovery that he

felt like teasing his daughter a little. "Well, well," he said. "Perhaps you could give me some idea what sort of a son-in-law I may expect."

"Oh!" cried Melanie. "That's easy, really. Someone much older than me and much cleverer: someone big and handsome and strong; someone who would have jokes with me and laugh at the same things: *someone like you.*"

"Like me?"

"Just like you…but really and truly I don't want to marry anyone—not for years and years."

"You're quite happy," he asked.

"Very happy."

"All you want is pans."

She ran across the room and hugged him. "Two," she said. "Just two, Daddy. It will make such a lot of difference to have them—but I'm afraid they'll be terribly difficult to get."

"I'll send Fraser into Wandlebury tomorrow. If anyone can get them he will."

They were very happy together all the evening.

It was half-past ten and the Meltons were getting ready for bed when there was a knock on the front door. The colonel went downstairs in his dressing gown and found Bobby Appleyard on the step.

"I'm awfully sorry to bother you, sir," said Bobby. "The fact is we've caught the fellow that's been hanging about the place."

"Well, what of that?" said Colonel Melton.

"Major Cray sent me to tell you about it, sir."

"What's he like? Where did you catch him?" asked the colonel.

Bobby realized that the colonel was not pleased. "I'm awfully sorry," repeated Bobby. "The fellow's making rather a fuss. We've got him in the guard room, of course. He's small and rather dirty, dressed in a dark-blue suit—Major Cray thought you should see him."

"What, *now*?" asked the colonel. "Surely it would do if I saw him in the morning."

"I don't know," replied Bobby. "Major Cray said…and the fellow is making rather a fuss…Major Cray doesn't know what to do with him."

Colonel Melton went upstairs and dressed. As he laced his boots he murmured uncomplimentary things about Major Cray. Cray was afraid of taking an ounce of responsibility; he was too fond of "passing the buck." This was not the first time Colonel Melton had thought hard things about his senior major; it was merely the last straw. He decided that he was not going to take Cray on active service…Cray wasn't the sort of fellow…too windy…no use having a fellow like that…

The night was dark and wet (a fact that helped to seal the fate of Major Cray). Colonel Melton and Bobby groped their way down to the guard room with the aid of an electric torch. Major Cray was there, waiting for them, so also was the guard—three large red-faced men in battledress—so also was a small, white-faced man in a navy-blue suit.

"Where was he found?" asked the colonel.

"In the lines, sir," replied Major Cray. "He was—"

"I worn't," said the man huskily. "I worn't in no lions. I wor lookin' in at the 'ut where the suppers wor cookin'. I wor 'ungry that's wot. I've as much roight ter be there as you."

"Have you taken down a statement?" asked the colonel.

"He won't make a statement," said Major Cray in anxious tones.

"What's your name?" asked the colonel, looking at the man as he spoke.

"No bisniss of yours," replied the man.

"He won't say anything," declared Major Cray.

"Come now," said Colonel Melton. "What's the use of going on like this. You're only making things harder for yourself. You've been hanging about the place for days—what's the meaning of it?"

"I 'aven't," replied the man. "I 'aven't bin 'anging about. I got 'ere this arternoon—come down in the bus—I got bisniss 'ere."

"What sort of business?"

"It's Mrs. Abbott I wants ter see."

"He can't see Mrs. Abbott tonight," said Bobby hastily.

"Of course not," agreed the colonel. "He can spend the night in the guard room. Give him something to eat; I'll see him again in the morning."

"'ere!" cried the man. "'ere, I say! Wotter you gettin' at? You ain't got no roight ter keep me locked up. You'll get inter trouble fer this. Wot 'ave I done! You carn't keep people locked up when they ain't *done* nothin'."

"I can," replied Colonel Melton, smiling at the little man's indignation. "You were in the lines without authority and you refuse to give an account of yourself."

"I'm in a aircraff factory," said the man. "That's goverment service jus' as much as a soldier. I came down 'ere on private bisniss, ter see Mrs. Abbott. I ain't sayin' a word maw—not ter you, any'ow."

"He ought to be shackled," said Major Cray in an undertone. "He's a desperate character—a spy—we were warned about him, sir."

"Nonsense," said the colonel. "The guard will look after him. I suppose you've disarmed him."

"He wasn't armed," said Bobby quickly.

The colonel hesitated at the door. "Come on," he said (not unkindly, for the man had plenty of spunk and spunk was an attribute that appealed to the colonel). "Come on. Why not make a clean breast of it? What have you been doing here?"

"I ain't bin doin' nothing. I tol' you I come down 'ere this arternoon. They give me two days off fer privit bisniss—strike me pink if it ain't the trooth."

Somehow or other Colonel Melton felt that it was.

Chapter Twenty-Two
"Where Did You See Your Father?"

E arly the following morning Wilhelmina was washing the doorstep at Ganthorne Lodge when suddenly she heard footsteps behind her and saw Colonel Melton coming up the path. She was very pleased to see him, for she liked the colonel; their acquaintance had started when Wilhelmina was merely Elmie Boles. Several times when Elmie was on her way home from school the colonel had stopped her and talked to her kindly and given her a sixpence—one did not forget things like that.

"Good morning, Wilhelmina," said Colonel Melton, smiling. He knew her history, of course, and, although he was of the opinion that it was exceedingly wrong—in fact positively criminal—to keep the child at Ganthorne without telling her parents, he was obliged to admit that good had come out of evil. Most extraordinary, thought the colonel, looking at her. Almost incredible, the change in the girl.

The girl had been a miserable, wispy, furtive little creature with tousled hair and a peaky face—now she looked healthy and happy and she wore an air of importance that sat quaintly upon her childish shoulders.

"You look very pleased with yourself," said Colonel Melton in a friendly manner.

Wilhelmina nodded. "I got my wages," she replied. "I've earned them, too. Miss Marks said that."

"Good work. What are you going to buy?"

"A skirt," said Wilhelmina. "And a jumper—a green one like Mrs. Abbott has."

"You couldn't do better," said the colonel gravely. He hesitated and then asked, "Is Mrs. Abbott in?"

"No, sir," replied Wilhelmina, straightening herself and assuming an official air. "Mrs. Abbott's out exercising the 'orses—the horses, I mean. May I take a message, sir?"

Colonel Melton decided she was quite capable of delivering a message, as indeed she was. "Yes," he said. "You might tell Mrs. Abbott that the sentries caught a man in the lines last night. He was brought into the guard room but he refused to give any account of himself beyond saying that he has business with Mrs. Abbott. I think perhaps Mrs. Abbott had better see him and, if she doesn't mind, I'll bring him up to the house after lunch— say about two. Can you remember that?"

Wilhelmina was staring at him wide-eyed. "Yes," she said breathlessly. "Yes, I'll tell her."

He turned to go, but she ran after him and caught him by the sleeve. "Please, what's 'e like?" she said.

Colonel Melton noticed the slip and he could not help smiling. "Oh, he's a very harmless sort of fellow," said the colonel. "Small and ferrety-looking, dressed in a dark-blue suit. You needn't be alarmed..."

Wilhelmina did not wait to hear any more. She turned and ran back to the house and dashed into the pantry, where Miss Marks was engaged in cleaning the silver.

"Miss Marks!" she cried. "Miss Marks, 'e's come!"

"He...has...come," said Miss Marks firmly, taking up another spoon and polishing it industriously. "And, please Wilhelmina, do not caper about like that. You nearly upset the table."

"*He has come!*" said Wilhelmina, her eyes starting out of her head. "*He has come*, Miss Marks—Oh, Miss Marks wotever shall I do?"

"Who has come?" asked Miss Marks, dropping the spoon and gazing at her protégée in alarm.

"It's 'im—it's Dad—'e's come to fetch me 'ome," cried Wilhelmina, her aitches flying in all directions unheeded. "It's 'im, I know it's 'im—small an' ferrety—that's wot 'e sed—in a blue soot—that's 'is best."

"Wilhelmina."

"Ow dear, ow dear!" cried Wilhelmina, squeezing her hands together. "Ow, Miss Marks! I won't gow—I won't leave you nor Mrs. Abbott neither. You sed I needn't—an' *she* sed I needn't—an' I won't."

"Compose yourself, Wilhelmina," said Miss Marks, patting her on the back.

"'Ow can I?" she wailed. "'Ow can I? 'E'll take me—I'll have ter gow—I'll never be 'appy agen. I'll throw myself in the river—that's wot—"

"Come now," said Miss Marks. "I told you that you were never to say such a wicked thing again."

"But I'll 'ave ter gow—"

"You need not stay," said Miss Marks in significant tones.

Wilhelmina was no fool—and she and Markie understood each other pretty well by this time—so she stopped crying at once and looked at Miss Marks.

Miss Marks nodded. "There now," she said. "Be a sensible girl. There is nothing to be gained by tears and lamentations."

"You'll 'ide me!" exclaimed Wilhelmina with dawning hope.

"I shall not hide you," replied Miss Marks. "It would be foolish—for you would probably be found and a great deal of trouble might result. Tell me exactly what happened. Where did you see your father?"(Markie paused for a moment. She had a feeling that these words were familiar, they had a familiar ring, but there was no time to pin down the quotation now.) "Where did you see your father," repeated Miss Marks. "What did he say? Pull yourself together and explain the matter clearly."

Wilhelmina did as she was told and Miss Marks was soon in possession of the facts of the case.

"You are sure it is your father?" asked Miss Marks.

"Small and ferrety-looking."

"I know," said Miss Marks hastily, "but there might be others answering to the same somewhat vague description."

"It's 'im," declared Wilhelmina, with emphasis.

Miss Marks nodded. "Very well, then…"

"Wot am I ter do?" asked Wilhelmina, but this time she asked it hopefully, her eyes upon her protector's face.

"Sit down and help me to clean the silver," said Miss Marks firmly. "It will take me a little time to explain…"

⁂

At two o'clock precisely Colonel Melton walked up the path to the door of Ganthorne Lodge followed by Sergeant Frayle and the small ferrety-looking man in the blue suit. Jerry was waiting for them—she had been given Colonel Melton's message in his exact words—but she was a little taken aback when they walked in.

"Oh, it's Mr. Boles!" exclaimed Jerry in dismay.

"You know this man?" asked Colonel Melton.

"Yes, of course. It's Mrs. Boles's husband—that used to be at the cottage—he came down to see them once or twice."

"Three toimes," said Mr. Boles in a husky voice.

"Oh, it was three times?" said Jerry, helplessly. "I didn't—er—remember."

Now that the cat was out of the bag Colonel Melton saw the

whole thing and all its implications at a glance, for he had a quick and lucid mind. He saw Jerry's predicament, and, although she was in the wrong, he was very sorry for her. If he had had any inkling of the man's identity he might have arranged things differently (perhaps the man had guessed as much, perhaps that was the reason he had refused to speak) but it was too late now. Mrs. Abbott was in for an unpleasant half hour and he could do very little to help.

"State your business, Boles," said Colonel Melton. "Mrs. Abbott is busy. We can't presume upon her time."

"That's easy. I want my Elmie."

"Elmie!" repeated Jerry, vaguely.

"Elmie," said Mr. Boles. "My Elmie's 'ere. She's 'ere without 'er parients' permission. I've come ter take 'er 'ome."

"But she doesn't want—" began Jerry and then she saw Colonel Melton shaking his head at her and stopped.

"Mrs. Abbott understood—" began Colonel Melton.

"I don't want no talk," declared Mr. Boles in a truculent manner. "I wants my kid, that's all. She's my kid an' I wants 'er. Where is she?"

At this moment the door opened and Wilhelmina walked in (it almost looked as if she had been listening outside); her entrance was so unexpected and raised so many different sensations in the bosoms of the room's occupants that there was dead silence for a few moments. Wilhelmina was not discomposed. She stood there calmly, looking from one face to another and smiling to herself. She was dressed in her best frock—it was dark green serge—and her hair, which was smooth and shining, was tied at the side with a green ribbon.

"Elmie!" said Mr. Boles at last.

"Yes, Dad?" said Wilhelmina in questioning tones.

Mr. Boles did not reply. He was breathing heavily; he was gazing at his daughter with his mouth slightly open.

"Yes, Dad?" repeated Wilhelmina.

"Well!" exclaimed Mr. Boles, giving himself a shake and straightening his back. "Well, this is a noice thing, this is. Wot d'yer mean by it—eh? Walkin' out of the 'ouse an' never comin' back, froightnin' us out of our wits! That's a noice thing ter do, ain't it?"

Wilhelmina said nothing.

"Too good fer yer 'ome, ain't yer?" continued Mr. Boles, warming up a little. "Too good ter wash up dishes fer yer ma! Livin' on the fat of the land, ain't yer? Dressed up fit ter kill—ribbings on yer 'air an' wot not! Think yer a bit of okay, don't yer?"

Wilhelmina did not reply.

"Charity!" said Mr. Boles. "Livin' on charity, that's a noice thing, that is! That's a bit of a come down, ain't it?"

"I've got a job," said Wilhelmina briefly.

"Got a job?"

"I'm a housemaid."

"Ho, a 'ousemaid! A pide servant!" said Mr. Boles in disgust.

"Like you," said Wilhelmina sweetly. "You get paid, too, don't you?"

"We are all paid servants," said Colonel Melton, who had been listening to the conversation with a good deal of interest. "In fact Mrs. Abbott is the only person in the room who works hard and gets no pay."

"She's a *capitalist*," declared Mr. Boles.

"I wish I were!" exclaimed Jerry. "As a matter of fact—"

"I didn't come to talk," said Mr. Boles, interrupting her with scant ceremony. "I come 'ere to taike Elmie 'ome. She don't want no jobs as 'ousemaids."

"But I do!" cried Wilhelmina.

"Your ma wants yer," said Mr. Boles, trying another tack. "Yer pore ma wants yer. She's bin porely."

"I would rather stay here," replied Wilhelmina but, for the first time, her voice faltered a little.

"You'll come 'ome, my girl. You'll come 'ome with me—an' no nonsense."

"No."

"I'll taike yer," said Mr. Boles rising as he spoke. "I'll taike yer now, this minit, an' I'd loike ter see anyone stop me."

Jerry half-expected to see Wilhelmina turn and fly, but she stood her ground manfully. "I suppose you could," she said, measuring her parent thoughtfully. "You could take me 'ome by force, couldn't you?"

"Yes," replied Mr. Boles, but he said it doubtfully.

"You couldn't keep me there, could you?" said Wilhelmina with a little smile.

"Couldn't keep yer?"

Wilhelmina shook her head.

"Wot d'yer mean?"

"You couldn't keep me at 'ome—not unless you kep' me locked up all the time," explained Wilhelmina.

Mr. Boles gazed at her in dismay. "Kep' yer locked up?"

Wilhelmina nodded.

"Strike me pink!" exclaimed Mr. Boles, envisaging the inconvenience of this drastic expedient.

"I'd just come back 'ere," continued Wilhelmina, whose aitches were becoming a trifle shaky with excitement. "I wouldn't stay at 'ome—not one moment longer than I could 'elp."

"But Elmie."

"I got a job," declared Wilhelmina. "I like it an' I get paid fer doin' it. You can take me 'ome if you want to—but I won't stay."

Father and daughter stood and gazed at each other and suddenly Jerry saw that they were alike. Mr. Boles was pale and sharp featured and Wilhelmina was a very nice-looking child but there was a likeness all the same...they were both full of "spunk"; they were both strong-minded and independent. They stared at each other for several moments, measuring swords, and then Mr. Boles laughed...Everybody joined in the laughter, partly with relief and partly because it really was very funny indeed.

"Strike me pink!" cried Mr. Boles, between his spasms of mirth. "There's a kid for you! Knows 'er own moind, don't she? Well, it beats me—beats me 'ollow—I carn't get around it, no'ow!"

After that everything was easy and pleasant. Colonel Melton and the sergeant vanished and Markie appeared carrying a tray upon which were set out a bottle of beer, a glass and two sandwiches. Mr. Boles had no use for the sandwiches—he had dined already—but the beer was a different matter. He drank to his daughter, remarking that she was a chip off the old block and worth two of Arrol, and he drank to Mrs. Abbott, and to "the 'ouse." He was about to drink the health of Miss Marks when he discovered that his glass was empty. Mr. Boles turned the bottle upside down and gave it a shake...and then he looked at his hostess, but she did not seem to understand.

"Oh well," he said. "It was good while it larsted."

As Wilhelmina had been given the afternoon off to go to Wandlebury and do her shopping, and, as Mr. Boles was obliged to catch the six o'clock train home, the two went off together in the bus.

"I suppose it's quite safe letting her go with him," said Jerry as she and Markie watched them walking down the drive.

"Perfectly safe," replied Markie. "Wilhelmina can see him off and come home before dark. One need have no apprehensions."

"It was clever," said Jerry thoughtfully. "You put her up to it, of course, you naughty old thing."

"I made a few little suggestions," admitted Markie with a satisfied air.

"You might have warned me."

"No dear," said Markie firmly. "It was essential that you should know nothing at all."

Wilhelmina came home in good time, but she came empty-handed, and when Markie inquired into the matter she replied in a somewhat shamefaced way that she had not bought the skirt. "Never mind," said Markie, kindly. "You can buy it next month. You are quite right to send the money to your mother, dear."

Chapter Twenty-Three
Miss Marks Goes for a Walk

Markie was sleeping badly. The pain in her side, which had abated for a while, had now returned nagging like toothache. She could not sleep and she did not want her meals. The pain was bad enough but the anxiety it occasioned her was a great deal worse and much harder to bear. Nobody knew better than she the devastating effects of a long agonizing illness. She had seen her father die by inches before her eyes—would Jerry have to go through the same Gethsemane with *her?* It must not happen, thought Markie. I cannot let it happen. I must keep going as long as I can stand on my feet. If only I could die, thought Markie. If only I could die now, before it gets worse, before Jerry finds out.

But Markie did not worry all the time, for sometimes the pain lessened and she was buoyed up by the hope that it was leaving her for good, and one afternoon when her spiritual barometer was pointing to "set fair," she decided to go out for a walk. I must get out more, thought Markie. I am much better—I need fresh air. She looked out of the window and what she saw confirmed her in her intention: it was a lovely afternoon, the sun was shining and a few white clouds were scudding across the bright blue sky.

Markie never went for a walk without dressing for the part. It never occurred to her to throw on a wrap and rush out onto the moor. She changed her shoes, donned her black cloth coat with the gray fur collar and a small black toque with white flowers in it, which had been the height of fashion when George the Fifth came to the throne. She put on a pair of suede gloves with buttons, took her bag and her umbrella, and sallied forth. She had intended to walk up the hill as far as the wood, but it was such a lovely day and she felt so well and happy that she decided to go farther. It would not matter if she were late for tea. She walked on through the wood, past the fallen oak where Archie and Jane had had their long interesting conversation, and came out onto the moor. Here she paused. Should she return or should she go farther still. She could strike across the moor by a footpath and come home by the Gostown road. It would not be too far. No, not a bit. Markie walked on.

How lovely it was! The air was cool and crisp with the first hint of autumn. The trees had been touched with frost—one here and one there—and burned as if with fire. The moors rolled away to the horizon, clothed with brown bracken and patches of sunlit grass. Dozens of rabbits scuttled about the moor, or sat at the doors of their burrows and watched Markie as she passed.

Presently the path ran up a steep rise and Markie puffed and blew as she breasted the slope, for she was out of training. She paused when she reached the top and stood there while she recovered her breath. It was a splendid view, a wide undulating expanse of moorland with here and there a wood or a cottage. To her left, a couple of miles away, lay Ganthorne Lodge and the cluster of Nissen huts where the soldiers lived, to her right lay the grounds and policies of Wisden House, below her was the Gostown road…and there was the bus that ran between Gostown and Wandlebury, bucketing along over the somewhat uneven surface in its usual headlong way. If Markie had been a little quicker she might have stopped the bus and got a lift home…but it did not matter, she was not really tired.

She walked down toward the road; it was only a few hundred yards, but to reach it she must pass through a wood; and the wood was a neglected sort of place, full of dead trees and choked with nettles and brambles and rhododendron bushes that had gone wild and straggly. There was something very unpleasant about the wood and Markie was suddenly a little nervous. It was absolutely ridiculous, of course, but she was— nervous. She had a feeling that she was not alone. Somebody was near.

Markie looked around. There was nobody to be seen…but she still had that odd feeling. "Perfect nonsense," said Markie firmly and she walked on a few steps, accelerating her pace a little…and then she stopped again. There *was* somebody else in the wood.

Markie could never explain why or how she knew. Whether she had heard something—which seemed unlikely—or whether she had seen something—which seemed unlikely, too. She just knew that she was not alone in the wood; something told her… and the same something, which told her she was not alone, told her to step over a ditch, scramble up a bank, and look through a tangled mass of brambles and rhododendron bushes.

Markie did these things and found herself gazing at a man, dressed in a tweed suit, who was sitting propped up against a fallen tree, fast asleep.

"Most extraordinary!" said Markie under her breath.

She looked at him for some moments and all sorts of ideas sped through her mind. Who was he? Where had he come from? Why was he here? He might be an officer from the camp who had come here for a little peace—but Markie knew all the officers and she had never seen this man before. Could he be somebody from Gostown? Could he be a guest from Wisden

House? He might be, of course, but somehow or other Markie felt doubtful, and the more she looked at the man the more doubtful she became. There was something very odd about him.

At first Markie could not decide why the man looked odd. She tried to crystallize her impressions. Was it his clothes? His suit was made of quite ordinary gray tweed, but it did not look comfortable and slightly shabby like most country tweeds. It was a new suit—and yet it was dirty, soiled with mud. That was odd, thought Markie, for what man in his senses would put on a brand-new suit to go for a ramble in the woods? His hair was queer, too. It was cut in a curious way. It was very short and bristly...his head was square.

"Most *extraordinary!*" said Markie again, but this time with quite a different inflexion, for she had reached the somewhat alarming conclusion that the man was not an English citizen; that his origin was Teutonic. Of course he might be a foreigner and yet have a perfect right to be here, for Britain was full of foreigners—it had become the most cosmopolitan spot on the face of the earth—but somehow or other Markie was sure that this man was not a friendly alien. She was sure of it even before she saw the gleam of the small revolver that lay beside him within easy reach of his hand...

Markie was breathing a little faster than usual as she withdrew from the hedge and climbed down the bank on to the path, but it was with excitement, not fear...she had found the spy. The man was a spy—they had been talking about a spy, and this was he.

Goodness! thought Markie, standing upon the path and literally gasping with excitation of feeling. Goodness, what had I better do? I cannot do anything myself, for the man is armed. I had better run back to the camp and tell Colonel Melton.

Yes, Colonel Melton was the person to deal with the situation. He would know exactly what to do...but Markie had scarcely taken two steps in the direction of the camp when she was assailed by a flock of doubts and misgivings: supposing her diagnosis was wrong and the man was not a spy! Supposing she got hold of Colonel Melton and brought him to the wood and the man proved to be quite a harmless person! *What a fool she would look!*

Markie stopped and thought about it. She had been sure of her premises, of course, but now she was not so sure. Now that her eyes were not fixed upon the man she could scarcely credit their evidence. And the whole thing was so extraordinary (thought Markie). It was not the sort of thing that happened to an ordinary person like herself. There was the revolver, of course. A harmless person would not walk about the woods carrying a revolver, nor go to sleep with a revolver placed close to his hand—only a man who went in fear of his life would take that precaution—but had she *really* seen the revolver? Could it have been something that *looked* like a revolver? His pipe, for instance!

I must make quite sure, thought Markie. I should look such a fool...I must have a closer view of the man.

With this aim in view Markie made a circuit of the bushes and finding a path that led in the right direction she came around behind her quarry through the trees. He was still asleep, but he seemed restless, breathing noisily and muttering...as Markie approached he flung out one arm and turned over on his other side. She waited till he was quiet again, and now she was perfectly certain of her man: his cephalic characteristics were unmistakable. She went nearer, stepping softly and carefully, and she saw his revolver lying by his side...

Moved by a sudden brilliant idea Markie stooped and picked up the revolver. It was cold in her hand, cold and heavy, and it had a grim ugly look—but the fact that she had disarmed her enemy gave her a good deal of satisfaction. He was not so dangerous now. Still dangerous, of course, thought Markie (backing away from him through the trees, and carrying the little gun very carefully as if it might go off at any moment and blow her up), still dangerous, but not *so* dangerous. Colonel Melton would be able to capture him quite easily without the risk of getting shot...

Chapter Twenty-Four
The Route March

Lieutenant Howe had arrived at Ganthorne Camp the night before. He was rather shy and he felt exactly like a new boy at school. He was so anxious to make a good impression and showed so much zeal that Major Cray deputed him to take "B" Company for a route march.

"You don't know the way, of course," said Major Cray. "But Sergeant Frayle can show you—and it will give you an idea of the lie of the land."

"Yes sir," said Jimmy Howe smartly.

The company was thirty strong—thirty-one including the colonel's batman, who, for some unexplained reason, had obtained permission to take part in the exercise. Jimmy Howe was young, and it seemed to him a good sight when "B" Company marched out of camp, smart, orderly, and fully attired for battle. It made Jimmy feel quite queer inside to see them and to know that for the next two hours this magnificent body of men would be under his command. Sergeant Frayle was most helpful. He suggested that they should take the track across the moor to Gostown and come back by the road. It was just the right length and there was plenty to see. The men liked it. Jimmy Howe agreed at once and away they went.

The moors were gorgeous, the bracken was a rich deep

brown—there was almost a purple tinge in it. The air was sparkling clear. Tiny white clouds raced across the sky. Jimmy Howe
striding along with his men felt as though the world belonged
to him. Presently the men started to whistle and Jimmy was
glad, for it showed that they were enjoying themselves too. On
they went, up hill and down dale, and at first Jimmy was so
enchanted with everything he saw that he thought of nothing
else, but after a bit he began to think of his mother and to wish
that she could see him now—how wonderful it would be if
she suddenly appeared and watched the company march past!
(Wonderful, but quite impossible, for his mother lived in York.)
And Aunt Deborah, thought Jimmy. Pity *she* couldn't see him.
She was a managing old lady, was Aunt Deborah; she managed
the whole family—including Jimmy, of course. Yes, it *was a*
pity she couldn't see him now.

The company marched to Gostown, swung left, and returned
by the road. It was a pleasant road and there was very little
traffic on it—not that there was much traffic anywhere these
days—a bus passed them at the top of the hill, and Sergeant
Frayle informed Jimmy that it was going to Wandlebury. They
were coming down the hill now, toward a wood, and beyond
the wood Jimmy could see Ganthorne.

They were nearly home, and Jimmy, who was still full of zeal
and ardor, was just beginning to wish that he had taken the men
a bit farther afield when a most extraordinary thing occurred.
Out of the wood rushed an old lady, and for a moment Jimmy
thought it was Aunt Deborah herself (for she was dressed in
the same démodé fashion, namely in a black coat down to her
ankles and a small round hat covered with white flowers) but
Jimmy's first thought gave place, almost at once, to a second
that was only slightly less alarming; the old lady was mad.

She rushed out of the wood and stood in the middle of the
road waving frantically and shouting, "Help! Help! Help!"

"What on earth," began Jimmy, turning to Sergeant Frayle, but he got no further. He was stricken dumb.

"B" Company was wavering and disintegrating before his eyes. The leading ranks went first and the others followed—in a moment the whole company of seasoned men was rushing pell-mell down the road. The whole company with the exception of Sergeant Frayle, and even he seemed somewhat demoralized. He ran a few steps and stopped and looked back at Jimmy, registering expressions of anxiety, mortification, and indecision that would have done credit to a film star.

Jimmy had been too amazed to give any orders—which perhaps was just as well—but now he recovered and said briefly—"We'd better follow them, I suppose," and took to his heels without more ado.

The old lady was surrounded by a solid wall of khaki when Jimmy arrived on the scene. It parted to let him through and closed up again behind him. He was now in the middle of the circle, face to face with Miss Marks.

"...the spy," she was saying in breathless tones, "a German...perfectly certain...in the wood...asleep...and here is his gun," she added producing a small revolver and holding it in an unpleasantly amateurish fashion so that it wavered around the little circle on a level with their belts. Fraser (who was standing quite near her, of course) disarmed her deftly; he opened the breach and half a dozen little bullets popped out into his hand.

"Oh, it was loaded!" exclaimed the old lady in alarm.

"Madam," began Jimmy politely.

"There is not a moment to lose!" declared the old lady, looking around at the men with shining eyes. "You must scatter and surround the wood. You must creep upon him silently and take him unawares."

Jimmy was about to protest when he felt a gentle touch on his arm. It was Sergeant Frayle. He had taken the revolver from

Fraser and was holding it out for Jimmy to see. "Look, sir," he said in an undertone. "It's a Jerry revolver, and the bullets are those soft-nosed things…"

Jimmy looked. He had not seen a revolver like it before—it was quite different from his own. "D'you mean it's true?" he asked incredulously.

The sergeant was sure it was true—he knew Miss Marks—but it was difficult to explain the matter to his officer. It was all the more difficult because by this time Miss Marks had recovered her breath and was giving her orders in a loud clear voice.

"Scatter!" cried Miss Marks, waving her umbrella. "Come upon him simultaneously from all sides. You, Shadwell, and you, Hollingford, to the south of the wood—Gheales, Barrington, and Willis to the north. Hide yourselves carefully and bar his escape, he cannot harm you, for we have taken his weapon. Quickly!" cried Miss Marks, brandishing her umbrella like a sword. "Quickly and quietly—he may wake at any moment and slip through our fingers…and you, Fraser," she continued, turning to her faithful friend. "And you, Benson," she added, picking out the champion boxer of the battalion. "Follow me, and I will lead you to him."

"Look here," began Jimmy, who had managed to find his tongue.

"And you," she added, turning to him. "Follow me, all of you; we will take him like a rat in a trap."

"Sir!" said Sergeant Frayle in agonized tones. "Sir, what would you—could we—shall I—"

Jimmy Howe swallowed something that seemed to have stuck in his throat. He said a little stiffly, "All right, Sergeant Frayle. Carry on."

"Thank you, sir," said Frayle. "I think we should do as Miss Marks suggests—unless you can think of a better plan, sir."

"Carry on, Sergeant Frayle," repeated Jimmy and this time he smiled.

"Thank you, sir," said Frayle with a sigh of relief. He really was unutterably thankful that young Mr. Howe had taken it so well. It wasn't many that would have—thought Frayle. It showed he was a bit of all right. He wouldn't lose by it, either. Frayle would see to that...

The men were scattering now, some to one side of the wood and some to the other. They were running along quickly with bent backs, creeping through hedges and vaulting over walls. Miss Marks herself, with the few faithful followers she had chosen, was waiting until her troops had taken up their position before advancing upon the enemy.

"Madame," said Jimmy—and this time "Madame" heard him for he had been warned by Sergeant Frayle that the lady was deaf. "Madame, I think it will be best if you leave this to me. Your dispositions are excellent," said Jimmy with the ghost of a smile. "I couldn't improve upon your plan of battle but I should prefer you to remain here with two of the men."

"Remain here!" exclaimed Miss Marks in surprise. "Dear me, no. I am not in the least tired."

"It isn't that exactly," said Jimmy, abandoning his high-flown language and coming down to brass tacks. "It isn't a question of whether you're tired or not. It's just that you would be better out of it. If he really is a spy—and I suppose he must be or he wouldn't have had that revolver—"

"He is a spy," interrupted Miss Marks. "Quite apart from the revolver his appearance is sufficient indication of his nationality—the cephalic structure is definitely Teutonic," added Miss Marks, clinching the matter once and for all.

"Oh!" said Jimmy vaguely. "Oh—well then—that's all the more reason why you should be out of it, because he'll be a pretty tough customer and there may be a bit of a scrap."

"Nonsense," said Miss Marks. "We must take him by surprise. You have no idea where the man is. If you start looking for him he will wake and hear you and have time to conceal himself—possibly to make his escape." She looked around and added, "Are you all ready?"

"Give them another two minutes," suggested Jimmy. "You want them all around the wood before we start."

They waited. Jimmy kept looking at his watch—two minutes seemed an endless stretch of time. He thought of all sorts of things as the hand of his watch crawled along. He had time to wonder, somewhat anxiously, whether the story would reach the mess—and in what form; to wonder whether he had been right to condone the breach of discipline—but what could he have done? He thought of Nelson's blind eye—and then decided that Nelson's blind eye was quite a different matter; it had been used not to condone but to disobey. He could think of no parallel at all. Whoever heard of an old lady appearing suddenly from the shelter of a wood and assuming command of a company? This brought him back to Miss Marks. He looked at her. She was standing in the middle of the road with her feet slightly apart and her umbrella grasped firmly in her hand. Her lips were set in a firm line and the light of battle shone in her eye. Jimmy had intended to make a further suggestion—a suggestion that Miss Marks should walk on toward Ganthorne and give the alarm— but he saw that such a feeble subterfuge would be useless.

"Time's up," said Jimmy at last.

"Good," said Miss Marks, who had been feeling the strain of waiting. "I shall go first and lead the way. You must follow, single file, for the path is narrow and—"

"I shall go first," said Jimmy.

"But I know the way."

"You can direct me."

"It would be much better—"

"Then you must take the revolver," said Jimmy, holding it out to her as he spoke.

Miss Marks looked at it. "Is it loaded?" she inquired.

Jimmy nodded.

"I have my umbrella," said Miss Marks a trifle uncertainly.

"No," said Jimmy, shaking his head. "The leader of the expedition must be properly armed."

"But you must not shoot him," said Miss Marks anxiously.

"I shan't shoot him unless I have to," said Jimmy and with that he stepped in front of her and led the way into the wood.

Miss Marks followed, directing him, and behind her came Fraser and Benson. They trod softly, avoiding dry twigs and trying to use the woodcraft they had learnt, but the crackle of leaves beneath their feet sounded very loud.

"This way," whispered Miss Marks. "Through here... along this wall...wait a moment. Yes, we turn to the right here. Yes, I remember now, this is the path. He is behind that hedge of rhododendrons."

Jimmy jumped the ditch, climbed the bank, and peered through the hedge. Then he turned his head and nodded... ("Thank goodness!" said Markie to herself.) He signed to the two men to divide and go around, one on each side. They melted away and left Markie standing alone on the path.

Just for a moment Markie wished she had not come. The woods were still and gloomy, and a few large raindrops began to fall. Markie could feel them pattering on the top of her hat. She began to unfurl her umbrella and then stopped...it seemed unsuitable.

The rain will waken him, thought Markie. He will spring up and find himself surrounded. Perhaps he will fight, or try to get away! Oh, I do hope they will not shoot him! All the glory and excitement seeped out of Markie as she stood there on the path, and she saw her adventure as a poor affair...one miserable unsuspecting fox and thirty hounds creeping up to him through the bracken. She could bear the suspense no longer. She did not want to see, but she *had* to see what was happening on the other side of the hedge. She stepped over the ditch, mounted the bank, and took up her position beside Jimmy.

"Go back," he whispered. "Go back—you'll be in the way."

She did not hear him—it might not have made much difference if she had—and instead of beating a retreat she dropped on her hands and knees and peered between the black snaky stems of the rhododendrons.

The man was still there. He was wakening now…sitting up and looking around…groping for his revolver. He was still searching for it feverishly amongst the leaves when Fraser and Benson appeared from different directions and advanced upon him. Jimmy, seeing them there, pushed through the bushes, shouting, "Hands up! You're surrounded!" The man sprang to his feet and immediately Fraser and Benson closed with him, seizing his arms.

"Don't hurt him whatever you do—don't hurt him!" cried Markie and she, too, forced her way through the bushes and arrived upon the scene.

"What on earth are you fellows *doing*?" asked the man in perfectly good English. "I suppose I'm trespassing. If so, I'm sorry. I sat down for a few minutes and I must have gone to sleep…you gave me a damned good fright. I suppose it's your idea of a joke!"

He spoke like a gentleman—an English gentleman. Jimmy fell back and the hand that held the revolver dropped to his side. How frightful! he thought. Good Lord, this is the last straw! The whole company has spent an hour stalking the fellow—I shall never live this down—never.

But Markie had been watching the man's eyes—his tongue was glib enough but his eyes were darting hither and thither like the eyes of an animal in a trap

"Fear nothing," said Markie, in correct if somewhat stilted

German. She could read German with the greatest of ease, but speaking it was a different matter. "Fear nothing. You are trapped. All is discovered; but they will do you no harm if you come quietly. Any attempt at escape is useless." She waved her umbrella as she spoke and, as if it were a signal, half a dozen more khaki figures rose from the bracken at the edge of the clearing.

"Gott in Himmel!" exclaimed the man in dismayed accents.

"Be tranquil," continued Markie soothingly. "Fear nothing. I shall not allow them to harm you. This officer has your weapon but he will not use it unless you attempt to escape."

"What are you saying to the fellow?" inquired Jimmy, looking at Miss Marks in awe...he knew enough German to be aware that the conversation was being conducted in that language, and he had realized (with relief) that his prisoner was a prisoner and not a harmless individual after all. Miss Marks explained what she had said.

"Of course," agreed Jimmy. "He won't get hurt unless he makes a bolt for it—or at least *we* shan't hurt him—but if he tries any funny tricks I can't answer for the consequences."

"You have his gun," Miss Marks pointed out.

"Yes," agreed Jimmy. "It was pretty smart of you to disarm him...just run your hands over him, Fraser, and make sure he hasn't got another...No? All right, then, take him back to the road and we'll form up and march him into camp. Sergeant Frayle, you had better remain here with a few men and make a thorough search of the wood."

"Yes, sir," said Sergeant Frayle.

"The police will have to be informed," added Jimmy. "You will remain here until you are relieved."

"Yes, sir," said Sergeant Frayle, delighted to observe that young Mr. Howe was reassuming command in such a competent manner.

The remainder of the company was recalled by a few blasts

on a whistle. They fell in quickly and marched into camp. Miss Marks marched with them, toddling along beside Jimmy in silence (for the pace was a little too rapid and she had no breath for speech). She was torn between the conflicting emotions of pride and regret. Pride in the fact that she really had accomplished something definite for her country, and regret for her prisoner, walking disconsolate and sullen between his captors. He might have been quite a nice boy (thought Markie) if only he had not been born a German, with that regrettably square head.

Chapter Twenty-Five
The Doctor's Diagnosis

Markie was in bed. She had fainted in the middle of supper—had rolled right off her chair and collapsed in a heap on the ground—and she knew nothing more until she found herself lying on her bed and heard the terrific fuss going on all around her. "Not brandy," Jane was saying. "Not until the doctor comes. Don't cry, Wilhelmina—go and fill two hot water bottles."

"She's dead!" wailed Wilhelmina.

"Nonsense, go and do what you're told," said Jane sharply.

"But Markie is *never* ill!" exclaimed Jerry's voice. "Oh dear, she must have been doing too much—and look how thin she has got—two safety pins in her waistband!"

"It was the excitement," said Jane's voice soothingly. "And we've all got thinner. Don't worry, Jerry…smelling salts—*there*, on the dressing-table—I think she's coming around."

"I am perfectly well," declared Markie in a shaky voice, and she endeavored to rise.

"Lie still, darling!" cried Jerry.

"Just until the doctor comes," added Jane.

"There is no need for the doctor."

"We've sent for him."

"I won't see him."

"Darling Markie, you must. He's coming. He'll be here in half an hour."

"I won't see him," said Markie, but she said it feebly, for she felt so ill that nothing seemed to matter very much.

Dr. Wrench was small and thin and agile. He had a brown face, somewhat wrinkled, and a pair of very brown eyes; it was therefore a foregone conclusion that his intimates should call him Monkey. He arrived at Ganthorne in his car before Jerry had expected—though not before she had hoped to see him—and instead of ringing the bell he let himself in and came bounding up the narrow stairs, two steps at a time. He was in Markie's bedroom, standing at the end of the bed and looking at her before she knew he was in the house.

Having heard of Markie's exploit—the news of which was already spreading rapidly throughout the district with the usual additions and variations common to news of this nature—Dr. Wrench had expected to find his patient suffering from nervous reaction, and he had come prepared to administer a little gentle badinage and a sedative, but one glance at his patient's face disabused him of these ideas. Miss Marks was really ill. She was in pain. The first thing to do was to clear the room; Jerry and Jane and Wilhelmina were banished and the door was shut.

"Now, what's all this?" demanded Dr. Wrench. "What have you been doing to yourself?"

"I walked too far," replied Miss Marks feebly.

"Where is the pain?"

"It is not bad."

"Let's see where it is."

"There is no need," began Miss Marks, clinging to the bed-clothes with both hands.

But the doctor was more than a match for her and despite her denials and prevarications she was examined thoroughly, prodded and poked and questioned until no shred of privacy remained to her, until every smallest detail had been revealed. Dr. Wrench sat down on a chair beside her bed and looked at her. "I thought you were a sensible woman," he said.

"I am," declared Miss Marks defiantly.

"A sensible woman would have taken advice months ago."

Miss Marks remained silent.

"Why didn't you take advice?" demanded Dr. Wrench.

"It was not necessary."

"Nonsense. That isn't the reason."

Miss Marks hesitated. "I suppose I was a coward," she said at last.

"A coward!"

"Yes, I was afraid you might say it was serious."

"So you just carried on," said Dr. Wrench with exasperation. "You just went on as usual—don't you realize that it's a very dangerous thing to do?"

"I hate being a bother," explained Miss Marks.

There was a short silence.

"What is it?" asked Miss Marks at last. "Is it serious?"

"Of course it's serious," replied Dr. Wrench. "You don't have pain without a cause. Pain is simply nature's way of warning us that something has gone wrong."

"Very serious?" asked Miss Marks anxiously.

Dr. Wrench looked at her. "What did you think it was?" he inquired.

"I thought perhaps," she began. "I wondered…"

"Oh, so that's what you thought!" he exclaimed. "You've been worrying yourself sick—and all for nothing. Appendicitis is the name of your complaint."

"Appendicitis!" exclaimed Miss Marks in amazement. "But surely…are you certain…is that all it is?"

"That's all," he replied, smiling for the first time.

"I can have it removed, then?"

"Most certainly," he replied. "You must have it removed as soon as possible. You'll be as right as a trivet in a fortnight or three weeks."

"I can't believe it," declared Miss Marks. "It is too good to be true...are you perfectly certain, Dr. Wrench? I thought appendicitis was a sudden acute pain accompanied by a high temperature."

"Yours is a chronic condition."

"I have lost weight," Miss Marks reminded him.

"What do you expect? People who worry themselves silly over nothing usually lose weight...What put the idea into your head?" he inquired as he rose to go.

"My father died of it...carcinomata of epithelial origin."

"You'll probably die of old age," said Dr. Wrench comfortingly—and he departed. Markie turned over and shut her eyes. She began to say her prayers but she was asleep before she had reached the end of them.

⁂

Jane and Wilhelmina stood on the doorstep of Ganthorne Lodge and watched the ambulance drive away. It was taking Markie to Wandlebury Hospital, and Jerry had gone with her to see her safely into bed. Markie had been in excellent spirits, talking and joking and giving all sorts of instructions and warnings to her deputies—in fact one might have thought that Markie was looking forward to her operation with delight. When the ambulance had disappeared from view Jane and Wilhelmina went back into the house and looked around.

"It feels funny without either of them," Wilhelmina said.

"Yes, but Mrs. Abbott will be back tonight," replied Jane. "As a matter of fact I thought of turning out the sitting room. It seems a good opportunity."

"I thought I would wash the curtains in Miss Marks's room,"

declared Wilhelmina, "and I was thinking we might make macaroni and cheese for supper."

"But Wilhelmina—"

"I've seen Miss Marks make it ever so often," said Wilhelmina, interrupting hastily. "You make the macaroni first, with potatoes and flour and fat and a dried egg, and you roll it out and cut it into strips and drop them into boiling salted water. You make the cheese sauce while the macaroni is cooking—and then you put the macaroni in a pie dish and pour on the sauce and brown it under the grill."

"It *sounds* easy," admitted Jane.

"Easy as anything," said Wilhelmina earnestly. "If you'd give me a hand we could do it beautiful. I know we could...and it's Mrs. Abbott's favorite."

This clinched the matter. "We'll make it," said Jane. "We'll start directly after tea. I'll turn out the sitting room in the afternoon."

Jane had profited considerably from Markie's tuition and she made a very good job of the sitting room. She cleaned it thoroughly and polished all the furniture—and as she worked she thought of all sorts of things. She thought of Markie. What a splendid person Markie was! Jane felt glad to have known Markie, for Markie's example had shown her that you could do humble things splendidly and be happy doing them—and make others happy. Jane thought of her own problem, she thought of Helen. She had behaved badly to Helen and she must make amends. She began to think of Archie—and then decided not to think of Archie...

Jane was just putting the finishing touches to the room when the door opened and Archie walked in.

"Oh!" exclaimed Jane, looking at him in dismay. She was conscious of untidy hair, dirty hands, and a crumpled overall. She wondered whether her face was clean—probably not.

"What's happened?" inquired Archie with anxiety. "I heard the most extraordinary tale. What are you doing?"

"Cleaning," replied Jane. "Markie has got appendicitis. They have taken her to hospital and Jerry has gone with her."

"Poor old Markie!" exclaimed Archie, sitting down and looking at Jane with rather a curious expression.

"I'm frightfully untidy," said Jane.

"Untidy but by no means frightful—go on, tell me the whole thing. What's all this about a spy?"

Jane told him about the spy, she told him everything, and Archie listened and nodded and made the right sort of response, and presently Wilhelmina brought in a small tray with tea and bread and butter and they had it together, sitting by the fire.

"So you aren't going away!" said Archie, suddenly.

"Not until Markie is better. I promised her I would stay and help Jerry—but it's a little worrying," said Jane with an anxious expression. "I feel I ought to write to Helen. I could write, of course—only, if she knew where I was, she might come over and make a scene."

"That's easily settled," replied Archie. "I'm going to London tomorrow for a few days. I'll post your letter in town." This was an excellent idea; it was clever of Archie to think of it.

"Write now," said Archie. "You needn't say much, need you?"

Jane got out her writing pad and sat down at the desk. She could have composed her letter more easily if she had not been so conscious of Archie's presence in the room. He sat by the fire, smoking, and looking at the flames...

"You seem to be saying a lot," said Archie at last.

"I'm not, really," replied Jane. "It's difficult. Where's the wastepaper basket?"

"I should put it in the fire if I were you."

"Perhaps I'd better."

The letter, when it was finished, was very short. It contained the news that the writer was well and happy and would return to Foxstead in about three weeks. Jane had tried to explain what her feelings were, her feelings about Janetta, but had given up the experiment in despair.

"That will have to do," said Jane, handing the missive to Archie. "I shall explain everything when I see her."

"Everything?" inquired Archie significantly.

"About Janetta," replied Jane firmly.

More might have been said but at this moment Wilhelmina appeared at the door. "What about the macaroni?" she inquired.

"You can't get macaroni, now," said Archie, who shared his sister's passion for this form of food. "Macaroni is not to be bought for love or money. I've tried everywhere."

"We make it," said Wilhelmina simply.

"I didn't know you could!" exclaimed Archie in surprise.

"It hasn't got holes in it, of course," Wilhelmina told him. "It's just long thin strips."

Archie rose. He said, "I'll come and help and I'll stay to supper—that will be all right, won't it?"

Jane and Wilhelmina assured him that it would.

Wilhelmina had laid out everything very neatly on the pantry table and weighed the ingredients with care. The potatoes had been boiled; they were divested of their jackets and mashed into a bowl with fat and flour and dried egg. Archie seized the bowl and a wooden spoon and proceeded to beat up the mixture. He was anxious to show Jane that he was a capable person, versatile and resourceful, and glancing at her he was glad to see that he was creating the right impression.

Jane was not to be outdone, and when the mixture had been thoroughly beaten and turned out onto a floured board she took up the rolling pin.

"Yes, you roll it out," said Wilhelmina, who was enjoying herself. "You roll it out and then you roll it up into a sort of swiss roll and then you take a knife and cut the roll into slices and that makes long thin strips of macaroni."

"I see the idea," said Archie. "It's very clever, isn't it? Roll it out, Jane."

Jane started to roll it out, but the dough was cloggy and, instead of forming a nice neat mat on the baking board, it stuck to the rolling pin.

"It's all right," said Archie. "We've forgotten to knead it, that's all. You must do it with your hands—I've just washed mine." He turned up his sleeves and plunged into the struggle.

The dough clung to his fingers, enveloping them in a white sticky mess. He tried to squeeze it off but it clung to him more lovingly than before.

"Good lord!" he exclaimed. "The stuff is like glue. Can't you do something about it, Jane?"

Thus appealed to, Jane tried to do something about it, but without success, for the dough wound itself around her fingers too. Their hands were covered with it. They were helpless.

"You should—have floured—them," gasped Wilhelmina, leaning on the table and shaking all over with laughter. "Oh dear—it's as good as the pictures—oh dear!"

"We should have floured them, Jane," said Archie gravely. "You realize that, don't you? If we had floured our hands the dough wouldn't have stuck."

"But what are we to do!" cried Jane.

After some difficulty they managed to scrape off the dough and return it to the board—there was less of it now, and it was still very cloggy.

"We can't roll it up," said Archie, eyeing it warily.

"We must cut it," declared Jane. "We must cut it up into neat pieces. We can't *waste* it."

They cut it into pieces—not neat pieces, for that was impossible—and dropped them into the pan of water boiling on the stove.

"It will taste the same," said Wilhelmina without conviction.

"Oh, of course," agreed Archie with enthusiasm.

Jane said nothing. She was looking at the pan, watching the queer bloated lumps that had begun to rise to the surface. After that the cooking operations went quite smoothly and according to plan, and when the dish was ready and nicely browned on the top it looked exactly like macaroni and cheese.

"Have we got to wait for Jerry?" inquired her brother. "I mean it smells so good and it's a pity to spoil it. Things like that ought to be eaten when they're ready."

Jane decided not to wait—her decision might have been different if she had been sure that the macaroni was a success—if Jerry came in later she could have an egg, and the macaroni experiment could be repeated another day.

"More flour and less potato," said Wilhelmina nodding. "We'll know better the next time."

Having agreed upon this Archie and Jane settled down to supper together and discussed the fruits of their labors.

"It's extremely good," declared Archie in some surprise. "The stuff doesn't taste like macaroni, of course, but you could hardly expect it. You know, Jane, things always taste nicer if you cook them yourself—even boiled eggs. Have you noticed that?"

"No, not really," replied Jane.

"Have some more," suggested Archie as he took a second helping.

"I'm not very hungry," said Jane—nor was she, for she could not forget those strange bloated lumps rising slowly to the surface of the water and turning over and over as if they were alive—as if they were some horrible sort of fish.

Archie could not stay long—he took his departure soon after supper—and, as he had left his horse at the stables, he persuaded Jane to walk down to the stables with him and see him off. She was all the more ready to be persuaded because she had been working indoors all day and because it really was a most beautiful night with a bright moon and a cloudless sky and a soft breeze that went whispering through the trees. They walked along together, not saying much, for Jane was never very talkative and Archie was busy with his thoughts. His thoughts were rather strange. If it had been wet or misty or if the moon had not been quite so gorgeous Archie might have proposed to Jane again (for, thanks to the macaroni, they had moved on a good deal further in their relationship), but Archie had just finished reading *Her Loving Heart* by Janetta and, in this extremely romantic tale, Cyril had proposed by moonlight...*the moon was sailing in a cloudless sky and the treetops were silvered by its light. All the world seemed to be made of silver and black velvet and the air was heavy with the perfume of nightstock*...it was an admirable setting for a proposal and Cyril had won his heart's desire.

Archie might have tried his luck if it had not been for Cyril. The treetops were silvery, and the world was made of silver and black velvet, but Archie could not do a thing about it because Cyril had spoiled the market. Archie understood Jane; he knew that she was sick of sentiment and romance. She would recover, of course, and in time she would realize that romance was a good thing in the right place. It was not the whole of life—as Janetta had made it—nor was it entirely foolish, as Jane seemed to think. It was like chocolate cream, thought Archie, a certain amount of it was good for you and extremely palatable; too much of it made you sick.

Chapter Twenty-Six
Queen Elizabeth's Room

A week passed. It was rather a curious week; it was a very unpleasant one for Jerry. She had known she would miss Markie, but she had not expected to feel so absolutely lost, so bereft, so completely deserted. There was Jane, of course, but even Jane could not fill the gap. Markie had her operation on the Sunday, and, although it was fairly serious, Dr. Wrench assured Jerry that all would be well. "Go and see her whenever you like," said Dr. Wrench. "It will do her good. Don't tire her, of course."

Jerry went and saw her. She sat with Markie for a little every day…and, to accomplish this, she was obliged to neglect a good deal of other work, and to leave all the household duties to Jane and Wilhelmina.

On Friday when Archie returned from London and rang up to inquire for Markie, Jerry was able to give him a good report. "She's *much* better," declared Jerry. "She looks better and feels better. I'm not worried about her anymore."

"Could you come over to tea?" asked Archie in a casual sort of voice.

"Come over to tea!" echoed Jerry.

"Why not?" asked Archie. "I mean if Markie is better—it will do you good to have a bit of an outing."

Jerry was surprised at this attention on the part of her brother, for it was most unusual. They were good friends, of course, but they were not in the habit of inviting each other to tea. When Jerry wanted to see Archie she rode over to Chevis Place and saw him, and when Archie wanted to see her he turned up at Ganthorne.

"But Archie, aren't you busy?" Jerry inquired.

"Yes, of course. I mean I've always got plenty to do—but I haven't seen you since I got back from town, so I thought you might come over. I can't work all day long, can I?"

"No," said Jerry, but she said it doubtfully, for as a matter of fact Archie was in the habit of working all day long.

"I've got to have tea, haven't I?" said Archie a trifle fretfully.

"Yes, of course," agreed Jerry.

"Of course if you're too busy."

"Oh no," said Jerry. "No, I'd like to come..." and then, suddenly, a thought struck her and she added, "Shall I bring Melanie Melton?"

"If you like," agreed Archie. "And bring Miss Watt."

"It would be too many," began Jerry. "I mean Jane won't mind."

"You'd better bring her," said Archie firmly. "I can't send the car for you, but perhaps."

"We can easily come in the bus," declared Jerry.

Jerry had expected that she and her two friends would be the only guests at Archie's tea party, but when she walked into the gun room she found Barbara there, ensconced in a comfortable chair near the fire. Jerry looked around the room to see whether Barbara had brought Lancreste, and was thankful to see that she had not done so. She disliked Lancreste intensely and could not understand why Barbara encouraged the youth. Last time Jerry had visited Barbara at the Archway House Lancreste had been there, and had spoilt the whole afternoon, and Jerry had been so annoyed about it that she had avoided Barbara's society for more than a week. But one could not continue to be annoyed with Barbara—at least Jerry found it impossible—so Jerry forgave her instantly and the two Mrs. Abbotts fell into each other's arms with cries of delight.

"What *have* you been doing!" Barbara exclaimed. "Why haven't you been over? I haven't seen you for ages...and so much has happened! How is poor Markie?"

"Better," said Jerry, who was glad she could answer the last question and ignore the first two. "Much better, really. She had it out on Sunday—it was rather more serious than they expected; the poor darling had let it go on so long—not saying a word about it because she didn't want to be a bother."

"You must miss her."

"Yes, frightfully. But of course I've got Jane."

"I must go when Markie is better," said Jane. She looked at Archie as she spoke, but, finding that Archie was looking at her, she looked away again.

The tea table was groaning with food, for Archie's idea of hospitality was to stuff his guests with the best of everything. His farms furnished him with cream and butter and eggs, and his bees with honey. Mrs. Frith had put her best foot foremost and had spent most of the day baking scones and cakes—it was a perfectly marvelous feast.

"I haven't seen anything like it for years!" declared Barbara, looking at the table in amazement.

"I haven't either," said Archie hastily. "I mean I don't live in luxury all the time—I mean—"

"Of course not," agreed Barbara. "You've just done it for us. It's *very* kind of you, Archie."

"I don't have a tea party every day...now, sit down. Where would you like to sit? Ah, here's Mrs. Frith with the eggs!"

"Goodness!" exclaimed Barbara, gazing at the large brown

boiled egg suddenly placed before her. "Goodness, is it really an *egg!*"

"Eat it and see," said her host in delighted tones.

"I don't feel as if I ought to eat it," she replied, taking up her knife and hesitating.

"Put it in a glass case," suggested Jerry, who had started to eat hers. "I think you ought to, Barbara. I mean you would be able to show it to your grandchildren."

"Yes," nodded Melanie. "You could show it to them and say, 'That is a hen's egg, my dear. We used to eat them, you know.'"

"They would be horrified, of course," continued Jerry, taking up the tale. "They would say, '*Eat* them, Granny! How disgusting! Didn't you have nice clean egg powder in those days?'"

Barbara laughed (she was always ready to laugh at herself) and Jerry was so pleased with her and loved her so much that she was able to master her repugnance and inquire after Lancreste's health in quite a pleasant tone.

"Oh, he's gone," said Barbara. "It's rather funny, really. I thought he would have come and said good-bye."

"Didn't he?" asked Melanie in surprise.

"I expect he was busy," said Barbara hastily.

"He went off in a great hurry, of course," said Melanie. "They wired for him to report immediately—but I'm surprised that he didn't find time to go and see you, Mrs. Abbott. He's very fond of you."

"It was horrid of him," put in Jerry.

"Didn't he leave a message or anything?" asked Melanie.

"No, but it doesn't matter."

"He was a bit fussed, you know," declared Melanie, trying to make things better. "It was a frightful scramble, really—and then, when he arrived at the airfield, he found they weren't expecting him until next day."

"Oh, you've had a letter from him?"

Melanie nodded. "Just to say he had arrived and everything was marvelous. He seems perfectly happy and contented. He's delighted to be back at work."

"Must have been trying for him hanging about here with nothing to do," suggested Archie.

"Oh, it *was*," agreed Melanie. "He was getting quite worried. Poor Lancreste, I was *so* sorry for him."

By this time Jerry was regretting the generous impulse that had moved her to inquire for Lancreste—what a fool she had been to mention his name!

"Wasn't it clever of Markie to catch the spy?" asked Jerry, changing the subject firmly.

"Tell us about it," said Barbara. "We heard all sorts of rumors. You know how stories get changed and twisted."

"And magnified," added Archie. "Wandlebury is a wonderful place for stories—it always was."

"But it isn't just a story," declared Jerry. "It's all true. He really was a spy and a very dangerous spy—wasn't he, Jane?"

"And Markie caught him?" asked Barbara incredulously, for although she had always admired Markie tremendously she could scarcely believe that Markie had captured a dangerous spy.

"Markie disarmed him," said Jerry. "She took away his revolver while he was asleep—and of course he was helpless—and then 'B' Company surrounded the wood and captured him. It was rather a muddle really because they had left off looking for him."

"Why?" asked Archie.

"Because of Mr. Boles. It was like this, you see," said Jerry, frowning in her effort to explain. "They had been warned about the man and they found Mr. Boles and they weren't sure whether he was the man or not. Of course I knew it wasn't Mr. Boles because he said it wasn't—and Colonel Melton agreed— but some of the others thought he was telling lies and it *was* him all the time."

There was a short silence.

"Sounds rather muddled," said Jerry apologetically.

"It sounds like double Dutch to me," said Archie in a resigned voice.

"Don't be silly, Archie," said his sister. "You could understand it if you tried."

"I never was any use at acrostics."

"Listen, Archie. They were warned about a spy and they caught Mr. Boles, but Mr. Boles wasn't the spy at all."

"Why did they think he was?"

"They didn't," said Jerry wearily. "They just thought the whole thing was a washout—at least some of them did—they thought that people had seen Mr. Boles and thought he was a spy."

"I'm beginning to see daylight."

"I should hope so," said Jerry sternly. "Everyone else saw it ages ago."

"They're sure this man is the real spy?" asked Barbara, who was anxious to be reassured on this point.

"Absolutely real. Sergeant Frayle found all sorts of gadgets in the wood. A little wireless set with a transmitter, and a thing with lights for signaling, and a sort of stove for cooking his food. Colonel Melton says he must have been there for at least a week—perhaps more—sleeping in the daytime and wandering about at night."

"Horrible!" exclaimed Barbara with a shudder.

"Yes, it is rather. He took things out of the larder," said Jerry. "I mean we missed things and Markie couldn't think where they had gone—it must have been him."

"Horrible for him, too," said Melanie, thoughtfully. "Think of being isolated in a strange country and knowing that everyone was trying to kill you!"

"He knew the country," said Jerry. "He used to come to

Wandlebury quite often before the war—and he can speak English as well as I can."

"Probably a good deal better," said Archie dryly.

"Markie is wonderful," continued Jerry, who was inured to brotherly insults. "There's practically nothing that Markie can't do if she puts her mind to it—and it just shows that people shouldn't laugh at Markie for being interested in skulls because it was the shape of the man's skull that put Markie on his track." She looked very hard at Archie as she spoke, for Archie was by no means innocent of the crime of laughing at Markie. Archie was often very naughty about Markie, and it was one of Jerry's sorrows that these two—both of whom she loved very dearly—did not appreciate one another as she could have wished.

"He should have disguised his skull," said Archie. "He should have fixed on bumps in the right places. I expect he *would* have done it if he had known he was going to meet Markie."

"Must you really go away?" said Barbara to Jane. Barbara hated people to quarrel and she felt the air growing sultry.

"Yes, I must," said Jane. "I've had a lovely holiday."

"We must make the most of you while you're here," declared Barbara. "Perhaps you and Jerry could come over to tea on Wednesday."

"I should love to, but I can't," replied Jane with regret. "I've got to go to the dentist on Wednesday afternoon."

"She's having a tooth stopped," added Jerry. "Mr. Clare is frightfully busy and Wednesday was the only day. I'll come if you like, Barbara."

"Of course," said Barbara, nodding. "Perhaps Jane could come to tea after the dentist, and you could go home together."

Archie had listened to these arrangements with interest. He now said with a serious air, "Barbara is quite right, Miss Watt. We must make the most of you while you're here. What would you like to do after tea? Would you like to see around the house—it's rather an interesting old house—or would you rather walk around the garden?"

"The house, I think," replied Jane, with a smile, for Archie's elaborate camouflage did not deceive her in the least and she was aware that she had been asked to tea for no other reason but to be shown the beauties of Chevis Place.

"Melanie would like to see it, too," said Jerry.

"Of course," agreed Archie, hiding his annoyance with a forced smile.

It appeared that everyone wanted to see around the house. Barbara and Jerry had seen it before, but neither of them wished to be left out of the expedition, so the whole party started upon a tour of inspection. This was not what Archie had hoped for, but he accepted the inevitable with a good grace, leading his guests from room to room, pulling up the blinds and opening the shutters and displaying the furniture and the pictures. Most of the pictures were portraits of members of the Chevis family—dead and gone—and they varied considerably in beauty and value. There was a Gainsborough and a Reynolds, for instance, and there were portraits scarcely worth the canvas upon which they were painted.

"You've altered the furniture," said Jerry.

"I've sold a lot of junk," admitted her brother. "It makes more room for the really good stuff...and incidentally I got quite a lot of money for it."

"You bought some more cows, I suppose," said Jerry.

"I used some of it to repair the roof," replied Archie with a smile.

"And the rest?"

"Wait and see, Jerry."

"It's a great improvement, anyhow," said Barbara, looking around in approval. "There was so much furniture that you couldn't see it properly."

"I've never seen the house looking so nice," added Jerry. She had never seen it looking so nice, nor had she ever heard its owner discourse about his treasures in such an interesting fashion. Archie was at his best. He went from piece to piece, fingering it lovingly and telling its history. He told them about the house, too, and this was quite as interesting in its way.

"It has been altered and enlarged," said Archie. "You can see where the new building has been grafted onto the old. I just wished I could take it all away—all the new part," declared Archie, waving his arms.

"The old part would be quite a nice-sized house," agreed Barbara.

"Amply big enough," said Archie. "It was old Sir Roger Chevis who did most of the building. He lived about a hundred years ago and had an enormous Victorian family so he had to make room for them. Unfortunately he had more money than taste."

"Perhaps you could alter it—take it down," suggested Jerry.

"It would cost thousands," said Archie with a sigh.

He talked on, showing them everything, and presently they arrived at the room where Queen Elizabeth had slept—or was said to have slept—when she visited Chevis Place. It was Archie's *pièce de résistance,* and like a good showman he had kept it to the last.

Jerry remembered this room as a cobwebby attic, filled with discarded furniture, so she was very much surprised when Archie threw open the shutters and disclosed the room to view.

"*There*," said Archie. "What do you think of it! I've removed everything except what *should* be here. I wanted to have it right. Of course it may not be quite right—I don't know enough about it."

The room was long and rather narrow with a low ceiling and an uneven wooden floor. It was paneled in dark wood, but it was not a dim room for it faced west and the setting sun filled it with a mellow light. In one corner there was a large fireplace with iron fire dogs standing in the grate. The furniture consisted of a four-poster bed with curtains, a huge oak chest, and several carved chairs with high backs and leather seats.

On the north wall hung a magnificent portrait of Queen Elizabeth herself, clad in rich brocade and decked with jewels.

"It's new!" exclaimed Jerry, in amazement.

"It's new, but it's old," replied Archie, smiling. "I bought it with some of the money I got for the furniture. Rather extravagant of me, but I wanted to have it here, in this room… and it really is rather interesting because one of the rings in the picture—you can see it on her finger—was given to my ancestor, Sir Godfrey Chevis, and has been in the family ever since. I'll show it to you."

The ring was in an old-fashioned jewel case, locked inside the chest. It was an emerald in a very heavy setting.

"Most attractive!" exclaimed Barbara taking it up and turning it this way and that so that the jewel sparkled in the light.

"It is," agreed Jerry. "Archie said I could have it but it ought to be kept at Chevis Place—besides it's too small for me."

"Try it on, Barbara," suggested Archie.

They all tried it on in turn but none of them could wear it—except Jane who found that it fitted her little finger. She was a trifle embarrassed at this discovery and removed it at once—as if it were red hot—and dropped it into Archie's palm. He was smiling to himself in a significant way as he locked it up in the box.

"The room has the right kind of feeling," declared Barbara, breaking the little silence that had fallen.

"She can't have been very comfortable here," said the practical Jerry. "No carpet, I suppose."

"Did they have rushes on the floor?" asked Melanie, looking around with interest and appreciation.

Archie was not sure. He had an idea that there might have

been a carpet or at least a large rug. "I'm going to find out," he said. "I hope the poor lady had a carpet, it would have made all the difference, wouldn't it?"

Jane had not said anything, but now she sighed, like a person waking from sleep. "There's atmosphere in this room," said Jane in a dreamy voice. "It's the sort of place where one could write a historical novel...if one could write, of course," added Jane hastily.

"Exactly," agreed Archie with fervor. "It's what I thought myself, when I was arranging the room. It would make a splendid study for an author. It's so quiet and peaceful and, if I could get the right kind of carpet, it would be quite comfortable. One would want a large table, a solid table, near the window—and a wastepaper basket, of course."

"You've thought it all out," said Barbara in surprise.

"What a pity you don't know any authors," said Jerry.

"Yes, isn't it?" agreed Archie smiling.

When they had all admired the room and discussed its arrangement they turned to go. Barbara and Jerry went first, followed by Melanie; Jane remained to help Archie to shut the shutters. Jane was sorry for Archie, he had behaved very well under somewhat trying circumstances and he deserved a little consideration. They shut the shutters, bolting them firmly with the heavy iron bar, and now the room was dark save for a narrow band of sunlight pouring through a slit.

"Like a sword," said Jane, pretending to grasp the blade.

Archie took her hand and held it, "I've been very good, haven't I?" he said in a low voice.

"You've been very kind indeed," replied Jane primly, withdrawing her hand. "It has been most interesting."

"And instructive," suggested Archie, imitating her polite tones. "I do hope you have found it instructive, Miss Watt."

Jane did not reply. She turned to go, rather hastily, for she felt anxious to overtake the rest of the party, whose voices could be heard in the distance, growing fainter and fainter. She turned to go, but her foot became entangled with the leg of a chair she had not seen in the dim light and she almost fell.

Archie caught her, and holding her in his arms he kissed her very gently but very firmly on the mouth. It was the second time, of course, and Jane was not so surprised. In fact she was not surprised at all.

"Don't, Archie," said Jane, struggling feebly.

"It's too late," said Archie, kissing her again.

"Too late?"

"Yes, your reaction came a few seconds too late. You liked it."

"No."

"Yes, you did. You liked it—and then you thought of Helen."

This was so true that Jane found it difficult to deny. She disengaged herself and tried to arrange her hat. "I wish you'd be sensible," she said.

"I am sensible," said Archie. "I want to marry you. I want you to come and write in Queen Elizabeth's room. She would like you to write here. She would like you to wear her ring."

"No, Archie."

"She would, really. She would come and whisper in your ear and tell you all sorts of interesting things."

Jane could not speak for a moment—it was so extraordinary that Archie should understand—but she pulled herself together and murmured that the others would be wondering...

"Let them wonder," replied Archie. "I've played the genial host all afternoon; I must have a few minutes to do what I want."

"It's no good, Archie. I've told you."

"I must speak to you, Jane. It's important."

"You can *speak* to me, of course," said Jane.

"All right, here goes—I've been thinking about it a lot. You can go back to Helen if you like."

"Thank you," said Jane with some sarcasm.

"You can go back and have a showdown," said Archie firmly. "Tell her the whole thing. That's the sensible way to tackle the problem. Tell her you're in love with me, and——"

"Am I?" inquired Jane.

"Of course you are. I wouldn't have kissed you like that if I hadn't been sure. What do you take me for?" asked Archie indignantly.

There was something so very touching about Archie at that moment that Jane very nearly said she would take him for a husband (the neatness of the retort appealed to her tremendously) but she bit the words back. She knew that she would never have another happy moment if she married Archie and left Helen in the lurch. Helen's influence on her had waxed, rather than waned, in the last six weeks.

"Tell Helen you're in love with me," repeated Archie. "Tell her I want to marry you. She won't stand in your way. Nobody would. It would be the most frightfully selfish——"

"You don't know Helen," said Jane firmly.

"Do you mean to say——"

"Yes."

"She must be an absolute gorgon!"

"No, she isn't. I wish I could make you understand. Helen is kind. She really is *very* kind—but she likes to be kind in her own way."

"I suppose she's one of those loonies who think marriage is wrong," said Archie. "My aunt was like that. She couldn't bear people getting married."

"Helen likes people to get married," replied Jane. "But she wouldn't like *me* to get married. I know that. She thinks I ought to write. She thinks writing is a sort of vocation."

"You would write much better if you were married," declared Archie with conviction.

Jane had a feeling that he was right—but that made no

difference. She said, "Helen brought me up. I owe her a great deal."

"I wonder why you ran away," said Archie, sarcastic in turn.

"I told you why," said Jane patiently. "I had to find myself. Now that I've found myself I must go back."

"To write books for Helen!" exclaimed Archie in disgust.

They said no more but went down the stairs in silence and joined the rest of the party in the hall.

Chapter Twenty-Seven
Barbara's Busy Day

Markie was better. Her condition was so much improved that she was able to receive visitors, and, hearing this news from Jerry, Barbara decided to go and see Markie and cheer her up. She armed herself with the *Geographical Magazine,* which seemed a suitable periodical for a person of Markie's erudition, and walked over to the hospital. It was a fine day and the walk was pleasant, and Barbara had time to think of all sorts of things as she walked along. If it had not been for the war and the petrol restrictions she would have gone in her car and it would have taken a quarter of the time, but walking was good for one…and what would she have done with the time saved? Barbara did not know the answer to that question. She had always been busy and she still was busy but, somehow, not any busier than before.

Markie was delighted to see Barbara. They were good friends. Markie respected Barbara because she ran her house well, made her husband happy, and had produced two satisfactory children. Barbara respected Markie's brains.

"How kind of you to come and see me!" exclaimed Markie.

"I'm so glad you are better," replied Barbara.

They shook hands solemnly. The nurse placed a chair beside the bed for Barbara to sit on, and went away.

Markie looked quite different, thought Barbara. It really

was most extraordinary to see Markie in bed…she was not the sort of person who makes a good show in bed: no lace cap decorated Markie's well-shaped head, no gorgeous creation of silk and wool was flung with careless elegance around her shoulders. She wore a gray flannel bed jacket, a truly sensible garment, and her gray hair, which was usually frizzled and waved, was perfectly straight and smooth, brushed back from her extremely good forehead. She looked like a man, thought Barbara, she looked like a very handsome man—and this was all the more strange because Barbara had always considered her rather a plain woman.

"You ought to wear your hair like that always," said Barbara impulsively.

"Do you think so?" asked Markie with interest. "As a matter of fact I have been considering the matter. It would be a great saving of time and trouble if I did not have to put curlers in my hair every night."

"And so much more comfortable," said Barbara, nodding. "Yes, I *do* think so, Markie. I like your hair much better straight."

"I shall consult Jerry about it," said Markie.

The subject was closed and Barbara was searching for another when Markie forestalled her.

"I shall soon be perfectly well," said Markie with a satisfied look. "I am feeling much better already and to tell you the truth I am quite enjoying my little holiday. The nurses are most kind and attentive. I had never been ill before and this illness has been an experience I shall not forget."

"Nurses are usually nice," put in Barbara.

"It is very curious how things work out," continued Markie. "One thinks a good deal when one is forced to lie in bed, and I have been thinking."

"About Jane?" inquired Barbara.

"How clever of you!" said Markie in surprise. "Yes, I was

thinking of Jane Watt. When she came to Ganthorne I was not very happy about it, for I was afraid her advent would change our lives, but now one sees that the whole thing was intended. It is most fortunate that she is able to stay on with Jerry while I am laid up."

"Yes," agreed Barbara, seizing the point. "Yes, how lucky! How lucky that Jerry happened to meet her on Mr. Tupper's doorstep! If Jerry had been a few moments earlier..."

"Or a few moments later," said Markie.

They looked at each other in complete understanding.

"It's a pity she's going away," said Barbara.

"Perhaps she will return," replied Markie with a smile.

Barbara had a feeling that more was meant by these simple words than appeared on the surface. "Return!" she inquired.

"Why not?" asked Markie hastily. "There is no reason why she should not visit us again—next summer perhaps."

"No, of course not," agreed Barbara.

"And then there is Wilhelmina," continued Markie. "I confess I was very much disturbed when Wilhelmina returned to Ganthorne—and now she has become so useful that I do not know what I should do without her."

"That wasn't good luck," replied Barbara with conviction.

"No?"

"No, it was an opportunity. It was bread upon the waters," said Barbara, struggling to convey her meaning. "If you hadn't seized the opportunity and *made* something of Wilhelmina she wouldn't be useful to you now."

"Perhaps you are right," agreed Markie with a sigh.

Barbara noticed the sigh, and, as she had been warned not to stay too long, she presented her small gift and came away. "Such a nice old lady," said the nurse as she and Barbara went down in the lift together.

"Do you mean Miss Marks?" asked Barbara in surprise.

"Yes," said the nurse.

Somehow or other Barbara had never thought of Markie as an old lady. She was by no means young, of course, and she was a lady in every sense of the word—but "old lady!"

"No trouble at all," the nurse was saying. "And that's lucky for me because my other patient's a ringer."

"A ringer?" asked Barbara.

"Yes, there goes her bell again. She'll just have to wait till I've seen you off," added the nurse defiantly.

Barbara hurried home, for she was having lunch early and immediately after lunch she was taking the children to Wandlebury to buy a present for Dorkie's birthday. Last year Barbara had taken Simon only, but this year Fay was considered old enough to join the expedition.

Tomorrow was Dorkie's birthday. Nobody knew how old she was, of course, for Dorkie maintained a discreet silence on the point. "As old as my tongue and a little older than my teeth," declared Dorkie when pressed. Simon guessed her age as thirty-nine. Fay had suggested eighty. "Somewhere between the two," said Dorkie in her usual placid way.

The children had hurried over their lunch but they took so long to dress—owing to their interest in Dorkie's age— that their mother was waiting for them in the hall when they came downstairs.

"Good-bye, Dorkie," said Simon. "We're going for a walk with Mummy," and he winked at Barbara in an impish manner as he spoke.

Barbara said nothing. She knew it was fun, of course—and she knew Dorcas was not deceived by the statement—but all the same she did not like Simon telling lies, and telling them in that very glib and competent manner. It made her a trifle uneasy.

They set off together; Fay trotting along with her hand tightly clasped in Barbara's, saying nothing but enjoying herself immensely; Simon hopping and skipping and talking hard as he always did except when he felt unwell.

"Dorkie didn't know," said Simon gleefully. "Dorkie thinks we're going for a walk. She doesn't know we're going to buy her a present. Let's get Dorkie a dressing gown. Her old one is awfully old."

"I'm afraid we haven't enough coupons," said Barbara regretfully.

"Bedroom slippers, then."

"We can't spare the coupons, Simon."

"A box of chocolates."

"Coupons, too," said Barbara with a sigh.

"What shall we buy her, Mummy? I know, we'll buy her a founting pen. *That's* not coupons, Mummy."

"We can try," said Barbara doubtfully. She was aware that for some reason or other, "founting pens" were practically nonexistent.

"What about a cup and saucer!" cried Simon, hopping with excitement. "A cup and saucer with a picture on it for Dorkie to drink her tea out of."

"We can try," said Barbara again.

"A little clock," said Fay, giving her hand a squeeze. "I think Dorkie would like a little clock."

"We'll see if we can find one," said Barbara, varying her reply but not her meaning.

She had known before the expedition started that it would be a long and wearying one, but she had underestimated the time and trouble it would cause. They went from shop to shop asking for the various things Simon and Fay had suggested and at every point they were met with the same reply.

"Oh no, we haven't had any for months." Sometimes the reply was polite and regretful; sometimes it was scornful and rude. Sometimes it was uttered in the tone of voice that really meant, "Don't you realize we're at war?" Barbara would have liked to explain that she knew about the war and that she was merely asking for cups and saucers and clocks and pens at the behest of her children, who could not be expected to know very much about the war owing to their tender age. The oddest thing was that the shops did not look empty. They looked quite well-stocked, but they were full of all the things one did not happen to want—just like *Alice through the Looking Glass,* thought Barbara.

"We'll get it at West's," said Simon, tugging at her arm. "West's have everything, don't they? Come on, Mummy. Here it is."

Barbara was dragged into West's. She was quite ashamed to voice her requirements by this time and murmured in apologetic tones, "I don't suppose there's the slightest hope, but have you by any chance got a founting pen?—I mean a fountain pen. No, I thought not. Have you such a thing as a clock. Quite a small one would do."

"We haven't had any clocks for months," said the assistant.

"Of course not," agreed Barbara hastily. "I didn't really think you would. What about a cup and saucer?... No, I'm afraid a plain white cup without a handle wouldn't do. It's for a present, you see. '

"Nail scissors, Mummy," said Simon hopefully.

"You won't get nail scissors," said the girl.

"Mummy!" said Fay, tugging Barbara's skirt. "Dorkie would like a little lamp for beside her bed."

"We have no bedside lamps," said the girl.

They were about to leave the shop in despair when Barbara had a sudden brilliant inspiration, namely that the problem should be tackled from the other end.

"I know," she exclaimed. "You can walk around the shop and see if you can find anything that Dorkie would like. How would that do?"

Simon and Fay received the suggestion favorably and went

off hand in hand, with the assistant following in their wake, and Barbara was standing watching them and thinking how perfectly sweet they looked when she felt a touch on her elbow. She looked around and found Mrs. Marvell standing beside her.

"Oh, it's you!" exclaimed Mrs. Marvell vaguely. "I thought it was Mrs. Dance."

Barbara was not pleased. She was aware that Mrs. Marvell was short-sighted but she had never suspected her of being stone blind.

"Why don't you wear spectacles?" asked Barbara with less than her usual pleasantness of manner.

"They don't suit me," replied Mrs. Marvell frankly.

"But if you need them."

"I can see all I want without them."

The inference was not very complimentary, but Mrs. Marvell did not mean to be rude. It was just her way.

"I was watching you," continued Mrs. Marvell. "You seemed to be asking for things. It isn't any use asking for things in shops. It just makes them angry."

"But how can you get things if you don't ask for them?" Barbara inquired. As usual, when she spoke to Mrs. Marvell, Barbara had begun to feel as if they inhabited different planets and were shouting at each other across millions of miles of space.

"It's no use," Mrs. Marvell said, and left it at that.

"How is Lancreste?" asked Barbara.

"He's gone," replied Mrs. Marvell.

"I know, but how is he? Have you heard from him?"

"He's all right," said his mother. "He's in the north somewhere. I can give you his address if you want to write to him. Newcastle or Hull or somewhere."

"He went off in a hurry, didn't he?"

"It was rather a rush. He left a message for you," added Mrs. Marvell with a surprised air.

"A message?"

"Oh, just the usual sort of thing."

"What was it, Mrs. Marvell?" asked Barbara firmly.

Mrs. Marvell looked slightly annoyed, for she hated having to use her brain. "You know the sort of thing," she replied in fretful tones. "He hadn't time to say good-bye and thank you for being kind to him. I was to tell you he felt much better and that he would write."

"Thank you," said Barbara smiling. She felt glad that Lancreste had remembered to send her a message in the hurry and bustle of his departure.

"He looked better," continued Mrs. Marvell. "Lancreste has been very difficult lately but he was better before he went away. More cheerful, somehow..."

"That's good," said Barbara happily.

"Mummy, we've found a box!" cried Simon. "It's really and truly *here,* and we don't have to pay coupons for it, the lady says. I think Dorkie would like it to keep things in. Look at it, Mummy!"

"Yes!" exclaimed Barbara. "Yes, it's simply splendid. How clever of you to find it!"

The box was large and solid, it was carved oak with a brass lock and key, and Barbara, who knew Dorkie's tastes, was perfectly certain that she would love it.

Could we have it wrapped up with paper and string?" asked Simon hopefully. "It's a present, you see, and Dorkie might see it before tomorrow."

"No paper or string," said the assistant firmly.

"Oh *dear!*" said Simon in dismay. "Oh dear, that's dreadful. Dorkie will *see* it."

"No, she won't," declared Barbara, paying for the box and putting it under her arm. "We won't let her see it. We'll have to hide it, Simon. You will go and scout and see if

Dorkie is out of the way while Fay and I carry it in. It will be fun, won't it?"

Simon's face brightened. He was perfectly happy again. All the way home he talked of different plans for secreting the box, and Barbara listened and agreed and wished with all her heart that her children had chosen something a little less weighty to give to their attendant. The box had not seemed very heavy when she lifted it off the counter but it grew heavier at every step and its unyielding corners bit into her arm in a most painful manner. Her arm was numb and she was worn out and dying for a cup of tea when at last they reached the haven of the Archway House.

Dorkie was nowhere to be seen. Being aware of the reason for the expedition she had taken care to be out of the way when it returned, and the conspirators were able to creep in and stow their treasure in the large seventeenth century chest that stood in the hall without let or hindrance.

"It's a pity, really," said Simon with a sigh. "It would have been fun to get Dorkie out of the way."

"*There*," said Barbara, locking the chest. "It will be quite safe until tomorrow morning."

"Dorkie won't know," said Fay gleefully.

"You mustn't tell her," said Simon.

"Fay won't tell her," declared Barbara, who was aware that if anyone told her it would be Simon. Talkers are never the best repositories for exciting secrets.

"You told her last year," said Fay.

"She guessed."

"No, she didn't—you told her."

"I didn't."

"You did."

They were still arguing, and Barbara was trying to make the peace, when the drawing room door opened and Miss Pearl

Besserton appeared. Her appearance was so sudden and unexpected, and so extremely unwelcome, that Barbara stood and gaped at her, unable to say a word.

"I heard you talking," said Miss Besserton, offering her hand to Barbara and behaving exactly as if she were the hostess and Barbara her guest. "I'm ever so pleased to see you, Mrs. Abbott. I hope you're quite well—and the kiddies. Such sweet little kiddies, aren't they?"

"Oh—er," said Barbara shaking hands.

"Been out for a walk with Mum?" asked Miss Besserton, smiling at Simon as she spoke.

"Yes," said Simon, eyeing her warily.

"They said you were out," continued Miss Besserton, turning back to Barbara. "So I said I'll wait till she comes in—even if it means me missing my train, I said."

"I see," said Barbara. "Yes—well—I was just going to have tea. Perhaps you'd like to have it with me?"

"I don't mind if I do," replied Miss Besserton.

The children went upstairs and Barbara followed her guest into the drawing room, where tea was ready and waiting on a little table drawn up near the fire. Barbara had formed the habit of making tea herself, for she could make it as she liked and when she liked, and it saved a good deal of trouble. She proceeded to make it now while Miss Besserton looked on and talked.

"It looks cozy," Miss Besserton said. "I was just thinking that while I was waiting. I must say I like a nice fire on a cold afternoon. You don't bother about the coal rations, I suppose. I mean you just have a fire when you want."

"We burn wood," replied Barbara indignantly. "We don't use any coal for this fire. My husband cuts down a tree and we saw it up ourselves. We're very particular about the fuel target."

"Sorry, I'm shore," said Miss Besserton. "I didn't notice it was wood." She sat down and took off her furs.

"Are you staying in Wandlebury?" asked Barbara.

"No, I'm here for the day. Came down on purpose to see you—if you want the truth."

"To see me!"

"I thort you might know where Lanky's gone," said Miss Besserton in a casual sort of tone.

"He got his orders and left in a hurry," replied Barbara, looking at Miss Besserton in surprise.

"I knew he'd gone. I said, 'Where's Lanky gone'—that's what I said."

"I don't know," said Barbara. This was perfectly true, for in the excitement of finding the box she had omitted to ask Mrs. Marvell for Lancreste's address. She did not regret the omission.

"P'raps not, but you could find out, couldn't you?" replied Miss Besserton. "I mean you could ask his mother."

"Why don't you ask her?"

"Because it wouldn't be a bit of good. Lanky's family haven't much use for me. They're not my sort—stuffy old beasts," she added beneath her breath.

"I couldn't," said Barbara, who had decided that her only hope was to be frank. "I mean I couldn't ask them for his address and give it to you. I expect he'll write to you," she added, softening the blow.

"You'd think so," agreed Miss Besserton. "It's funny, reelly. I haven't had a letter from Lanky for a fortnight. I wasn't worrying much, because—because—but a fortnight's a long time...Lanky generally writes nearly every day. In fact he was a bit of a nuisance like that," added Miss Besserton in a burst of confidence.

"Oh...yes," said Barbara, who did not know what else to say.

"I mean to say letters are all very well but you can have too much of that sort of thing. It gets on your nerves. I used to scream almost when I saw his writing. I wouldn't mind seeing it now."

"He'll write soon," said Barbara.

"Yes...yes, I expect so. Of course we had a bit of a tiff—but that was nothing new. I mean to say we're always having tiffs and making it up again. There's nothing in that, is there?"

"Do you take sugar, Miss Besserton?"

"I like a little shoog if you can spare it."

"Oh yes, of course," said Barbara.

"It's funny," said Miss Besserton, accepting her cup of tea and stirring it thoughtfully. "I mean I got a bit of a shock when I found he hadn't written for a fortnight. I wrote to him— quite a nice letter it was—and he never answered so I thort I'd better come down and see what had happened. You could have knocked me down with a feather when I heard he'd gone."

"He left in a great hurry."

"He could have written if he'd wanted to. People always can," said Miss Besserton, who was no fool.

"Will you have some jam?" asked Barbara.

"I don't mind," replied Miss Besserton, helping herself lavishly. "They're pretty stingy with jam at the boarding house where I'm staying." She hesitated and then looked at Barbara and said, "I thort perhaps you'd know what's come over Lanky."

"No, I'm afraid I don't know anything about it."

"I don't know what to do," declared Miss Besserton. "I mean Lanky and I have been friends for ever so long—I mean you could depend on Lanky. The girls used to tease me about Lanky and call him Old Faithful—that shows you, doesn't it? Of course I got a bit bored with him now and then but I always knew he was there."

Barbara said nothing.

"You don't think he's making up to another girl, do you?" asked Miss Besserton anxiously.

"I don't know," mumbled Barbara.

"You would know if he was, wouldn't you? I mean he tells

you things, doesn't he? I mean I wouldn't like Lanky to—to find someone else."

Barbara made a noncommittal sound. She was terrified of opening her mouth in case she should say the wrong thing.

"Well, it's funny," said Miss Besserton. "I mean of course we had tiffs now and then, but…"

There was silence. Barbara looked at Miss Besserton and was dismayed to see that her lips were quivering. She was horrified when two large tears formed upon Miss Besserton's eyelids and rolled down her cheeks.

"Oh dear!" exclaimed Miss Besserton, brushing them away. "I don't know why I'm so unlucky, I'm shore."

Fortunately for Barbara there was a train to London at five-twenty and, as Miss Besserton was obliged to catch it, the dreadful interview came to a hurried conclusion. Barbara accompanied her guest to the door and watched her walk down the drive and disappear. She had a feeling that Miss Besserton had passed out of her life forever. Poor soul! said Barbara to herself. It's her own fault, of course, but you can't help being sorry for her.

Chapter Twenty-Eight
The Dentist's Waiting Room

It was Wednesday afternoon—market day in Wandlebury—and although the market was a mere shadow of its former self it still carried on and a certain amount of business was transacted. Archie had driven in early to sell some of his produce. He had lunch at the Apollo and Boot and met a good many friends—farmers with whom he had had dealings in better days—and he chatted with them and groused with them and bewailed the egg rationing scheme that seemed to be going from bad to worse. At first, when Archie had started to farm his own land, the neighboring farmers had been a little difficult; some of them had been definitely hostile, others had laughed at him behind his back and had prophesied disaster, but Archie was a friendly soul with no airs about him and gradually he had worn down the barrier of prejudice. He was quite popular now, his success was admitted, and his opinion carried weight.

After lunch Archie went into the lounge and sat down near the window. He took this seat because he wanted a good view of Wandlebury Square, not because he wanted to talk to old Mr. Brown of Fairfarm, who was sitting opposite. Archie took up a paper and pretended to read, but not one word of its contents penetrated to his brain; for this was the day Jane Watt was going to the dentist, and the dentist pursued his somewhat grim business in Wandlebury Square, and Archie had decided to head Jane off and have another talk with her while she was waiting for her appointment.

A dentist's waiting room may seem a curious place to choose for a talk with Jane, but Archie had no choice in the matter. Jane was leaving Wandlebury almost immediately and this was his only chance of seeing her alone. If he went out to Ganthorne the place was always stiff with people, and Jerry spent all her time endeavoring to pair him off with Melanie. Of course it was just as well, in a way, that Jerry had got this particular bee in her bonnet, for the last thing he wanted was to be thrown at Jane's head—that would ruin everything—but it was annoying that he could never get a moment with Jane. He wanted to talk to Jane, not to propose to her again, but merely to keep himself in front of her eyes, to show himself to her and let her get used to him...for of course he knew Jane much better than she knew him. He knew her through her books—and this was why he was a bit further on than she was, this was why she was lagging behind. She loved him, of course (she had practically admitted that she loved him) but she did not see—as he saw—that they were absolutely suited to each other; she could not envisage the future. Archie was quite willing to give her time. He had proposed to her twice and both times she had refused him, but he was not in the least cast down. He would let her go back to Foxstead. He would leave her alone for a little—for a fortnight perhaps—and then he would ride over and see her and propose to her for the third time. It might not work, of course. He might have to wait longer; he might have to propose to her four or five or six times before she said yes, but ultimately Jane would say yes, and all would be well.

She loves me, thought Archie, so it's bound to be all right in the end. The only snag is Helen. Helen will have to be tackled. When I see Helen I shall know how to tackle her—whether to coax her and wheedle her or take a strong line—and, once I've got Helen where I want her, I can go ahead. I shall have to go carefully, of course. I've got to remember Edward—and all the other fellows in her books—mustn't propose to her in the garden, like Julian, or on the top of a mountain like Harold, or on a moonlight night like that ass, Cyril. It's a pity (thought Archie), it really is a nuisance that Jane has written so many books with so many proposals in them—cramps one's style a bit...and I mustn't say, "Darling, I can't live without you," or anything like that. Funny (thought Archie, smiling to himself), that's exactly the sort of thing I want to say to Jane—that's exactly what I feel—"Darling, I adore you! You're the most beautiful thing on earth!"

"Yes, Chevis-Cobbe?" said Mr. Brown, leaning forward with his hand to his ear. "What were you saying?"

"How are your pigs doing?" asked Archie loudly.

Mr. Brown began to give Archie a detailed account of his prize sow and her latest litter, and at that moment Jane appeared, walking briskly across the square to the dentist's. She walked well, with a springy heel and toe movement and a spring from the hip—and Archie, who really was desperately in love, felt his heart go surging out toward her. No time must be wasted, of course (for although Mr. Clare was an extremely busy man and not very good at dovetailing his appointments, it was just possible that he might be ready to see Jane at the proper time), so Archie abandoned Mr. Brown, threw down his paper and ran down the stairs and across the square. He arrived on Mr. Clare's doorstep just as the door was being opened to admit Jane.

"Archie!" exclaimed Jane in surprise.

"I was lunching at the Apollo," said Archie breathlessly. "I saw you. I'm coming in, too. We can talk while you're waiting."

"My appointment is at three."

"But you may have to wait," said Archie, and he followed her into the hall.

"But Archie—"

"You don't mind, do you?" said Archie, taking off his cap. "I mean I can cheer you up and take your mind off."

Jane did not mind at all. It was nice of Archie. She was only going to have a tooth stopped, of course, but still…

The page boy—who looked about ten years old—ushered them into the waiting room murmuring that Mr. Clare was "a bit be'ind 'and today" and left them to their fate.

Archie had expected the waiting room to be empty. He had forgotten that Mr. Clare shared the waiting room with his partner. He had forgotten that, being market day, the farmers' families would have seized the opportunity to get a lift into the town. His heart sank as he followed Jane into the room and saw the crowd. Six people were waiting to see Mr. Clare or his partner, three women, one old man, and two children—they were dispersed about the room, occupying all the comfortable chairs, and, while some of them were making a pretense of reading, others were sitting in disconsolate attitudes brooding upon the ordeal that lay ahead.

When Jane and Archie walked in six faces were turned in their direction and twelve eyes looked at them with furtive interest and then looked away again…and twelve ears will listen to every word we utter, thought Archie in dismay.

"Don't bother to wait," said Jane in low tones as she and Archie sat down at the table on the two remaining chairs.

"Nothing else to do," murmured Archie.

"No good," whispered Jane. "Awfully grim for you—may have to wait hours."

"Doesn't matter."

They said no more—it was impossible to talk when you knew that twelve ears were straining to hear your remarks—but all the same Archie decided to stay, for he had a feeling that Jane was glad to have him there, that she was touched by his solicitude. He offered her an illustrated weekly and took another himself and silence fell—complete silence, save for the ticking of the clock.

Archie's paper was an ancient number—he had given Jane the new one—he turned over the pages and looked at pictures of planes and tanks and warships and generals with boyish faces and steady eyes. If Jane won't have me I shall join up, thought Archie, who was suffering from a sudden wave of pessimism (which may or may not have been due to the atmosphere in the room). If Jane says no quite definitely I shall take the shilling and the farms can go to hell.

Jane's paper was new and crisp, but it contained much the same sort of pictures—tanks in the desert and planes and warships and generals—she turned over the pages without being able to take much interest in them; and then, quite suddenly, her eye was caught and held. There, in the column devoted to literary gossip, was a well-known name, blazoned in large type.

JANETTA WALTERS (read Jane, holding the paper up to the light so that she might see it better) JANETTA WALTERS, *the popular author, has completed a new novel to be published shortly. It is entitled* LOVE TRIUMPHANT *and Miss Walter's large circle of admirers need not be told to make a note of it for their library lists. The story is well up to her usual standard, it is sensitive and delicate and full of romance. Miss Walters has had a slight nervous breakdown, due to overwork, and has gone to Cornwall to recuperate. Her next book, which is already well on its way, is entitled* LOVE'S GARDEN *and we are informed on good authority that it will have a Cornish setting.*

Jane read the notice three times before she could believe her eyes...and then, gradually, the meaning of it dawned upon her and she smiled to herself with amusement. She had thought of all sorts of ways in which the problem of Janetta might be solved, but she had never thought of this...and yet, of course, it was the obvious way and the very best way of all...Helen had donned Janetta's cloak.

Jane could not help wondering in what circumstances Hector had proposed—probably in the rose garden on a moonlight night—and she wondered whether Phyllis had accepted him at once or kept him on tenterhooks for a page or two. She wondered how Helen would get on with *Love's Garden* and whether the lovers in it would do much bathing; whether they would go sailing or merely wander along the cliffs and watch the birds...these were the sort of things one did when one went to Cornwall, or so Jane believed.

"Cornwall!" said Jane to herself. "Why Cornwall? Helen might have chosen somewhere less hackneyed."

Jane smiled more broadly than before. She almost laughed—but a dentist's waiting room is no place for laughter—for now she was beginning to realize the whole thing clearly and all its implications. She passed the paper to Archie, putting it down in front of him on the table and pointing to the paragraph she wanted him to read.

He read it carefully—and then he looked at Jane. There was a question in his eyes. Jane nodded.

"Miss Watt next, please," said the diminutive page.

The door of Mr. Clare's house burst open and out rushed Archie. He was hatless and there was a wild air about him, an air of madness. He went straight across the square to the fountain and sat down on the edge. The fountain was not playing, of course. If it had been playing he could not have sat down on the edge of it without getting wet. He sat there for a moment in a dazed sort of way and then he got up and walked around... he could not sit still. No, it was impossible. He was too excited. He felt as if he wanted to shout and dance the hornpipe or to seize hold of somebody and say, "It's all right! Of course I knew it would be, really, but still..."

Archie walked around the fountain three times without stopping. He laughed aloud—why shouldn't he laugh. "I've something to laugh at," said Archie, addressing the stone boy who stood ankle-deep in the pool and supported the large stone jar from which, in normal times, limpid water was wont to gush. "By gosh, I have," declared Archie. "And I don't care if all the farmers in Wandlebury are watching from the windows of the Apollo and thinking I'm drunk. I *am* drunk. I'm walking on air. Oh gosh, it's wonderful…couldn't be better…I needn't have worried about Cyril and Edward and Co. Not one of them thought of proposing in a dentist's waiting room. Neither did I as a matter of fact. I didn't propose unless you count raising your eyebrows as a proposal. Do you?" inquired Archie, gazing at the stone boy. "Do you count it or not? It's rather important, really." The stone boy made no reply.

"Well, never mind," said Archie. "I don't blame you for not being able to answer offhand. Think it over and let me know."

Fortunately there was nobody else in the square, so nobody except the stone boy witnessed Archie's behavior…he was able to work off his madness in comfort. It was absolutely necessary to work off his madness before Jane emerged from the dentist, so that he could greet her in a matter-of-fact way. The madness was working off gradually but Archie still felt that he wanted to do something desperate. He explained this to the stone boy but the stone boy did not reply. He looked sad and dusty and hopeless.

"Poor wretch!" said Archie, shaking his head. "What do you know about love! You've never felt like this. You haven't got your heart's desire. You haven't got anything at all. There you stand, day after day with your empty jar. I suppose the town council have decided that it would be wrong to have a fountain splashing in the middle of the square when there's a war on… it's silly, really, because the water comes from the stream and the stream flows on just the same whether there's a war or not. Poor wretch—why shouldn't you have your water?"

There was nothing selfish about Archie's happiness, he wanted everyone to be happy—and especially the stone boy who had listened so patiently to all he had said—and seeing a large rusty handle beneath the surface of the pool Archie pulled up his sleeve, leaned over and grasped it firmly. It was pretty stiff, of course, but Archie was strong. He turned it full on.

The effect was magical. In a moment the fountain came to life and a stream of water sprang from the jar the boy held upon his shoulder; it towered into the air like a silver pillar and rained down in sparkling cascades. Standing back and surveying the result of his illegal action Archie felt like a king. The sun blazed down upon the falling water, creating a thousand rainbows and amongst the rainbows stood the boy, no longer dusty and parched and hopeless, but clean and joyous.

It was gorgeous. It was magnificent. It was exactly what Archie needed to crown his joy. He was still standing there, feasting his eyes and ears upon the sight and sound of the fountain when Mr. Clare's door opened and Jane came out. He went to meet her and they met in the middle of the road.

"Let's go and tell Jerry and Barbara," said Archie, putting his hand through her arm.

"Yes, let's," said Jane, smiling.

Read on for an excerpt from

MISS BUNCLE'S BOOK

Available now from Sourcebooks Landmark

Chapter One
Breakfast Rolls

O ne fine summer's morning the sun peeped over the hills and looked down upon the valley of Silverstream. It was so early that there was really very little for him to see except the cows belonging to Twelve-Trees Farm in the meadows by the river. They were going slowly up to the farm to be milked. Their shadows were still quite black, weird, and ungainly, like pictures of prehistoric monsters moving over the lush grass. The farm stirred and a slow spiral of smoke rose from the kitchen chimney.

In the village of Silverstream (which lay further down the valley) the bakery woke up first, for there were the breakfast rolls to be made and baked. Mrs. Goldsmith saw to the details of the bakery herself and prided herself upon the punctuality of her deliveries. She bustled round, wakening her daughters with small ceremony, kneading the dough for the rolls, directing the stoking of the ovens, and listening with one ear for the arrival of Tommy Hobday who delivered the rolls to Silverstream before he went to school.

Tommy had been late once or twice lately; she had informed his mother that if he were late again she would have to find another boy. She did not think Tommy would be late again, but, if he were, she must try and find another boy, it was so important for the rolls to be out early. Colonel Weatherhead (retired) was one of her best customers and he was an early breakfaster. He lived in a gray stone house down near the bridge—The Bridge House—just opposite to Mrs. Bold at Cozy Neuk. Mrs. Bold was a widow. She had nothing to drag her out of bed in the morning, and, therefore, like a sensible woman, she breakfasted late. It was inconvenient from the point of view of breakfast rolls that two such near neighbors should want their rolls at different hours. Then, at the other end of the village, there was the Vicar. Quite new, he was, and addicted to early services on the birthdays of Saints. Not only the usual Saints that everybody knew about, but all sorts of strange Saints that nobody in Silverstream had ever heard of before; so you never knew when the Vicarage would be early astir. In Mr. Dunn's time it used to slumber peacefully until its rolls arrived, but now, instead of being the last house on Tommy's list, it had to be moved up quite near the top. Very awkward it was, because that end of the village, where the old gray sixteenth-century church rested so peacefully among the tombstones, had been all late breakfasters and therefore safe to be left until the end of Tommy's round. Miss Buncle, at Tanglewood Cottage, for instance, had breakfast at nine o'clock, and old Mrs. Carter and the Bulmers were all late.

The hill was a problem too, for there were six houses on the hill and in them dwelt Mrs. Featherstone Hogg (there was a Mr. Featherstone Hogg too, of course, but he didn't count, nobody ever thought of him except as Mrs. Featherstone Hogg's husband) and Mrs. Greensleeves, and Mr. Snowdon and his two daughters, and two officers from the camp, Captain Sandeman and Major Shearer, and Mrs. Dick who took in gentlemen paying guests, all clamoring for their rolls early—except, of course, Mrs. Greensleeves, who breakfasted in bed about ten o'clock, if what Milly Spikes said could be believed.

Mrs. Goldsmith shoved her trays of neatly made rolls into the oven and turned down her sleeves thoughtfully. Now if only the Vicar lived on the hill, and Mrs. Greensleeves in the Vicarage, how much easier it would be! The whole of the hill would be early, and Church End would be all late. No need then to buy a bicycle for Tommy. As it was, something must be done, either a bicycle or an extra boy—and boys were such a nuisance.

Miss King and Miss Pretty dwelt in the High Street next door to Dr. Walker in an old house behind high stone walls. They had nine o'clock breakfast, of course, being ladies of leisure, but the rest of the High Street was early. Pursuing her previous thoughts, and slackening her activities a little, now that the rolls were safely in the oven, Mrs. Goldsmith moved the ladies into the Colonel's house by the bridge, and the gallant Colonel, with all his goods and chattels, was dumped into Durward Lodge next door to Dr. Walker.

These pleasant dreams were interrupted by the noisy entrance of Tommy and his baskets. No time for dreams now.

"Is this early enough for you?" he inquired. "Not ready yet? Dear me! I've been up for hours, I 'ave."

"Less of your cheek, Tommy Hobday," replied Mrs. Goldsmith firmly.

At this very moment an alarm clock started to vibrate furiously in Tanglewood Cottage. The clock was in the maid's bedroom, of course. Dorcas turned over sleepily and stretched out one hand to still its clamor. Drat the thing, she felt as if she had only just got into bed. How short the nights were! She sat up and swung her legs over the edge of the bed and rubbed her eyes. Her feet found a pair of ancient bedroom slippers—which had once belonged to Miss Buncle—and she was soon shuffling about the room and splashing her face in the small basin which stood in the corner in a three-corner-shaped washstand with a hole in the middle. Dorcas was so used to all this that she did it without properly waking up. In fact it was not until she had shuffled down to the kitchen, boiled the kettle over the gas ring, and made herself a pot of tea that she could be said to be properly awake. This was the best cup of the day and she lingered over it, feeling somewhat guilty at wasting the precious moments, but enjoying it all the more for that.

Dorcas had been at Tanglewood Cottage for more years than she cared to count; ever since Miss Buncle had been a small fat child in a basket-work pram. First of all she had been the small, fat child's nurse, and then her maid. Then Mrs. Buncle's parlor maid left and Dorcas had taken on the job; sometimes, in domestic upheavals, she had found herself in the role of cook. Time passed, and Mr. and Mrs. Buncle departed full of years to a better land and Dorcas—who was now practically one of the family—stayed on with Miss Buncle—no longer a fat child—as cook, maid, and parlor maid combined. She was now a small, wizened old woman with bright beady eyes, but in spite of her advancing years she was strong and able for more work than many a young girl in her teens.

"Lawks!" she exclaimed suddenly, looking up at the clock. "Look at the time, and the drawing-room to be done yet—I'm all behind, like a cow's tail."

She whisked the tea things into the sink and bustled round the kitchen putting things to rights, then, seizing the broom and the dusters out of the housemaid's cupboards, she rushed into Miss Buncle's drawing-room like a small but extremely violent tornado.

Breakfast was all ready on the dining-room table when Miss Buncle came down at nine o'clock precisely. The rolls had come, and the postman was handing in the letters at the front door. Miss Buncle pounced upon the letters eagerly; most of them were circulars but there was one long thin envelope with a London postmark addressed to "John Smith, Esq." Miss Buncle had been expecting a communication for John Smith for several weeks, but now that it had come she was almost afraid to open it. She turned it over in her hands waiting until Dorcas had finished fussing round the breakfast table.

Dorcas was interested in the letter, but she realized that Miss Buncle was waiting for her to depart, so at last she departed reluctantly. Miss Buncle tore it open and spread it out. Her hands were shaking so that she could scarcely read it.

ABBOTT & SPICER
Publishers
Brummel Street,
London EC4

—th July.

Dear Mr. Smith,

I have read *Chronicles of an English Village* and am interested in it. Could you call at my office on Wednesday morning at twelve o'clock? If this is not convenient to you I should be glad if you will suggest a suitable day.

Yours faithfully,
A. Abbott

"Goodness!" exclaimed Miss Buncle aloud. "They are going to take it."
She rushed into the kitchen to tell Dorcas the amazing news.

Miss Buncle's Book

D. E. Stevenson

Who knew one book could cause so much chaos?

Barbara Buncle is in a bind. Times are harsh, and Barbara's bank account has seen better days. Maybe she could sell a novel…if she knew any stories. Stumped for ideas, Barbara draws inspiration from her fellow residents of Silverstream, the little English village she knows inside and out.

To her surprise, the novel is a smash. It's a good thing she wrote under a pseudonym, because the folks of Silverstream are in an uproar. But what really turns Miss Buncle's world around is this: what happens to the characters in her book starts happening to their real-life counterparts. Does life really imitate art?

A beloved author who has sold more than seven million books, D. E. Stevenson is at her best with *Miss Buncle's Book*, crafting a highly original and charming tale about what happens when people see themselves through someone else's eyes.

Praise for *Miss Buncle's Book*:

"Love it, love it, love it! There are no vampires, no faeries, no weird creatures, just a sweet story about real people living in a world I've always dream of." —*Reader Review*

For more D. E. Stevenson books, visit:

www.sourcebooks.com

Miss Buncle Married

D. E. Stevenson

A marriage and a sudden move to a new town won't slow this mischievous writer down!

Barbara Buncle: bestselling novelist, new wife...new neighbor? In this charming follow-up to *Miss Buncle's Book*, the intrepid writer moves to a new town filled with fascinating folks...who don't even know they might become the subjects of her next bestselling book.

Miss Buncle may have settled down, but she has already discovered that married life can't do a thing to prevent her from getting into humorous mix-ups and hilarious hijinks.

A beloved author who has sold more than seven million books, D. E. Stevenson is at her best with the stories of Miss Buncle.

Praise for *Miss Buncle Married*:

"Completely charming and funny, in a way that's intelligent without being difficult, and cozy without turning sticky-sweet." —*Reader Review*

For more D. E. Stevenson books, visit:

www.sourcebooks.com

About the Author

D. E. Stevenson (1892–1973) had an enormously successful writing career: between 1923 and 1970, four million copies of her books were sold in Britain and three million in the States. Her books include *Miss Buncle's Book*, *Miss Buncle Married*, *The Young Clementina*, *The Listening Valley*, *The Two Mrs. Abbotts*, and *The Four Graces*. D. E. Stevenson was born in Edinburgh in 1892; she lived in Scotland all her life. She wrote her first book in 1923, but her second did not appear for nine years. She published *The Two Mrs. Abbotts* in 1943.